IGNITE ME

USA TODAY BESTSELLING AUTHOR
HEATHER RENEE

Ignite Me

Heather Renee

Published by HRB Publishing LLC

Copyright © 2022 HRB Publishing LLC

Immortal Vices and Virtues Universe Copyright © 2022 Kel Carpenter LLC.

Edited by: Jamie with Holmes Edits and Amy McNulty

Cover design by Yocla Designs

ISBN: 978-1957731094

For the family I've found along the way.
Thanks for never giving up on me.

CHAPTER ONE

Coming home to a package on my doorstep didn't give me the same joy it once had. A decade ago, when I'd begun offering my services in trade for the things I needed, there'd been a thrill that the hunt had given me.

As I stared at the black envelope waiting for me, I'd much rather have pretended I didn't see anything and headed inside my cabin. It was in the remote parts of No Man's Land, a place where the wise people left me alone and the stupid ones provided me with target practice.

As I reached for my metal doorknob, magic from the envelope that had found its way to me sent charcoal tendrils of energy up until they wrapped around my wrist.

Well, that wasn't normal for a package.

The power encouraged me to bend down and take the invitation inside, overruling my stubbornness. I could have disregarded the spell with my own strength, but someone had taken extra efforts to make sure I considered this request. That piqued my interest.

When I bent over, the magic dissipated, and my fingers grasped the thin envelope. I stepped into the doorway, then listened and scented for anything that didn't belong, just like I did every time I came home.

I wasn't part of any of the Houses, and I preferred it that way, but that didn't mean they weren't aware of who I was.

Grayson Barrett. A wolf shifter tracker who had never failed a mission. Also a sometimes-assassin when the reward and justification were tempting enough.

Though, there was one little secret of mine that nobody knew. The source of my success, yet, some days, the bane of my existence. The dark part of me that gave me additional abilities and that very few knew existed.

Once I'd confirmed nothing was out of place inside my one-bedroom cabin, I moved past the entryway. I eyed the small wooden table to my right, then the couch and fireplace to my left. Given the sender had used higher-level magic to deliver the letter, I decided a seat in front of the fire would be better for whatever I was about to read.

My heavy-booted feet carried me toward my worn, brown leather couch. I sat on the middle cushion, kicking my legs up onto the already dented, metal coffee table.

With a flick of my thumb and middle finger, flames lit the logs in the fireplace, then I settled in to open up the offer.

The ebony paper was thick with no writing on the front, but when I flipped it over, there was a wax seal, crimson in color, with no logo, just a circular imprint over the flap. I swiped the pad of my thumb over the soft substance, and something pricked my skin.

Pulling back, I considered throwing the envelope right into the fire, but then it floated out of my grip, hovering above the coffee table as it began to unfold.

Interesting. *That* had never happened before.

The aged parchment seemed to be attached to the black envelope as everything came undone at the same time. There were no words on the tanned paper, but swirls of white mist grew around the would-be message until a distorted man's voice began to speak.

"Mr. Barrett, my name is Johnathon. I require not only your services, but your discretion as well. As you may be aware, the House of Fire and Fluorite has suffered immensely over the last year. Due to their lack of proper leadership, a witch has been able to infiltrate them. Powers have been stolen, and children have been sacrificed."

That was quite the accusation and would require proof before I believed it.

The voice continued speaking while the mist seemed to grow bigger and thicker around the paper. "We would like the target dealt with quietly and swiftly. If you can return her to No Man's Land, we can take things from there. If that's not possible, death is a viable solution as well. We merely require her body to be brought back with you as proof of completion of the assignment."

"And what do I get out of this?" I asked, assuming the magic was capable of answering back. Though, I was already intending to decline the job regardless of what they offered.

My ability to tell fact from fiction wasn't sensing any lies, but omissions and carefully worded sentences were always something of a red flag.

The mist shifted, and an image of a silver ring with a clear stone in the middle appeared. "This would be your compensation."

I scoffed. "I don't wear jewelry."

The voice's haunting laughter echoed around the room. "But this is no ordinary piece of jewelry, Mr. Barrett. This is a shifting House ring."

I watched as intricate lines changed directions with each transformation and the colors of each House flashed at the center. Red for Blood and Beryl, the home of vampires and misfits. Green for Earth and Emerald, another popular place for witches and people that like to be left alone. Then, there was an iridescent color for Fire and Fluorite, the House currently most likely to fall apart, filled with hot-headed shifters.

The ring disappeared before it finished showing me each of the Houses that had once been what the humans called states and countries.

"This ring will allow you to move through the Houses without hassle," Johnathon said. "It is the only one of its kind and will be yours upon completion of the contract, should you accept."

My eyes stared at the mist where the ring had been pictured. No Man's Land had its problems, but I'd done enough damage to be left alone for the most part. While the idea of being able to slip in and out of the Houses without making noise was tempting, I still wasn't sold.

Just as I was about to reject the offer, the mist shifted again, showing more images. First, it was a burning building with blue flames, then it was a young woman with light-blonde hair blowing behind her. I couldn't see her face, but the energy she was shooting around was dark and ravaging everything in its path.

The third was of three small children, all younger than the age of ten. Two boys and one girl with tattered clothes and dirtied, bruised faces. Their lifeless bodies were tangled around each other inside a metal box, eyes thankfully all closed.

The image changed to a video. The witch was holding a little girl in her grasp, one with rosy cheeks and dark hair just like my little sister had.

My jaw cracked, and every inch of me burned with fury as I blinked, reminding myself that the girl in the video wasn't my Addie, but she was still someone's daughter and maybe sister. An innocent soul that hadn't deserved to have energy sucked from her as I watched the witch do.

As the color faded from the young girl's face, the witch carelessly dropped her to the ground. Just before she turned around, the scene faded away.

"These are just a few examples of the disasters we've stumbled upon," Johnathon spoke darkly, his tone matching my decreasing mood.

I sat up from the couch, my shoulders stiffening, and my feet dropped back to the carpeted floor. I didn't know these children. They were nothing to me. But that didn't matter, not after what happened to my sister. Anyone who would harm children deserved to die. Mercilessly.

"Where do I find her?" I demanded.

The glee in the disguised voice wasn't to be missed. "She's hidden in a coven. Her story is that she has hardly any magic, but do not believe her lies. No truths pass between her lips."

After seeing all those children, that wasn't going to be a problem. My hands squeezed shut so tightly that my knuckles popped.

"Send me the coven information and I'll leave straight away," I said, my voice gravelly.

"Very well, Mr. Barrett." Another image began to appear. "One last thing. This is the witch you will be looking for."

Within the mist was a portrait of a woman in her late twenties—maybe early thirties—with long hair that wasn't as blonde as I'd thought before. It was more of a platinum-white, ending just above her hips.

Her red lips were full and cheekbones sharp, giving her an exotic look when combined with her glowing, beige skin. Lastly, her eyes captured my attention. A light blue with a darker outer ring framed by long, thick lashes.

I wouldn't deny she was stunning to the eye, but I also knew her image could have been concocted. False beauty to further help the witch's search for power that didn't belong to her.

The mist began to retreat, and the edges of the parchment started to burn.

Whoever had sent this request had gone through a lot of effort to keep their identity hidden. That was normally a hard pass for me, but seeing those children had flipped a switch inside me.

This witch had to pay.

"That is all we have for you," the voice said. "The coordinates, along with any pertinent details, will replace this message. We'll be in touch once you've returned home."

As soon as he'd stopped speaking, ashes fell onto the floor between my legs, then a piece of paper floated down on top of the pile. I stared at it for several moments.

As much as I'd wanted to leave this alone, I knew I wouldn't be able to sleep after seeing what I had. I needed to figure out what the hell was going on.

Not for me, but for the memory of Addie.

I'd find the witch who had killed those kids, and I'd deliver the suffering that was rightly deserved.

CHAPTER TWO

KINSLEY

I sat at the edge of my coven within the House of Earth and Emerald, staring up at the bright moon. The surrounding trees hid me from the view of the coven, and I closed my eyes, trying to soak up the energy I could feel moving around me.

After all these years, one would think I'd have accepted my lot in life, but I hadn't been able to. Well, not entirely.

There were pieces I'd grown used to, like accepting how people had first seen me as nothing more than the orphan witch to be pitied. When I'd grown older, their view of me had changed to the weak…*broken* one to be kept at a distance.

Nobody wanted to be friends with a witch whose parents had abandoned her and who couldn't fully access her magic. After being kept at arm's length from my fellow coven members, I'd finally learned to stop caring what they thought and focus on what I believed.

Hiding in the woods, staying home by myself, training in the gym, talking to the moon as if it was my only friend… I had to discover what else was out in the world.

Though, my lack of a House ring prevented me from leaving anytime soon. Unless I wanted to risk No Man's Land on my own.

I'd been told that I wasn't allowed to have a ring for my own protection. That it wasn't safe outside of the protection of our coven for a nearly no-powered witch. That I was best with the ones who protected me.

There seemed to be a thin line between protection and captivity.

Though, No Man's Land was no joke. I wasn't naïve enough to think I could survive that cesspool on my own, and I'd yet to make any friends I could rely on that would watch my back when I finally fled the coven.

With a heavy sigh, I pushed up to my feet and gave the moon one last glance. "I guess it's time to go back to my cell…*house*."

If I were being honest with myself, I'd admit that the coven hadn't treated me *badly*. I'd been given food and clothes and always had a roof over my head, but there had never been a "home" for me.

No pseudo parents who gave a shit about me, merely rotating care-givers who made sure I never got into trouble. Once I'd become an adult, and it became clear that I wasn't going to be some remarkable witch, I'd been transitioned from living with different families every few months to a small studio space above the coven's gym.

My feet began carrying me back toward my apartment, and I shoved my hands in the pockets of my jeans as I trudged through the grassy field.

When I'd made it a dozen or so feet from the treeline, something stirred behind me. My shoulders stiffened and I glanced up, spotting the main part of the coven a mere fifty yards ahead of me. If I was a normal witch, I could simply teleport back to my house, but of course, I couldn't even conquer the most menial of magic abilities.

Knowing that and hearing whatever was behind me getting closer, I tilted my chin up, hung my arms loose at my sides, and strode forward as if I didn't have a clue that someone was lurking in the shadows.

If I was attacked, I wouldn't be completely defenseless. A benefit to failing all of my magic teachings was that I'd at least used those disap-pointments to excel in combat classes. Plus, living above the gym gave me all the after-hours access to training that I could want.

Physically, I could take down a couple-hundred-pound man, so there was at least that.

Another ten feet closer to the coven and my chest was feeling a little lighter. Maybe I'd just been imagining whatever I thought I'd heard in the trees…or maybe not.

"Kinsley Ash," a deep man's voice said from behind me.

I couldn't have heard him correctly. Nobody would ever be out here looking for me specifically.

A random attacker, sure, but someone using my full name? Not likely. I kept walking.

"Stop," the same voice demanded.

My left foot paused in the air, almost as if his command were laced with magic, but it didn't quite stick.

I slowly turned around, widening my stance and preparing myself for a fight.

If this guy wanted me, I wasn't going to be taken easily.

He stepped out of the shadows from the forest, and I sucked in a breath when my eyes took in his dark glare.

My heart momentarily stopped before it began racing again, and I felt myself being drawn toward the rigid stranger.

Mate.

This man… He was… *Mine.*

Feelings erupted inside me that I'd never experienced. My skin heated and my mouth ran dry while my heart felt like it was going to beat right out of my chest.

Was he going to take me away from this lowly existence I'd been living? Was this the answer I'd been searching for all these years while standing under the night's moon?

"I'm going to kill—" His words cut off as I assumed he'd finally realized the same thing I had.

We were mates. A bond created by the fates that could tie us together for life.

Yet, I hadn't missed the malice in his previous words or the way the moonlight showcased dark, menacing eyes directed right at me.

"You've got to be fucking kidding me," he snarled. Then he quickly added, "I reject you, Kinsley Ash."

Five words. That was all it took to cut me down.

To smother the softer emotions I'd so easily clung to for those brief seconds.

To shred any hope that I'd had for a life more than what I'd always known.

Still, my head shook. "No."

His head reared back, and I tried—yet failed—not to be enamored by his roguish features. He had thick, ebony hair that naturally seemed to swoop up by a couple of inches on the top and was just slightly shorter on the sides.

His arms were covered in black and grey tattoos starting above his short, black sleeves and ending at his fingertips. Hell, I could even see more of them peeking out from above the V in his T-shirt.

His lips begged to be nipped at, and his dark brows furrowed so tightly that I wouldn't have been surprised if there was a permanent wrinkle between them.

"No?" He growled. "What do you mean *no*?"

I took a step back and held my hand out. If he wasn't outright attacking me, I'd at least pretend like I had magic to maybe scare him with.

"I mean *no* to your rejection," I retorted with rising bravado. "You were about to say that you were going to kill someone, and I can only assume by your twisted, snarling face that you meant me. Well, I'm not in the mood to die. So let me repeat myself more clearly. No, I don't accept your rejection. Whoever you are."

A rumble built in his chest, and he shook his head as if he still didn't understand. "Quit playing your magic tricks on me, Witch."

Well, this guy might have known my name, but he obviously didn't *know* me.

Just as I was about to refute his statement, the sexy brute came charging at me. Acting on instinct, thanks to all those nights spent in the gym, my foot lifted and connected with his gut. His shoulders pushed forward from the impact, and I took the opportunity to allow my fist to meet his jaw.

The echoing crack made my lips curl upward, and again when I grabbed his neck and slammed my knee into his handsome face.

Such a pity.

Just when I was starting to think I had the upper hand, he recovered from whatever shock he'd been in and wrapped his arms around my waist, attempting to take me down.

His heated skin burned mine, and sorrow filled me at the realization that this man—supposedly the one meant just for me in this world—could be trying to kill me, but I shoved those feelings down and focused on not allowing my face to be pummeled.

When he began pushing me toward the ground, I wrapped an arm around his neck and used my body weight to press down on his head. His six-and-a-half-foot frame started to timber forward, but he reached for my thigh and flipped me up and over him.

I landed on the ground hard, the impact rattling my bones and sending stabbing sensations through me from head to toe.

"Fuck." I groaned. "Was that really necessary?"

He snarled in return and sat on me before I could get up. "Was it necessary to kill those kids?"

Now, it was my turn to be shocked…

"What are you—" Before I could finish my question, he punched me just beneath my neck. Like really fucking punched me.

Sure, I'd hit him first, but still, I was a little more than shocked by the impact.

Before I could physically respond, his hands covered my throat, but they only squeezed hard enough to keep me pinned. "You're not my mate. You're just using magic to trick me."

He spoke with conviction, but I could see the uncertainty in his cognac eyes that were darkening by the second.

"Listen, psycho stranger. I don't know who you think I am, but I hardly have any magic." My words were garbled, and the longer I spoke, the more my vocal cords burned from his touch, but I kept going. "And I wouldn't hurt a child, let alone multiple of them."

Flickers of something I didn't recognize appeared in his eyes, then he blinked several times before finally squeezing them tightly shut. The weight of his body wasn't leaving my neck, and even though I knew the truth, he seemed to be struggling a little too much with our predicament for me to allow him to keep me in this position.

With my not-mate distracted, I bucked my hips up and punched his kidney before attempting to roll out from under him. "Seriously. What is your problem?" I demanded, ignoring the stabbing pain in my cheek from his previous punch.

He grunted in reply and got up before me. The black boot on his right foot was coming right for my head. Instead of hoping I got out of the way in time, I raised my forearm, blocking the kick, and reaching up with my other hand to press on his knee.

A fun trick I'd learned throughout my years of training.

He winced, trying to stay upright, but there wasn't a chance in hell of that unless he wanted to risk breaking a bone or two.

With a triumphant smile, I watched as he fell back on his ass. Though, my glee only lasted a mere second before he was scrambling back to his feet.

The flickers I'd seen in his eyes before turned to flames, and I was pretty sure his skin was darkening with every step forward.

I'd sworn this guy was a wolf shifter from first sight, but no shifter I'd ever seen visit the coven could do anything like that.

Thanks to the distraction, he was able to grab a hold of me again. His fingers dug into my biceps, pressing my arms into my sides and forcing me to remain immobile. "Who are you?" he spat.

"Kinsley Ash. A powerless witch that's never left this coven," I answered.

His head shook roughly. "Lies."

I tried meeting his fiery gaze, but he wouldn't focus on my stare. "Maybe you can tell me why you wanted to kill me in the first place, and we can answer some of each other's questions?"

Reasoning with a psychopath didn't seem like the best solution, but I didn't see any other way out of this. Sure, thanks to the shitty-but-should-have-been-amazing mate connection between us, he couldn't kill me, but that didn't mean he couldn't hurt me if he wanted to.

And I was more than sure he wanted to.

CHAPTER THREE

GRAYSON

I'd fucking known better. I should have listened to my instincts. I shouldn't have taken this job. What was supposed to be a simple *snatch, grab, and maybe kill* had turned into something more, something I wasn't sure I could believe.

Normally, it was easy for me to decipher the truth from any lie, but when Kinsley spoke, my mind felt foggy as it fought between believing what I was told and what she was saying.

The mate bond, if it was even real, was the last thing I needed.

I'd always known the possibility of meeting my mate was there, but I'd hoped that day would never come.

Now, looking everywhere but at Kinsley's tempting, cerulean eyes, I tried to reject her again.

"If you accept my rejection, I won't kill you," I bargained.

The job didn't actually require me to take her life, so I wasn't lying. Though, taking her life had been preferable after seeing the photos of those children.

She scoffed in my face. "Bullshit. You can't even look me in the eyes when you say that. How about we back up a hot minute and you tell me why the hell you're here?"

The sincerity of her confusion only served to make matters worse for me.

Nobody knew of my extra ability to tell truth from lie. At least, none who were still alive. Well, aside from D, but he wouldn't have anything to do with this. I knew that without a single doubt.

And this mate bond… Could it have been fabricated by a powerful enough witch?

I hadn't thought so, but the more muddled my thoughts became, the more I believed—and hoped—that might be the case.

I secured her wrist and jerked her toward me. Her chest collided with mine, but I ignored the heat that scorched through me from the contact.

"You don't get to ask the questions here," I snarled. "You are my prisoner and nothing more. Keep your mouth shut and this will go a lot easier for the both of us."

She surprised me when she used her other hand to punch me right in the neck, causing my throat to ache instantly. It was just another thing to add to my confusion. She kept using physical defensive moves instead of magical ones.

Thanks to my shock, she broke free of my hold and began running in the opposite direction, back toward her coven.

With a growl, I lengthened my stride and wrapped both arms around her waist. "I said you're coming with me. Whatever magic you're using might prevent me from killing you, but that won't stop me from taking you where you belong."

She struggled against me, and once again, I was impressed by her strength. "And where would that be?"

"No Man's Land. To pay for your crimes."

She went limp in my hold, possibly trying to use dead weight to throw me off again, but that wasn't going to work with me.

"What crimes?" she asked with a heavy sigh when I began walking toward the treeline again.

My chest rumbled. My instinct was to answer her question, but I didn't trust this woman. Not after what I'd seen.

With the pull between us, I knew it was better to keep my mouth shut.

"Seriously?" she scoffed. "That's how you're going to do this? Show up here, accuse me of something heinous you won't even give me details on, and then stay silent?"

Yep. That was exactly how it was going to be.

I wasn't sure if it was because my silence was the best choice for the situation or for myself. There were too many conflicting thoughts, and until I felt more confident about the situation, silence was my friend.

Having her pressed against me wasn't ideal when my body and heart were longing for her only minutes after having met her. A part of me wanted to lift her up until our faces were level so that I could capture her lips before claiming her as mine.

With a hard shake of my head, I increased my speed and pushed the disgusting thoughts out of my mind. I needed to get the fuck out of here and away from this seductress.

I'd thought she was too beautiful from the picture, and I'd been right.

I chuckled darkly as I continued to drag her next to me. She probably looked like an old hag in reality and this was her disguise to get past others.

Well, not me. Not today.

"What's so funny?" she demanded.

I raised a brow and *tsked*. She still didn't get how this was going to work.

I was in charge here. She didn't get to ask the questions.

"If you don't shut your mouth, I'm going to shut it for you," I deadpanned. "I can still hurt you when I feel inclined, and I get closer to that every second."

Besides the initial punch—which I'd immediately regretted—there wasn't a part of me that wanted to actually hurt her anymore. I wasn't sure what to do about that fact besides do my best to keep her quiet and get back to my Jeep, which was waiting just outside the boundary line of Earth and Emerald.

A vice tightened around my core, and my chest rumbled. Fabricated or not, the bond was affecting me more than I was willing to admit aloud.

My grip around Kinsley's waist tightened, and I ground my teeth together as I considered my options and what I did know. I knew that I hadn't sensed lies from Johnathon nor Kinsley, but one of them had to be lying.

I was leaning toward the latter because Johnathon had those images, but then again, my abilities worked on words, not pictures...

Fuck. This really wasn't good, and this would also be the last time I didn't listen to my instincts. Fucking magic was too devious. I'd let my curiosity and emotions get the better of me.

She whimpered and began reaching for my shoulders. "I take it you're feeling inclined to hurt me now."

Apparently so.

The more disappointing fact was how I loosened my hold without thinking twice.

Instead of me continuing to drag her along at my side, Kinsley managed to get her feet back under herself and walk.

I released her waist but kept a tight grip on her forearm. "If you run again, I will catch you and it will be painful."

Her mesmerizing eyes flicked up and caught mine in their hold. They glazed over, and she turned away, looking toward the ground. "I should have known better."

I didn't fucking care what she should have known. I didn't fucking care that she looked like I'd just killed her dog.

Fuck!

Why couldn't I sense her magic? Why was the only thing pulsing through me the maddening bond that I didn't want to believe was real?

She sniffled and used her free hand to swipe angrily at her cheeks. Her nearly-white hair fell forward as her head lowered more and hid her face from me.

Though I should have been happy about that, I stupidly found myself filled with more disappointment.

Grunting, I picked up speed, not realizing that she'd have to run to keep up with me until she began breathing heavily and my dick got excited from all the panting noises she was making.

This wasn't fucking good.

I stopped abruptly, and her shoulder slammed into my rigid arm, knocking her to the ground. Well, almost.

She'd gone from badass fighter to this pathetic thing. I wasn't sure what to think about that, either.

My hold on her arm was still tight, so she more dangled above the dirt instead of laying in it. She didn't make a move to right herself as I stood there, glaring at her twisted, yet tempting body and taking deep breaths to get my shit together.

I'd never failed a mission. Hell, I hadn't even had one go wrong to the point where I was scrambling, but this… This was new territory for me.

I'd fought witches, vampires, fae, and more. Fought them all and survived because that was what I was best at, but for the first time, a voice inside me wished this one target would overpower me and run.

No. I wouldn't let that happen. No matter my previous reservation about this assignment. I'd seen the pictures. I'd heard the truth in the words Johnathon had spoken.

A witch had killed those children.

This witch.

Right?

My shoulders stiffened, and I reached down without looking at Kinsley so that I could throw her over my shoulder. I couldn't wait for her to act like an adult and walk on her own. I needed to get to the Jeep and start the drive back to my house.

The trip would require me to sit next to her for sixteen hours while I sped down the interstates toward my cabin's location in the middle of No Man's Land.

I should have bargained for a fucking portal spell to get us back sooner, but I'd thought she would be a corpse by the time I'd started driving. Not a temptress seated next to me.

Maybe I could knock her out and tie her to the back seat.

Shit. The only thing appealing about that thought was tying her up.

With a loud huff, Kinsley punched me first in my side, then right at the center of my spine.

That shit didn't feel very good.

I pulled her forward and cradled her against my chest, squeezing tightly until she was boxed in against herself.

Her sharp eyes glared up at me. "You're a dick."

I glanced down at her briefly, keeping all emotion from my face and tone. "I had no idea."

She made a grumbling sound from her chest that piqued the interest of my wolf, but I ignored his longing for this moment.

She wasn't our mate.

She was a murdering witch who needed to be put down.

Only, I couldn't be the one to do that like I'd hoped.

At least when she was dead, the bond would end.

If it was even real.

My lip lifted, but I kept my snarls to myself as I trudged forward through the dense forest. The moon shone high above, lighting the path I needed to take back to the Jeep.

"What's your name?" she asked, her voice calmer than it had been before.

Still, I ignored her.

"Fine," she said a little chipperly. "If you won't tell me, I'll call you…Richard. Seems fitting, wouldn't you agree?"

No, I wouldn't, I thought.

"So, Richard. Are you like an assassin or something?" she mused. "I bet it pisses you off that you can't kill me. Luck hasn't really ever been on my side, and I thought maybe that was changing when I saw you…until you attacked me like a fucking psychopath. But then I realized maybe I was right to believe you were my ticket away from the coven. I at least still have a chance to figure out who the hell you think I am."

She paused, and I absolutely didn't watch while she licked her plump red lips and swallowed, then continued to ramble.

"You might know my name, but did you know that every step you take is the farthest I've ever been from that coven back there?" she asked genuinely, though she didn't wait for an answer. "Well, at least that I know of. I was apparently left here when I was a baby, and since nobody knew where I'd come from, the coven bounced me from home to home, but they never gave me a family. I'm not even a member of this House."

That last bit gave me pause. There were no lies I could taste from her words, but how could she live here and not be part of Earth and Emerald?

My eyes quickly roamed over her neck and hands. There was no ring or necklace to be seen. Either she'd hidden the House object, or she was telling the truth.

I'd have felt better if I believed the former.

She continued to ramble, and I had to admit, it wasn't a tactic anyone had used on me before. She didn't seem the least bit scared of me. Though, that was probably because of the mate bond. Her mind was telling her she was safe when that was the furthest thing from the truth.

At least, that was what I kept trying to tell myself.

"So, I feel like I should be more upset that you're kidnapping me, but maybe this is what my life needed," she said brightly. "A little shakeup, you know? I've been going to the edge of the woods for years now, staring up at the moon and wishing for more, just like I had been tonight. Then, *bam*! There you were. Sure, I'd rather you didn't try to kill me or think I'm a monster, but maybe I need to be grateful for the situation, regardless of all that."

I finally broke. I couldn't take her nonsense. "You are either the dumbest person I've ever met or the smartest."

She smirked, staring up at my face, but I wouldn't fully look at her. I couldn't.

"I bet the fact that you don't know which I am pisses you the fuck off." Her words were a punch to the chest, because she was absolutely fucking right.

But like hell was I going to admit that out loud.

CHAPTER FOUR

KINSLEY

Firstly, what the fucking shit was happening with my life? Secondly, this guy was like ice. I'd tried to break him with my fighting moves, then by playing broken, followed by talking his ear off, but still, he gave me nothing about why I was being taken from my so-called home.

Though, I hadn't been lying about anything I'd said. After he'd stopped trying to actively hurt me, I realized, while this wasn't the best-case scenario, he was giving me what I'd been wanting.

I was leaving the coven, walking away from Earth and Emerald, and I had protection. Of course, that last word was used lightly and he would probably gladly let someone else kill me if given the chance, but I wasn't worried.

Well, I was trying not to be.

Hence my rambling.

"How far are we walking?" I asked. "Where are we going? Oh, yeah. No Man's Land, but isn't that place, like, huge? Are you going to carry me the whole time so that I don't run away, or do you have a portal spell? I'd make one, but I can't."

I paused briefly, but he still wasn't in the mood to chat. Thankfully, I wasn't easily deterred.

"Not that you asked, but I don't really have any magic," I said. "I can heal quickly, run faster than most of the witches, and my hearing isn't too bad, but outside of a few sparks, magic isn't really my thing. I've been told that's probably why my parents abandoned me. Pretty fucked-up, huh?"

His jaw at least tensed at that last bit, confirming he wasn't completely heartless.

"So, Richard. I'm pretty sure you won't answer any of my questions, but since you know a little about me, let me pretend I know something about you." My voice deepened as I pretended that I was him, hoping to further annoy him into conversation. "'I was an only child. I get my shit attitude from my parents, who failed to teach me any manners. I hate people and animals and anything good left in this fucked world. I get off on—'"

He growled so deeply, I felt the vibrations in my own chest. "Shut the fuck up, Kinsley."

I winked at him. Probably not the smartest thing, but I was on a roll. "Or what?"

His head lowered and turned until his dark eyes with flickers of forest-green flames glowered at me. "Or I will *make* you."

"How?" I pressed.

His brows furrowed. "How what?"

"How are you going to make me shut up? Because I don't have any intention of stopping my blabbering until you answer some of my questions." My face was dead serious. I had very little to lose at this point.

If I didn't find out exactly what he thought I'd done, there was no way I was going to be able to save myself. At least, not one I could see yet.

His gaze moved until he was staring up at the dark sky. "Fuck."

The singular word was spoken so quietly, I almost wasn't sure he'd said it, but triumph filled me anyway. I was getting to him. That meant there was something in him that saw me as a person and not a target or whatever I'd been to him when he'd first shown up.

I could work with that.

For the first time in my life, I was grateful to the coven for never really accepting me. My upbringing just might be the very thing that saved me from this man, because there was no way I was going to be the damsel in distress.

I would fight until my last breath to defend myself in whatever manner was necessary.

My next play was the connection I felt to him.

He might have thought I'd been able to fabricate it, but I knew that wasn't true, which meant whatever empathy he was feeling was real. I needed to use that against him.

"*Okaaaay*." I drew the word out slowly with a heavy sigh. "We seem to be at a stalemate, but what if we started over? I mean, I'm all snug as a bug in a rug in your arms. That seems rather personal, don't you think? Let's pretend you didn't want to kill me before you realized you couldn't, and we can get to know each other. You know, since this bond isn't going anywhere quick."

His tightening hold on me—which thankfully didn't hurt any longer—and resounding grunt was my only reply.

"Richard." I repeated his made-up name. "Doesn't quite flow off the tongue for someone like you. Are you ready to share yet?" Silence and a stony-yet-handsome face were his answer. "Fine. We'll stick with 'Richard' for now, then. Where are you from? I didn't see a House ring on your hand, and I don't feel a necklace beneath your shirt. Are you all gruff and tough because you've been surviving in No Man's Land?"

A twitch appeared in his jaw. Huh. Maybe that was his tell. I might have been on to something.

"That's pretty badass," I said, going for a little ego stroking. Not that he probably needed it. He was sexy and strong and there was no way that fucker didn't know it. "I considered running away to No Man's Land, but the last...*foster mom*, you could call her... She convinced me that I'd sooner die. So I spent the last eight years training my body to fight back since, as I said before, magic had failed me."

Still nothing from him.

Damn, he was good.

I lifted a hand and concentrated on the tiny bits of energy I had inside me. When nothing happened, I squeezed my eyes tightly, begging the magic to come forward and show this dick how little power I actually had. He needed to believe I was telling the truth.

When nothing came, I growled in frustration and reopened my eyes. When I did, he was staring at me again with his head tilted to the side, and his jaw was slightly relaxed.

"What?" I asked.

"What were you just trying to do?" he asked, his voice filled with… maybe surprise? Or it might have been confusion.

I shrugged within his arms. "I wanted to show you that there is no way possible I could have used my magic to commit any kind of crime. I'm nearly powerless. A broken witch."

While I was still attempting to tap into whatever emotions the bond should have been trying to persuade him to feel, my words weren't a lie, and neither were the feelings they evoked inside me.

Not-Richard went back to looking ahead and briefly, so did I. I'd never been to these parts of the forest. The stories of women taken as slaves and all the murders in No Man's Land that I'd been told hadn't seem too farfetched. Though, if this guy had survived there—assuming some of what I'd said earlier was right—then maybe it wasn't all bad.

The large oaks began to thin, and I could see a road ahead. "What happens when we get out of the trees? Will we be out of Earth and Emerald, then?"

"We left your House five minutes ago," he answered, shocking the hell out of me.

Maybe my plan wasn't so asinine after all.

"How do you know that?" I asked. "Was there a sign I missed while I was talking or had my eyes closed? Or have you been here plenty of times before and just know?"

His head turned toward me once more. "I'm having a difficult time believing you're that stupid."

The tone of his words was flat, making it hard for me to decide if I should be offended by his statement or not…

"I don't think I'm stupid," I said. "Sheltered. Naïve. Inexperienced. All of those, yes. But not stupid when given the opportunity to learn."

Another delicious rumble built from deep inside his chest, but he seemed to be all out of verbal responses.

Just when I was ready to go on my next tangent, I caught sight of the Jeep he'd mentioned. There wasn't a top on it. Just a black roll cage above the navy-blue body.

He eyed the front of the vehicle, then the back, before setting me down. His hands grabbed my biceps, positioning me until I was standing in front of him. "Don't piss me off or I will tie a rope around your waist before securing it to the top bar and let you drag behind the Jeep while I travel at eighty miles an hour down the freeway."

I glanced quickly behind him, then back at his face. "Oh. Was that you being nice back there? Cool. Super good to know," I droned.

He might have been a mostly unfeeling prick, but even he wouldn't have missed my sarcasm there.

Though there was no insight as to what he thought of my words because in the next second, he spun me around, lifted me up by the hold he still had on my arms, and tossed me into the front seat. "If you sit there and keep your mouth shut for at least thirty minutes, I'll tell you my name."

Oh, he was negotiating. I could work with that.

"Does that mean every half-hour I get to ask a question?" There was no hiding my grin. I could possibly agree to this.

His lip lifted into a lovely snarl, then he stormed around the front of the vehicle.

I was totally winning here.

Never mind that I was still being taken somewhere against my will.

Well, mostly against my will.

Richard pressed a button on the dashboard, and a thrum of energy ignited around us. The motor turned over, a low, rumbling sound echoing from the exhaust.

He turned the wheel and maneuvered the jeep around while I put on my seatbelt. Something I'd only ever read about in books.

My stomach churned as his speed increased, and I pressed my hands over my face, doing my best to hold in the groan that badly wanted to escape.

One of his fingers poked my shoulders hard, likely leaving a bruise. "What do you think you're doing?"

I gagged, keeping my eyes closed. "Trying not to throw up in your car."

He slammed on the brakes, and my boobs were hugged a little too tightly by the chest strap.

"What the fuck did you do that for?" I snapped, but before he could answer, I turned my head until it was hanging over the door, thankful there were no windows on this thing, and vomited. Hard.

"Fucking hell," he grumbled before I heard his door open and close.

My head was pounding, and my mouth tasted like rotten food.

Okay, maybe I should have been more grateful to have never been in a moving vehicle before.

I could see his black boots a few feet from where my puddle of disgustingness was glistening under the moonlight. Once I was done gagging, his finger pressed against my clammy forehead and pushed my head back up. "You're faking that."

My eyes rolled, and I sighed. "Who the fuck would fake needing to throw up? It's not the most pleasant thing to do. If I were faking anything, I'd have pretended to pass out."

His eyes darkened, and he stared so long at my face, I was sure he was seeing straight into my soul. *Fuck.* Why did I want to reach forward, grab the back of his neck, and find out what he tasted like? Though, maybe now wouldn't have been the best time. Vomit breath probably wasn't all that attractive, but what would I really know about that?

I was twenty-eight years old, and I'd never been kissed. That was what being the pariah of your coven did, made it so you had very little social skills and zero life experiences.

Though, I'd read books. I could picture a smolder, and this dude had his perfected with a sprinkle of asshole.

He stepped forward, avoiding my mess, and reached past me into the jeep. His fingers lifted the latch on the storage box in front of me, then pulled out a napkin, shoving it at me. "Clean yourself up. I don't want to smell you the entire drive back."

I forced my lashes to flutter at him. "You're my very own Prince Charming."

His eyes squinted as if he didn't get the reference. To be expected, though. I didn't presume a psycho like him read too many books.

Maybe we could both teach each other a thing or two about life…

Hell. What was wrong with me?

Mate or not… Sexy as fuck to look at or not… Dude still tried to kill me.

But he didn't do it in the end, a hopeful voice whispered in my mind.

Maybe not, but that had nothing to do with him thinking I was telling the truth and everything to do with fate.

That fickle bitch.

She'd done me dirty this time.

CHAPTER FIVE

GRAYSON

Exactly thirty minutes after I'd gotten back into the driver's seat, Kinsley cleared her throat while keeping her eyes on the center of the road, which I'd advised her to do so she wouldn't get sick again. Not because I was being nice, but because we didn't have time for her weak stomach.

"How close was I with 'Richard'?" she asked, a bit of glee in her tone and a smile playing on her cherry lips.

"Grayson, so not even a little close," I muttered.

Her fingers danced over her knees, and she chanced a glance my way. "What about a last name?"

"No." If she didn't already know it, she didn't need to.

The fact that she seemed truly inept about all things of the outside world had me second-guessing everything that I was doing. I hated to admit that I was worried the only reason I was questioning anything was because of the bond. The longer she sat next to me, the more it was building.

Uncertainty wasn't something I was familiar with, and I fucking hated it.

Had I been sent to kidnap, and possibly kill, an innocent woman?

Had I missed the omissions from Johnathon's words, or had I heard what I'd wanted to once I'd seen those kids?

I didn't think anyone knew about my family since their deaths had occurred before I'd made a name for myself, but if Johnathon had figured out my past and used that to motivate me, did he also know who I was beyond the wolf shifter I portrayed?

That question was quickly rising on my list of priorities.

Kinsley gasped. "Stop!" I ignored her and she reached over to punch me in the arm. "I said, *fucking stop.*"

My foot slammed on the brakes, not because I was listening to her, but because it was time to teach her a fucking lesson in manners.

"You can't just—" Before I could finish my sentence, she was already unbuckled and had leapt from her seat, not bothering to use the door handle, and landed on the road.

She ran for the forest, and I growled loudly. Was she seriously fucking running from me again?

Once I was out of the jeep and headed in her direction, I realized she hadn't made it far. Not only that, but I saw the reason for her panic.

A white horse—no, wait. That was a damn unicorn lying in the grass.

Kinsley was leaning over the fallen being, her hands covered in its dark-blue blood. She looked back at me, tears in her eyes. "We have to help her."

Fuck. No, we really didn't.

"She's as good as dead, based on that amount of blood," I said harshly. "Now, let's get out of here before I have to kill the people who did this because they're still looking for a fight."

I reached for Kinsley's arm, but she jerked away from my touch. "I'm not leaving until she's passed or we help her somehow. Nobody should die alone."

Her sincerity felt like a smack across the face.

The more she spoke—at least, when she wasn't trying to annoy me to death—the more I realized that whoever had sent me after her was wrong. Though, there was still more to this story, and I needed to decide if sticking around was worth potentially starting something I didn't want to finish.

Kinsley stroked the animal's matted white fur. It appeared as if something had slashed a sword down her front flank, but then I noticed that crimson also coated the pale purple horn protruding from her head.

I glanced around, and about ten feet behind the unicorn, there was a dead body with a sword lying next to him.

My head tilted down toward the mystical animal I'd previously believed was extinct. "Can you shift?"

Her eyes blinked twice, and she blew air through her nose that made me think she was frustrated, so I took that as a *no*.

"If you care so much about her wellbeing, then heal her," I said to Kinsley, hoping this would be the moment she revealed herself.

Her light-blue eyes looked up at me with continuous tears falling down her cheeks. "I would if I could, but I… I'm a broken witch."

That wasn't the first time she'd said that to me, and I hated that my instinct was to believe her. I hated even more that I'd been duped and still couldn't be sure who was lying.

The unicorn nuzzled Kinsley's hand and made a softer whinny noise.

Shit. Maybe I had my answer right there.

From what I knew about unicorn shifters, they were some of the most powerful beings in the world, born from a strong shifter that mated with a fae or angel, unless they were a dark unicorn born from a demon. Regardless of their heritage, they could tell good intentions from bad, could hide their true identities, could glimpse the future, and hell, I was pretty sure they could even heal…

My gaze flicked back to the dead man. He was a wolf shifter. I could scent as much. While he might have been a good hunter, there was no way he should have been able to get the jump on this particular supernatural.

"You're not even hurt, are you?" I asked with a slight growl to my words.

Kinsley gasped at me. "Look at her…or him. Of course it's hurt."

"Unicorns are only female. So, it's definitely 'her' and no, she's not," I said with absolute certainty. "You can quit the act and shift, but you better be prepared to tell us why you were waiting for us."

Kinsley's shocked face was another thing that had me beginning to finally accept that she really was who she was saying, but I shoved those thoughts aside for the moment.

The unicorn actually rolled her turquoise eyes while silver energy shimmered over her body. The gaping wound stitched itself back together before she got up on four legs. Kinsley was up and moving a few steps closer to me as the opal-white unicorn swished her iridescent colored tail back and forth.

"Shift," I demanded.

Her head lowered, pointing the tip of her horn at me.

"You don't scare me," I droned.

She made a weird noise, then her body covered with that same silver power. Within the blink of an eye, she was standing on two feet, dressed in black leggings and an oversized, light-pink T-shirt.

She glared at me, then moved her still-turquoise eyes to Kinsley and stepped forward.

Before I could stop anything from happening, the unicorn hugged her and squealed. "Oh, I'm so excited to finally meet you!"

I had no fucking clue where this glee was coming from, but one thing I knew was that an already fucked situation just got even more complicated.

Kinsley's arms hung there loosely. "Uh…you, too. I'm glad you're okay."

The unicorn backed up a pace. She flicked dark blue, nearly midnight-colored hair over her shoulder and the moonlight made her brawny skin seem as if it were almost sparkling. There was a round, youthfulness to her face, but the way her turquoise eyes assessed me made me think she was much older than her twenties.

"Of course, I am," the unicorn said cheerfully. "I'm Lia, and you're Kinsley." Then, she pointed at me and glared. "And you're Grayson Barrett."

Fucking hell, this wasn't good.

Kinsley glanced between the two of us, again seeming confused as hell about everything happening. "What happened to you, and how do you know us?"

Lia smiled softly and raised a flippant hand in the air. "Oh, nothing happened to me that's important now you're here." Then she looked at me again, ignoring Kinsley's second question. "Have you figured it out yet?"

I glowered at her. "Figured what out?"

"Do I have to do everything?" she muttered, more to herself than to either of us, then pressed a hand over Kinsley's chest.

A bright light grew over Kinsley, and her mouth went slack, but she wasn't tensing up, so I didn't assume she was in pain. And I didn't want to admit that was something that would have bothered me immensely.

When Lia stopped whatever she was doing, she asked pointedly, "And now?"

I ignored the cocky unicorn and focused on Kinsley. When I'd first seen her, I'd thought it was weird I couldn't sense much power from her, but I'd thought a smart witch who was stealing the lifeforce from children probably wouldn't flaunt that around.

Then, I'd just dismissed the lack of magic for…well, for nothing. I'd been too fucking distracted by her to pay close attention to anything that seemed off.

Now, though, I was still sensing energy coming from Kinsley, but there was something else there that hadn't been before—or just not as obviously, because there was no way I would have missed that.

"You're a wolf shifter?" I asked, distrust lacing my darkly spoken words.

Kinsley laughed right in my face. "You're hilarious."

"Oh." Lia's eyes widened, and then she grabbed both of Kinsley's shoulders before bending her forward so their foreheads could press together.

Kinsley's eyes turned to saucers then darted my way, but I wasn't stepping in. I wanted to know what the hell was going on and what I'd gotten myself into.

Lia made a humming noise, but no other visible energy showed like it had before. They stood together until Kinsley finally relaxed and closed her eyes. Another minute after that, she finally gasped and stumbled back. "How…? No." Her head shook furiously. "That's not possible."

The unicorn nodded. "There is very little that's impossible in this world now, something you're going to be learning a lot about soon."

"What does that mean?" I demanded.

Lia turned and stepped toward me, but I backed up, my chest rumbling loudly. "Don't fucking touch me."

She sighed and brushed thick strands of hair behind her ear. "Listen to me, Grayson. I'm not here to trick you or get in your way." She pointed back to Kinsley. "I'm here to protect her. Unfortunately, you're a part of her now. So, you can either accept that I'm not going anywhere and make this easier on all of us. Or we can have it out right here and now, then move on. Either way, the three of us are going to get in that jeep and head west."

Fucking future-seeing supernaturals.

When I merely glared at her and crossed my arms over my chest, she smirked in return. "You know I'm telling the truth."

Sure as shit, I did, but then again…maybe not. Maybe the powers I kept mostly hidden from the world weren't working the way they should have been. I'd allowed my emotions to be distracted by the image of the dead children, then the bond appearing, and Kinsley not being anything like I'd expected. Now, we'd been joined by a fucking unicorn.

For the first time in forever, I wasn't sure what to believe, and that did something to my insides that I didn't care for.

"Prove it," I said.

She didn't hesitate to reach out and lay her palm on the center of my chest. As soon as she'd touched me, I sucked in a breath and closed my eyes.

Images of me with my baby sister, Addie, flashed through my mind, and then of me shifted into my flaming-green wolf while Addie giggled from her spot in the grass.

Her dark curls bounced over her shoulders, and her dimpled cheeks puffed up as she smiled brightly.

With a roar, I shoved the unicorn away from me. "I said not to fucking touch me."

"Do you believe me?" she asked without missing a beat.

I had to turn around before I answered her, because I was tempted to lash out with my darker half. It was the one part of me that I was equally thankful for yet also hated.

The demon in me that had come from my father.

The curse that had killed my family and left me alone in this godforsaken world.

The powers that allowed me to channel my rage by searching for piece-of-shit people who didn't deserve to continue breathing.

"Um, can we come back to me for a minute?" Kinsley asked with labored breath. "Who the fuck wants to explain to me how I wouldn't have sensed a wolf inside me after all these years?"

She was rubbing her chest so hard that a red spot formed on her skin beneath her fingers.

The bond I hadn't wanted to accept as truth tugged on my emotions, but I stopped myself. I wasn't the one who was going to console her.

I wasn't the person she needed, even if she wasn't a magic-stealing murderer.

Lia sighed at me. "You're being ridiculous."

I watched as the unicorn went to Kinsley and quietly whispered to her. I observed closely how Kinsley nodded softly, pressing her lips together while her eyes remained wide.

Then, I forced my feet to take me back to the jeep. I needed a minute—or forever—to figure out what the fuck I was going to do now.

CHAPTER SIX

KINSLEY

There should have been a point long before I'd spotted a dying unicorn on the side of the road that I'd begun to freak the fuck out, but clearly, I was more broken than I'd realized. Well, maybe not broken, but twisted, for sure.

How was it possible that I wasn't a witch? I'd been raised in a coven. I could make sparks—on occasion—with my hands. I could… Well, fuck. That was about it.

But wouldn't someone have said something to me? Wouldn't they have kicked me out of the coven instead of passing me around from house to house until they'd finally given me the apartment?

I didn't understand how any of this could have been true. Yet… there was a new warmth inside my chest. I'd always thought I imagined the feeling and had only felt it when sitting beneath the moon and wishing for something more out of my life.

Had I known deep down?

No, that wasn't possible. Being anything else besides a witch had never crossed my mind, but I'd been sure I was meant for more than the coven I'd been locked away in.

Lia came back to me. Her touch was gentle and soothing while her bright eyes held my stare. She whispered to me quietly about how everything was going to be okay now and that there was no reason to freak out.

That was fucking easy for the unicorn to say.

When I'd first seen her lying on the side of the road, I'd thought she'd been a horse. Those are from the human days and rare nowadays, but no, she'd been so much more than that. A supernatural that I'd thought was more of a myth than anything else.

A mother-freaking unicorn.

"I won't let anything happen to you, Kinsley," she said. That finally broke me out of my stupor, along with watching Grayson walk back to the jeep. Though, he'd yet to give me any real answers, so I didn't concern myself with his distance.

My brows furrowed at Lia. "What do you even mean by that? How do you know who I am? *Who* are you?"

She looped her arm through mine and guided us farther away from where we'd found her and closer to where the jeep was parked in the middle of the road. Grayson was now leaning against the passenger's door.

"Like I said before, my name is Lia. I'm a unicorn shifter and the last of my kind. I've been hidden for years, but then, one day, I knew I had to come find you."

"How?" I swallowed thickly.

Her cheeks darkened. "Well, I began dreaming about you."

Well, that wasn't fucking creepy at all.

"But we're getting ahead of ourselves here," she continued. "Do you know anything about unicorns?"

I shook my head. "After seeing them in the old children's books, I thought they were make-believe."

She leaned her cheek against my shoulder like we were long-lost friends. "That was what we hoped people would believe after we escaped from our portal to here, but my time for hiding has ended. At least, to a point."

"What does that mean?" I asked as we kept walking.

At that point, we'd made it past the jeep and were a dozen or so yards away from Grayson. I was surprised he wasn't raging about his prisoner being away from him, but I tried not to think too much about him. As much as the connection to him would allow me.

"It means that centuries ago, my kind lived in Arcadia until we were hunted to near extinction," she said softly. "I came here with my grandparents about sixty years ago and never saw anyone else from my family again. We hid amongst the humans for a long time until Pappy fell ill. I never knew what happened to him, but when he died, Gammy didn't last much longer."

I reached a hand up and wrapped my fingers around her hand, which was holding on to my bicep. "I'm sorry, Lia. I can understand what it's like to not have family, but I've never had to lose anyone I cared about."

She sniffled lightly. "And I hope you never have to. Well, at least not for a long time." Her steps slowed, and she turned to face me. "One of my abilities is to glimpse the future. I saw you were going to be here, and I knew I needed to be as well."

My eyes cast back to where we'd found her. "But you were attacked. I'm so sorry."

Lia's dark lips tugged downward. "That was actually intentional. I didn't know how else to get you to stop without resorting to standing in the middle of the road, which didn't seem safe, given who I knew would be driving. Though, I hadn't expected that I'd need to kill the shifter. He'd scented my blood after I gave myself the wound and didn't take my warning pokes for what they were."

I wanted to be irritated that she'd purposefully gotten herself hurt, and subsequently killed someone, but there wasn't a single part of me that was. Mostly because if what she was saying was true, the guy deserved to die for hunting a fellow supernatural.

"But why me?" I asked.

She shrugged and glanced briefly behind us. "You need to know who you are, and I need to save you from something. Outside of that, the details are rather fuzzy. Well, besides knowing we need to go to Fire and Fluorite. That's where we'll find more answers."

Grayson was suddenly standing next to me again. "I'm not stepping foot in that cesspool of idiots. Plus, the place is probably burned down by now."

I tilted my head at him. "Why? I thought they were one of the stronger Houses?"

"Stupidity sometimes looks a lot like bravery, but that doesn't make them strong," Grayson answered gruffly. "The last two leaders were dumb enough to get themselves killed and now there are factions within the House creating a war that's bound to affect more than just Fire and Fluorite. I'd rather stay out of it."

Lia twirled a lock of midnight-colored hair around her finger. "Well, you're welcome to stay out of it, but I'm taking Kinsley there."

Grayson's fingers wrapped around my wrist, and he pulled me tightly against his side. "You're not taking her anywhere."

Rage rose up inside me, a feeling unlike I'd ever known. My chest burned with fire, and my muscles coiled. I badly needed to exert whatever this was before I risked combustion. I didn't like the aggressive way Grayson touched me or his attitude toward Lia, and for the first time in my life…I felt confident enough to do something about that without suffering severe consequences.

My other hand slammed down on where he was holding me, and then I raised my knee right into his crotch. "Don't fucking touch me when you're angry."

He groaned and wobbled backward but didn't drop to his knees like I'd been hoping he would.

When his head lifted, the dark flames in his irises were back and Lia stepped between us. "I didn't think you were who I needed to save her from, but don't think I can't take you down, Demon Wolf."

My audible gasp had both of them looking at me. "You're a demon?" I whispered.

Could this night get any fucking weirder *or* worse?

Never mind. I hadn't meant to ask that, Universe, because I knew things absolutely could and I'd really rather they didn't.

Lia moved out of the way as Grayson finally stood straight again, looking me dead in the eyes. "I'm a wolf shifter and demon hybrid. A big difference from being full demon. I promise you that. And if you think to tell anyone that information, you'll be wishing I'd have been able to kill you when I found you. I would have been more merciful, then."

The darkly spoken threat didn't bother me nearly as much as wondering what demon abilities he might have had. I'd heard whispers of demons gracing this Earth before, but thankfully, most of them kept to their world, which had two names I couldn't ever remember...

Shit, I never thought I'd meet one, let alone be mated to one.

Then again, I never thought I'd be a wolf shifter instead of a broken witch, either.

Was I really a wolf shifter? How could I have never transformed before? I might not have ever been out in the real world, but I didn't think a wolf could be suppressed for years without the human losing their mind.

"Why don't we get in the vehicle?" Lia suggested. "It might not be safe out here for much longer."

Grayson sneered at her. "What do you know?"

She winked at him. "I know what I've already said. You can either choose to believe me or walk away from your mate like you previously intended. It's not like you need whatever they offered you to bring her in."

"Who told you about me?" I asked him. Not that the answer really made a difference. Grayson couldn't kill me, and I no longer had to go with him.

Though, that didn't mean I wanted to flee from the psychopath just yet.

I knew I should have just told Lia to take me to Fire and Fluorite, but thanks to whatever magical pull I felt toward this deliciously dark demon, I wanted him to want to come with us.

His hands fisted at his sides, and he ground his teeth, first looking at Lia. "I do things because I want to, not because I need anything. And I'm not walking away. We're going to No Man's Land, and I'm going to figure out why I was lied to."

Oh, thank fuck. He finally believed me. Though, that didn't seem to change his raging vibe, so I wasn't hopeful that anything else was going to change other than he'd be done wishing he could kill me. That was the minimum I was hoping for.

Lia *tsked* and waggled a finger at him. "No, we're not, but it's cute you think you're still in charge."

It was more like sexy, but "cute" worked too.

"What if we—" I tried to say, but Grayson's growl cut me off.

"You're not taking her to Fire and Fluorite," he spat. "She's mine."

My head reared back, not liking the possessive tone of his words. I might be attracted to him and curious as fuck about our bond, but nobody was going to control me now that I'd escaped the coven. Not even someone who was supposed to be my mate.

"Crazy demon wolf, come again?" I retorted. "I'm *yours*? With just a few words spoken, I could change that unless you're taking back your rejection."

He glared. "We're not discussing that right now."

I reached for his black T-shirt and jerked him closer. "I think we are. If you're going to use this bond as the reason you think I should do what you want, then you better have a lot more to fucking say. Like answering my previous question. Who sent you after me in the first place?"

His lips parted ever-so-slightly and I couldn't stop myself from glancing at them. Damn it. I didn't need to be wondering what it would feel like if they were pressed against my heated skin or if my toes would curl like I imagined they would when he touched me in places nobody ever had…

His hand covered mine over his chest and squeezed hard just before he stepped a few inches closer. His breath was warm on my cheeks as he looked down on me, but I stared defiantly back.

"I take back my rejection." He grumbled the words that should have made my heart do a happy dance, but his tone…

"Maybe I don't want you to take it back," I quipped in return, raising a pointed brow.

His lips lifted just in one corner. The closest thing I'd seen to a smile from him yet. "Lying doesn't suit you, Kinsley Ash."

Then he released me and began walking back to the jeep.

That mother fucker.

I took a step forward to follow him, but Lia's hand pressed against my shoulder, halting my forward momentum. "Take the loss, girl. You've got bigger battles to win."

I shuddered, reality coming crashing down on me as I met her friendly eyes. "Who am I?"

"That's what we're going to figure out," she said. "Just as soon as we get to Fire and Fluorite. In the meantime, maybe Grayson isn't as bad as I thought he was. Let's see if we can come up with a compromise, shall we?"

I just shrugged because I didn't know what else to do.

I'd spent my life wishing for something more, and in one night, I'd gotten way more than I'd bargained for.

Like a mate, a unicorn shifter, and a fuck-ton of questions I'd yet to get any answers to.

That was going to change just as soon as I got my libido and emotions back in check.

CHAPTER SEVEN

GRAYSON

Fuck. That word in its many variations was on repeat inside my head as I drove west. Either way, if we settled on Fire and Fluorite or No Man's Land, that was the direction we needed to go. Given I'd already been up for nearly thirty-six hours, I was ready to stop, but I wanted to increase the distance between us and the coven I'd taken Kinsley from.

Based on what she'd said so far, I hadn't thought anyone would be tempted to come after her, but knowing she wasn't even a witch—that she was a wolf shifter—changed everything.

Changed my thoughts, my feelings, and what I thought we needed to do.

Someone had hidden her, and someone else had found her, which was where I'd come in, but why? Kinsley wanted to know who she was, and so did I.

She was sitting in the front seat next to me, and Lia was in the back, but the unicorn wasn't exactly sitting. She leaned forward, keeping her head right between Kinsley and me.

"So, who wants to go first?" she asked calmly.

Kinsley twisted sideways, her white hair blowing around from the lack of top on the jeep. "First for what?"

"To tell their story," Lia replied. "I'd volunteer, but I think the two of you have information that can fill in some of the gaps for me."

Like hell was I going to participate in story time.

Kinsley, however, didn't hesitate to begin rambling. Though I wasn't surprised. I might not have always liked where I'd come from, but at least I knew what I was.

"As far as I know, I was left at that coven when I was only six months old," Kinsley said. "My magic never came in, and, while nobody mistreated me growing up, I was often excluded from coven activities, which I guess makes more sense now. Nobody ever hinted that I might be something else. They just told me I was weak or broken and suggested that I just stay out of the way or that it was safest for me to remain where I was."

Out of the corner of my eye, I caught Lia's hand reaching for Kinsley's. "It *was* safest for you. I don't know why, but I feel confident about that."

Kinsley's smile seemed forced, and the ire that built inside my chest on this woman's behalf only added to my irritation.

She was supposed to be a mark. I wasn't allowed to care about her. It shouldn't have made a difference to me if she'd been deemed the pariah of her coven, left believing there was something wrong with her.

Yet I wanted to turn the jeep around and burn the whole damned place to the ground.

Fucking hell.

My hands tightened around the steering as my foot pressed harder on the accelerator. With the increased speed, wind whipped around the open interior loudly, making conversation hard, which I was more than okay with.

Lia, on the other hand, was not.

She lifted her hands up and a clear, yet metallic energy created a dome where the top should have been. The unicorn smiled triumphantly. "That's better."

Kinsley nodded as she attempted to tame her long, platinum strands. A few of them were stuck to her lips, and damn it if my hand didn't flinch, wanting to remove them myself.

"Your turn, Grayson," Lia said chipperly.

I ignored her. There was no way they were going to know about my past. That had nothing to do with what was going on here.

"You're her mate," Lia stated, as if she could read my mind and was countering my inner argument.

I glanced over my shoulder and glared at the dark-skinned unicorn. "So fucking what? I was also the man sent to capture or kill her."

She leaned back in her seat and crossed her legs.

Fucking unicorn.

I put my eyes back on the road, and silence filled the jeep. Uncomfortable and tension-riddled silence.

After a couple of minutes, I could feel Kinsley's gaze burning into the side of my face. "You never answered my question. You don't have to tell us about you, but I deserve to know why you accused me of killing children."

She wasn't wrong about that, especially now that I was sure at least one of us was being set up for something else.

"A man named Johnathon sent me a request to find you, or kill you, if necessary," I answered. "I don't know who he is, but he would have to be working with a witch to have sent the message the way he did."

Lia briefly touched two fingers to my neck, then jerked her hand away. "The message was tainted with dark magic. You had no choice in going after Kinsley."

I slammed on the brakes and whipped my head around so I could see the unicorn. "What the fuck did you just say?"

"You were magically influenced to take the job," Lia elaborated. "The dark energy is still there. That's why you still want to go to No Man's Land. That's where they want Kinsley. You're stronger than the energy, which helps you fight it, but the magic is still encouraging your actions."

She seemed so fucking sure of her answer. Her certainty further irked me. How could I have not known someone was screwing with my head? I was one of the strongest fucking supernaturals I knew. People didn't fuck with me. Ever.

The steering wheel bent slightly within my hands. "Can you take the dark energy out?"

Fuck, I hated asking that. If she could, that meant I owed her, which wasn't going to sit well with me.

She nodded. "But I'll have to touch you again. If you try to bite me, I will put you down without a second thought."

Our stares locked in a battle of dominance. I didn't know everything that unicorns were capable of, and they'd been hunted to near extinction, so they couldn't be all powerful, but something about the glee in Lia's eyes told me she truly believed she could "put me down" without straining a muscle.

"Do it," I demanded.

She raised a brow. "Say, 'please.'"

"Are you fucking kidding me?"

"Do I look like I'm kidding?" she quickly countered.

This was why I lived in the middle of No Man's Land. Alone.

With a slow exhale, I finally muttered, "Please."

I almost thought she wasn't going to accept that, but then she touched my forehead with her palm. A charge of something warm and quick-moving pierced through my skin, zipping through my body.

My body jerked in resistance from the foreign power, but Lia kept her hold on me for several seconds before she finally pulled away.

"You should be good now," she said, then she leaned back, a slight sheen covering her forehead.

I didn't need to ask to put the pieces together about my previous thoughts once I'd noticed her exhaustion.

Unicorns were formidable. They just didn't have a deep enough well to protect themselves for the long haul.

Kinsley glanced between us. "So, what now? We can go to Fire and Fluorite?"

Sure enough, my drive to go back to my cabin wasn't as strong, but I still wasn't set on going to a House that was destroying itself from the inside out.

Before I could answer, Lia spoke. "If you don't want to go to Fire and Fluorite yet, then we need to find somewhere we can go for Kinsley to get comfortable with her wolf. She'll need to make sure there are no compatibility issues with her other half before we confront the House."

Kinsley swiveled around in her seat. "You think I have a wolf after all this time? I was starting to assume that while I might not be a witch, I might still be broken. Why else would they have hidden me?"

Because she was fucking special. I already knew that and could see that even more now that Lia had removed whatever darker energy I'd been tainted with.

The unicorn met my gaze in the rearview mirror. She nodded, and I sighed out of frustration. Was I really going to agree with her?

Fuck. I was.

The problem was that I despised most people. There was only one other person I could trust who wouldn't say anything to anyone else or give a shit about me having supernaturals with me who may or may not be questionable in power.

"There's no way you don't have a wolf," I said to Kinsley, then I glanced back at Lia again. "Do you see any reason why we couldn't go to No Man's Circus?"

I didn't want to specifically mention the ringleader because his secret wasn't mine to tell, but I'd at least call and give him a heads-up if Lia was already aware of him.

Her turquoise eyes squinted, and she shook her head. "I can't sense any dangers there, but I'd advise staying away from as many people as we can until we know more."

"What does that mean?" Kinsley asked. "Don't you know every-thing that we need to?"

Lia frowned and blinked a few times. "No, but I know enough and the visions I have are never wrong. Though, they don't give direct information. They're more like images that give me a nudge in the right direction."

I scoffed. "'Right' doesn't always mean 'easy,' either." My gaze flicked briefly to Kinsley. "Don't take her help to mean you're safe. Whatever is happening is only just getting started."

"Well, aren't you just the epitome of sunshine?" Kinsley deadpanned.

At least I wasn't a liar. I'd never seen the point. Things were always easier when the truth was spoken, even if it was uncomfortable.

Lia's eyes were on me again, and I swore if that unicorn could read minds, I would end her life without blinking.

She moved her stare to Kinsley without showing any kind of tell. "Grayson isn't wrong, but we should be able to avoid the worst of the possible situations if we work together. I know that. Even if we don't understand what's coming, we're all on this path together for a reason."

Great. She wasn't only snarky, she was philosophical. Just what I needed.

"So, what *do* you know?" I demanded, fighting back a yawn.

Lia raised a brow. "Are you going to share anything about yourself first?"

"Not likely," I grumbled.

Kinsley chuckled. "I could probably fill in some blanks. Before I saw you, Lia, I was having the best conversation with myself about Grayson and me."

I hadn't missed her blabbering since we'd found Lia, and I hoped she didn't resume that particular trait anytime soon.

"I already know all I need to," Lia said hauntingly. "I was just hoping Grayson was ready to play nice. He will be eventually, though."

Her confidence severely grated on my nerves.

I didn't want a mate, and I certainly wasn't going to "play nice."

Though, as I thought the words, I knew I was full of shit. I could have goaded Kinsley into rejecting me back there. I could have left her with the unicorn and walked away from this bullshit.

I could have done a lot of things over the last thirty-six hours and yet…I hadn't.

As much as I hated to admit this even to myself, I wanted to know more about Kinsley. I wanted to see her safe and where she belonged. Most importantly, I didn't want to trust anyone else to make sure that happened.

"So, since it seems to be my turn for story time…let me tell you what I know," Lia said, staring only at Kinsley. "About three months ago, I began dreaming about Fire and Fluorite. Shortly after that, the stories of their leader being killed started going around. It seemed there was a chance for things to get better there. And then, with more betrayal came another downfall."

"What kind of betrayal?" Kinsley asked reverently.

"That's a story for another time." Lia frowned briefly before continuing, still only focusing on Kinsley. "I also kept seeing your face. You were alone and in a forest a lot until one day, you weren't." She nodded at me. "I saw Grayson, and, for weeks, I thought I was supposed to save you from him, but then things changed and I realized you already knew how to protect yourself physically."

Yeah, I hated to admit it, but even I had been taken aback by Kinsley's fighting ability when I'd first tried to take her.

"There wasn't much else for me to do in the coven when I couldn't practice magic and while living above a gym," Kinsley said with a small shrug.

Lia grinned. "It proved useful at least and I'm sure it will again. Anyway, I then saw the two of you driving and I recognized the road. That was when I came up with my plan to pretend to be injured. Though, I hadn't foreseen the wolf showing up and nearly ruining things. Two seconds earlier and the two of you would have seen me with my horn through his chest."

I might have liked her more then, but she didn't need to know that.

"Why wouldn't your own ability show you something to protect you from being attacked?" Kinsley asked.

Lia shrugged. "I only see what I need to. What happens between one event and the next is just part of life."

"Can you focus on other people to see more about them if you want?" Kinsley pressed.

"Not usually, but that doesn't mean I don't try when needed," Lia answered, "but mostly, it's intuition that guides me once I get the first vision."

Kinsley was fully invested in the conversation, judging by the way she stayed twisted in her seat so she could stare right at Lia. "What else can you do?"

Lia patted her arm. "Let's save that for later. I can't share all my secrets just yet."

I had a feeling she was waiting on me to share more about my demon past, but that wasn't happening.

Not fucking ever.

That was a part of my life that had taken everything from me, and I had no desire to revisit those days. The only benefits of my darker half were being able to tell truth from lie, and my flames when needed in a fight.

They made my wolf nearly indestructible, and I was more than okay with giving him that advantage. Most people who'd heard the stories of my flaming wolf assumed I was half-warlock and I was glad to let them think that. Those who had personally felt the heat knew better, but they hadn't lived long enough to dispute the rumors I'd carefully helped put into place.

As Lia continued to go on about her visions that had led her to finding Kinsley and subsequently me, I focused on driving, wondering if all the hard work I'd done over the last ten years to build the life I'd wanted was about to be set on fire.

Then I wondered if I actually gave a shit.

CHAPTER EIGHT

KINSLEY

The longer Lia talked, the more I felt as if I'd found a true friend. She was kind and forthcoming, and there was a sincerity in her voice that made me feel safe for the first time in my life.

Of course, I didn't think I'd been in danger at the coven, but I'd never been settled. Something had always been missing, and maybe it'd been the fact that I wasn't actually a witch, but I had a feeling that it had also been because nobody had ever taken the time to know me.

Lia, however, asked a million questions about the things I'd done while growing up and what I'd been doing with my adult life.

I told her about spending years trying to be something I never would be and then later transitioning to combat training. That was the only thing I'd ever felt part of within the coven. I'd always assumed it was because they got a thrill out of taking down the broken witch, but once I'd grown physically stronger than them, I couldn't deny there'd been a level of respect that I'd finally felt I had.

All the while, Grayson acted as if he didn't give a shit about our conversation, keeping his eyes focused on the road and his hands tight around the steering wheel, which was now slightly bent, but he couldn't fool me. He might not have been watching me, but my eyes didn't stray from him for too long.

I saw each time his knuckles turned white, like when Lia asked me about past boyfriends—a subject I avoided answering just yet—or the way his shoulders strained against his shirt when I talked about being on my own for the last eight years without anyone to have full conversations with.

When Grayson yawned for the third time, Lia placed a hand on his seat, less than an inch from his shoulder. "Do you want me to drive so you can rest?"

His jaw tensed. "No."

"Then do you trust me to give you a zap of energy?" she asked. I tilted my chin, curious how that would work, because I was getting tired as fuck, but I didn't want to sleep and miss anything.

"*I* do," I replied when Grayson didn't, then I held out my hand.

Grayson's fist blocked Lia from touching me. "No."

I shoved him with my palm, enjoying the extra strength I already seemed to have from whatever Lia had done to me earlier. "You get no say in the matter."

Our eyes locked in a challenge, and I waited for him to play the mate card, but he managed to refrain. That fucker could act as if he didn't give a shit, but the fact that he was still around spoke so much louder than anything else.

Or so I kept telling myself, hoping my instincts weren't wrong.

As we stared at each other, my chest heaved. Whatever bond was between us tightened around my core, awakening that part of me unlike any of the books I'd read ever had.

Without thinking, my tongue darted out to wet my lips, and I didn't miss how his darkening eyes followed the movement. I leaned further over the center console, unsure of what I was doing but wanting to know what he might do if I were just close enough.

Never mind that he was driving at high speeds down the highway or that my new friend was sitting just a couple of feet away.

All I could focus on was Grayson and how much I wanted to know what he tasted like.

His chest rumbled low and oh-so-sexily, but before I could explore what that meant, Lia had clearly had enough.

She grabbed each of our shoulders, and a chill raced through my body. "Something to cool the both of you off and to keep everyone awake until we get where we're going."

I sucked in a mouthful of fresh air and settled back into my seat. Yeah, maybe she was right.

Mate or not, this guy had just tried to kill me only hours ago.

I needed to think a bit more with my head and a lot less with my vagina.

Grayson's lip lifted in a snarl. "I didn't give you permission to touch me again."

"And nobody gave you permission to be a dick, yet..." she quipped, making me snort.

Maybe all of this was going to be better than I had hoped for.

Too many hours later, we'd traveled through the slums of No Man's Land. At one point, I'd been certain we were going to die. A pack of rogue wolves had started chasing us, but between Grayson and Lia showcasing only minute amounts of their power, the ragged-looking pack had quickly scampered back into the depths of the dying forests around us.

I'd been told we were almost to the circus where we'd have a place to regroup, but when Grayson started to pull over and I couldn't see any buildings, I had a feeling that wasn't exactly the case.

Grayson turned in his seat and glanced at Lia. "Can you help, or do I need to plan on killing the border watch team up ahead?"

My eyes widened. "I'm sorry. What?"

"No Man's Land is split up over here," Lia answered as she continued her staredown with Grayson. "To get to the circus, we have to travel through a smaller section of Earth and Emerald for a brief time."

"And how are we going to do that without drawing attention?" I asked rapidly. "What if my coven has reported that I'm a runaway and they try to take me back? I won't go back. Not fucking ever."

I shivered in my seat at that thought. I wouldn't be held captive, pretending I was something I never would be, again.

Lia reached for me, lightly gripping my shoulder. "I'm sorry, Kinsley. I didn't think of that. I was just going to enchant the guards if we ran into them, but let's not risk having more problems to deal with. I can use a portal since I've been by the circus once before. Though, I never did stay for the show. Too bad we won't have time to visit."

Grayson's lips thinned, but he stayed silent, turning back to face the steering wheel as Lia stood up in her seat.

Her magic reminded me of a witch's, but there was something more wild and free about the way her hands moved, and she hadn't cast spells or used potions. Whatever this unicorn was capable of, it came from within, and it was fucking badass.

A bright, turquoise circle formed in front of the jeep, growing in size as Lia's movements became faster. As the opening widened, an apartment building came into view with what looked like a large tent erected in the middle of the structures.

Grayson pulled forward, and I stared up, watching the bright-blue sparks flicker above us as we passed through the temporary portal opening.

"Who exactly is this friend of yours that we're meeting?" I asked when the portal closed behind us. Something wasn't sitting right with me when it came to not knowing exactly where we were any longer.

I also wasn't sure if I was more surprised that Grayson had a friend or that there was a *circus* out here in this godforsaken territory.

"His name is D," Grayson said gruffly when we parked in front of what appeared to be a construction site on the backside of the apartments. "And you don't get to ask questions about him or what he does here. That's his business, not ours. Do both of you understand?"

I nodded, but Lia didn't agree as quickly. "Is he like you?"

Grayson's eyes filled with flames. "Nobody is like me."

"Right." She rolled her eyes. "Let's go, then. We have a wolf to resurrect."

When I got out of the jeep, my knees buckled, and I had to hold myself up with the door. Apparently, sitting in the same seat for eighteen hours wasn't good for one's legs.

Lia leapt from the back and wobbled, too. She shrugged sheepishly. "Opening a portal takes a lot of energy out of me, which is why I didn't offer to do it before, but it's fine now that I know I'll get the chance to rest." She glanced around and nodded toward where we could hear people and music. "Are we going to have privacy?"

Grayson nodded as he came around the front of the jeep. "When I texted D earlier, he assured me that we wouldn't be bothered as long as we stayed in the construction section and used the forest area out back while the show was going."

Great. Nobody would get to witness my body being torn to shreds and changing into a beast of an animal. That made this whole situation heaps better.

Once I got my legs to work right again, I followed Lia and Grayson. We passed by piles of drywall, lumber, and other random things I didn't know the names for. Around the corner were a few finished sections. Grayson let himself into the one labeled "105" on the white door.

I stepped through the entryway and sighed at all the comforts here. There were what appeared to be a brand-new couch and a matching love seat in the living room. A metal coffee table sat between them that matched the stools I could see at the kitchen counter. To the right, there was a short hallway with three doors.

Considering that peeing on the side of the road wasn't my favorite pastime, I continued forward without waiting for the tour I didn't think was coming.

The first door was a bedroom with white walls and a mattress positioned at the center. The second was my saving grace. I locked the handle behind me and had my pants down in record time.

With a sigh, I peed and eyeballed the shower next to me. My skin was still itchy from the dirt and sweat I'd acquired in my initial fight with Grayson. A shower to wash away the shit night sounded like an excellent way to soothe some of my rough edges. Except my plans were swiftly interrupted.

A fist pounded on the door. "Hurry up."

"Fuck off," I muttered in return, not meaning for Grayson to hear, but…

He kicked in the door while I was still on the toilet. I bent forward to cover myself and sneered at him. "What the shit is your problem?"

"Don't talk to me like that." He growled.

I raised a brow at him. "Then get some fucking manners."

His dark eyes stayed on my face the whole time, but even still, the sexual tension we'd experienced in the jeep came back with a vengeance. Though, it was easier to break this time, because there was very little that was sexy about sitting on a toilet with an irritated, hot-as-fuck dude watching.

"Care to back up a step or three and close the door so I can 'hurry up'?" I asked with a flippant wave of my hand.

He snarled in answer, then slammed the door closed behind him. Though, it didn't quite close like before. I heard him grumble something, then another door slammed loudly.

I finished up and washed my hands, sighing when I noticed the lock was officially busted and we'd only been here two minutes. Hopefully, this D guy was forgiving and wouldn't kick us out thanks to Grayson's anger issues.

When I got back to the living room, Lia was lounging across the love seat with her hands behind her head. "He went to get D. Told us to stay here."

"Super," I droned, more disappointed that I didn't have time to take a shower and actually enjoy the hot water soothing my still-some-what-sore muscles. "How long do you think we're going to be here?"

She peeked over at me as I sat on the couch. "That depends on you."

I hadn't really asked much before about what it meant to be a wolf shifter. To be honest, I didn't really care. At least, that was what I told myself.

I'd rather pretend there would be nothing grand about this revelation than be disappointed when I remained a broken supernatural.

Plus, it wasn't like anything had really changed. I still didn't have a home or a family. Hell, I didn't even have a mate who wanted me.

What difference would knowing that I wasn't a witch make?

"Do I need to do something to make my wolf appear?" I asked, at least pretending to be interested since Lia was frowning at me.

She sat up, crossing her legs underneath herself, and looked right at me, almost as if she could see into my soul. "You need to believe in yourself. To know that you are incredible just the way you are. Most importantly, you need to forget how anyone else has made you feel in the past, because they were idiots."

I coughed and turned to look out the window for distraction, but there were curtains blocking my view. "Of course. That won't be a problem." The lie fell almost too easily from my lips.

She made an odd sound, but before I could ask another question, the door opened again. Grayson entered with a man behind him.

The man's copper eyes remained locked on Lia, but not in the romantic sense. More out of curiosity assuming Grayson told him she was a unicorn.

She smirked at him. "I'm not looking for a new home, big guy."

"You can't fault me for being intrigued," he said, then he quickly glanced at me but seemed to be talking to Grayson. "This is her?"

"Yep."

"I see." His fingers rubbed lightly over the smattering of dark facial hair around his cheeks and chin.

My back went ramrod straight while I shoved all thoughts of self-pity back into their corner. "You *see* what?"

I was allowed to talk shit about myself, but fuck anyone else thinking they could.

The two brooding men shared a look before D gave me his attention again. "I see that you're not what anyone else thought. But you'll be safe here to do whatever it is that you need. The rooms aren't complete, as you may have seen already, but the kitchen should have anything you need."

"We appreciate the privacy," Lia said, staring hard at the broad-shouldered and rather attractive man.

His lip twitched upward but only slightly before falling again. "I have a business to run, and guards who don't like when I ask them to stay behind. So, I need to get going, but Grayson knows how to find me if anything comes up. There is a forest just east of here, past the carnival area, that you can do whatever you need to in."

Grayson nodded stiffly, then stepped out the front door with D following right behind.

Once it clicked closed, Lia sighed and fanned her cheeks. "Seriously. If I didn't know there was something better out there for me…"

I cocked my head. "Are you holding out for your mate?"

"Gods, no." She made a disgusted sound. "I just know he's close by, and that fine specimen of man isn't him."

I blushed and nodded, then glanced down at my feet.

"Are you?" She gaped, moving to sit by me before I could look back up.

I shrugged. "Not intentionally. With the way I grew up, it wasn't like people were dying to take me out."

Lia held my hand, and her face turned dead serious. "A virgin? I so didn't see that, but don't worry. We're going to get you laid."

Grayson picked just that moment to walk back in the door, and I froze. His grip on the handle began to bend the metal, and the low growl rumbling from him turned my insides upside down.

Fuck. Why did I find his asshole-ness so damned attractive?

Stupid bond.

Yeah, I could totally blame this fiasco on the mate bond and not all the dirty novels the coven had hoarded away from when supernatural romance books had been considered fiction instead of fact.

"Bed. Now," he demanded.

My face blanched. Though, warmth pooled between my legs. "Excuse me?"

"You need to sleep before trying to shift later tonight," he muttered, clarifying his words that I'd taken in a very different way.

Holy hell. I'd thought he'd been… Well, we all knew what I'd *thought* and I wasn't even mad about it.

"Of course," I murmured. "I'll get right on that."

Right after I took care of my own business, because there was no way I was sleeping without a bit of relief.

Relief that I knew Grayson wasn't going to provide me and that he probably wouldn't allow anyone else to, either.

Lia waggled her fingers at me as I got up. "Happy sleeping."

I shot her a glare over my shoulder, then went into the bedroom farthest from the living room.

Then I snorted because the additional space between me and that demon wolf wasn't going to make a bit of fucking difference.

My body was suddenly all too aware of where he was and what he *wasn't* doing.

CHAPTER NINE

Kinsley was more than a wolf shifter. She had to be. When I'd first seen her image, I'd thought she'd been a temptress, but I'd had no fucking clue what it would be like to be in her presence. To hear she was a virgin and know that when she went into that bedroom, she was touching herself.

I'd had to leave. To get away from her scent that called to me…no, *demanded* me to satisfy her myself.

Fucking mate bond.

Behind the carnival area with its booths, Ferris wheel, and other things I didn't care about were the trees I sought solace within, shifting as soon as I got past the tree line. My silver wolf howled and stretched once he was on all four paws. It had been a few days since I'd let him run free, so I wasn't surprised when he began to sprint.

Green flames started to grow around his light coat, and I could sense he wanted to return to Kinsley, but that wasn't happening. I was still in charge, even if we were in his body.

Any aggressions or needs we had were going to be taken care of out here. I wasn't going to go back to that apartment and further complicate things. I couldn't.

He ran for miles, exerting the extra energy I didn't think we should still have, considering I couldn't remember the last time I'd closed my eyes to rest. Maybe Lia's boost hadn't been such a bad thing.

When we got to a point in the forest that I couldn't sense anyone else around, my wolf sat on his haunches and took a deep breath. Then, I let my demon powers seep out.

The green flames that were already present turned to a dark emerald, and my wolf's body grew from four feet in height to six feet. Without needing to see them for myself, I knew his eyes would be ebony and the previously silver fur would be like burnt charcoal.

I focused on our surroundings, stretching my energy as a way to expunge more of it. My wolf wasn't the only one who needed to be let out on occasion. If I didn't use my demon side, then there were often repercussions—like murderous rages—and I avoided those at all costs. So far, I'd been successful.

I wouldn't be my father. I could control the bleaker side of myself. I was stronger than the demon blood flowing through me.

My darker powers locked on to Kinsley's sleeping form, even from miles away. They could taste her innocence and the connection we shared. The temptations we both seemed to be feeling and the need to claim her as mine all grew by the second.

I pictured her crimson lips, sun-kissed skin, wide eyes…and those tits that I'd love to bury my face in.

My wolf growled and snapped his jaws, breaking the stupor I'd been falling into a little too deeply.

Fuck.

I needed to figure out what I was going to do with this woman, because ignoring her wasn't going to work for the long haul.

I knew that after spending less than a day with her.

As I pulled my demon energy back in, my wolf shuddered and let out one more howl into the night sky before we headed back to the apartments.

When I came out of the clearing, D was there with a few of his guards standing close enough to keep eyes on their ringmaster, but not so close as to be overwhelming with their presence.

I shifted back to two feet, soaking in the wolf's pure energy that brought my human side back, along with the amethyst stone that I kept tied to my wrist. The charm brought back all of the clothes I'd been wearing before.

It was a worthy trade I'd done with a witch after I tracked down her grandson, who'd been messing with dark shit that he'd had no business touching at only sixteen. Plus, fighting without my clothes on if I was forced to shift back to human hadn't always been ideal.

"How was your run?" D asked casually when I approached, keeping his hands in the pockets of his black slacks.

"Needed," I clipped. "Is everything okay?"

He raised a brow. "I was hoping you could answer that for me."

"What's that supposed to mean?" I demanded. D was someone with whom I shared mutual respect, but we didn't often get in each other's business, and I preferred it that way.

"It means you called me, needing somewhere to lie low, but you didn't tell me you were bringing a unicorn and a new mate with you," D said with narrowed eyes. "You're the most cautious man I know besides myself, Grayson. So, tell me how the fuck you ended up in this situation."

As much as I hated it, he had a point.

"Fuck if I know." I groaned, then went on to explain how I'd gotten the information to hunt Kinsley down and bring her back to No Man's Land.

"She's your mate and you brought her back to the one place where the fucker wanted her? That's savage, even for you," he said with a shake of his head.

Didn't I fucking know it.

"Where else was I supposed to take her?" I snapped. "To a House that's at war with itself like the unicorn suggested even though Kinsley doesn't know who she is? And nowhere else was going to let us in. At least I didn't go back to my cabin."

D rubbed a hand over the back of his neck and adjusted his stance. "I see your point, but I still don't understand how you agreed to all of this in the first place, even if they used dark magic on you."

I could understand. Though, it hadn't escaped me that there might have been something bigger at play than any of us realized.

My boot kicked at a stray rock. "He showed me pictures of dead kids."

D knew about Addie. He was the only person still living who did. Who knew my baby sister had been attacked by demons my father had sent looking for my mother, ones who hadn't known about me until I'd hunted them down myself.

She'd been home alone. Defenseless at only ten years old.

The demons could have waited for my mother to come home, but instead, they'd chosen to send a message.

They still hadn't gotten what they, or my piece-of-shit father, had wanted.

My mom had finally told me everything she knew about him. She'd made me promise to make them pay for Addie's life. To make them hurt how she had.

I'd done just that. I'd hunted them all through the depths of Soleil —or Celestia, depending on who you asked—the demon and angel portal. I'd ripped them slowly to shreds while their agonizing screams had echoed into the shadows they often hid in.

My father had been saved for last. He hadn't known who I was until he'd laid eyes on me. I'd done my best to make that happen, and it had been worth every moment I'd spent in the darkness when he'd realized I wasn't there to join him but to take his worthless life away.

When my fist had torn through his chest, nothing had ever felt more satisfying.

That changed when I'd gotten home.

After I returned, my mother had taken her own life. She'd left a note saying she was at peace with this life now that the demons were dead, but she couldn't survive any longer. That she needed to be with her baby girl.

I'd been so fucking angry with her for that choice after all we'd been through, but I'd channeled my aggressions into something I could live with. Like killing bastards who fucked with the wrong people.

"Do you think this Johnathon knows your weakness when it comes to kids?" D asked, shaking me out of the past I tried not to revisit often.

"It shouldn't be possible, but if they have a Seer at their disposal, they might. Or maybe I left one alive without realizing it. Hell, there are too many possibilities, no matter how careful I thought I was."

Magic had its advantages, but there were just as many hindrances, too.

"Well, you can't change the choices you've already made or what they might already know," he said. "Do you need help with your shifter mate?"

As the ringmaster to this circus, D had certain abilities that kept him in charge, but I didn't think his methods were what Kinsley needed.

Or that I could handle watching her possibly suffer just to see if we could get her to shift faster.

"I can take care of her," I replied. "We'll be out in the forest shortly. Are you still able to keep people out of there for the night? If all goes well, we'll be gone by morning."

He cocked his head to the side. "What place do you think will be safer for three supernaturals without a House than here?"

"I'm going to try to trust the unicorn." Fuck, that was hard to say. "Once Kinsley knows more than just physical fighting, then we can see what was guiding Lia to Fire and Fluorite in the first place. There might be answers there as to who sent me after Kinsley."

D glanced back briefly and then lowered his voice. "And what if those answers put you in deeper shit than you can handle on your own? Fire and Fluorite isn't the best place to be right now, and they're not taking too kindly to outsiders, given all that has happened."

He wasn't wrong, and those were all the reasons I hadn't wanted to go there in the first place. I could handle myself, but protecting Kinsley at the same time? That would be harder. I could tell myself I didn't care all I wanted, but nobody would get to her without going through me first.

I'd fucking torch that cursed House to the ground before I let them touch her.

"Do you know anyone who can get us an in?" I asked, hating that this would be the second favor I'd owe him if he did.

Thankfully—or maybe not so much—he shook his head. "Anyone

trustworthy there is fighting their own battles. They don't have time for anything else. Or they're in hiding, doing their best to keep their families safe." He paused and looked me square in the eyes. "You're going to be on your own."

Why was I not surprised to hear that?

"I need to get back to the apartment," I said. "I'm not sure if I'll see you before we leave. I don't want to stay long enough for anyone who doesn't need to know to find out where we are and bring trouble to your front door."

D reached a hand toward me. "Appreciated. Let me know how things work out."

"Will do." I accepted the shake, then he went walking back toward his men.

I'd been gone for a couple of hours. Hopefully, that was enough time for Kinsley to sleep, because it was time for us to find her wolf.

CHAPTER TEN

KINSLEY

When I woke up from my much-needed nap, I was hoping the sexual frustration that had been coursing through me earlier would have eased up some. Instead, it was reignited when I opened my eyes to find Grayson standing over me with his arms crossed.

Muscles bulged from under his tight, black tee, and there was a sexy tic right above his jawline that I could see through the light scruff on his face.

His dark eyes stared right into my soul, and I smirked. "I don't bite if you want to lie down."

He leaned closer, placing a hand next to each of my shoulders. His lips were within inches of mine. All I had to do was push up onto my elbows and I could capture his mouth, but then he spoke, reminding me why I'd been taking care of myself earlier instead of letting him touch me.

"*I* do bite. Now get your ass up. We have work to do." He began backing away, then paused and added, "You can sleep more later tonight."

My palm was aimed for his chest, but he got out of the way of my trajectory before I could make contact.

Stupidly fucking sexy demon wolf.

I rolled out of the bed and groaned when I stretched. I wasn't sure how much sleep I'd gotten, but since it'd been dark when I'd finally closed my eyes and the sun still wasn't up now, I didn't suspect much.

Still in the T-shirt and leggings I'd been wearing when Grayson had taken me, I padded my way to the bathroom.

My skin felt itchy, so the first thing I did was remove my clothes, then I bent over to turn on the shower.

Just as my fingers touched the metal knob, a loud growl echoed through the small room.

I peeked over my shoulder, and Grayson was standing in the open doorway with flames in his eyes.

His stare was locked on my bare ass, which was on full display for him.

I might not have been with a man before, but I sure as hell knew how to handle my hormones, and if Grayson wanted to tempt me, I was going to do the same to him.

My hand quickly turned on the shower, and I pushed the curtain open before turning to face him fully. "Do you only bite in the bedroom? If so, I'm not opposed to sharing the shower if you were hoping to use it."

The rumbling coming from him was so deep, I swore my toes felt the vibrations. "Put some fucking clothes on."

I chuckled. "How about you knock next time?"

"You weren't supposed to be naked so fast," he countered.

I nodded and placed a hand on my hip. "Right. Did you need something, Grayson?"

His eyes couldn't focus on any one place for very long, but he was still capable of words. "D offered to provide clothes. I didn't know your size or what you'd want."

Oh, God. This was priceless.

His hands were shaking at his sides, and his pupils had turned to slits. I could see his wolf begging to be released, but impressively, Grayson kept his control. Mostly.

"Jeans, size six. Boots, size seven, and shirt should be a large." I glanced down at my chest. "The twins don't like it when they're too constricted."

His jaw cracked from the hard grinding of his teeth, then he slowly turned away from me, closing the door behind him. I heard him mutter something about "Virgin, my ass" but I decided not to comment.

Just because I was comfortable with my body didn't mean I had been lying, but he could think whatever he wanted. For now, anyway.

I turned for the shower again and got in, quickly washing up and rinsing so I could see what I had missed since getting some sleep.

My skin still felt itchy even with a soft, cotton towel on my body, and my bones even seemed sore. Maybe fighting with Grayson yesterday had taken more out of me than I'd realized…

With the towel wrapped tightly around me, I exited the bathroom and went right out into the living room. There was a man standing there with two bags in his hands. Before I could get a good look at him, Grayson was suddenly in front of me, blocking my not-quite-naked body from the unknown visitor.

Grayson growled, and I heard two thuds before the door quickly closed.

I peeked around his arm and sure enough, the guy was gone, but the bags were just inside the doorway. "Was that necessary?" I droned, moving around him to find my clothes.

"Do you have no modesty?" he snapped back.

I laughed. "How was I supposed to know someone would be inside the apartment? Or that you'd storm in the bathroom as if you didn't know I was in there already?"

He clenched his hands into fists and stomped past me, but I grabbed his wrist. "Where's Lia?"

"Communing with nature," he spat, then he jerked out of my hold and went to the other bedroom, slamming the door closed behind him.

Wasn't he such a peach?

I kept the towel wrapped around me and grabbed both of the bags with one hand before heading back to the room I'd been sleeping in. I caught the time on the microwave. It blinked 11:24pm. Great, I'd only gotten two hours of sleep. I was going to need Lia to give me another boost.

When I entered back into the bedroom and closed the door behind me, I didn't bother to lock it. Grayson would just break it anyway, and his mood swings were driving me mad.

My chest did this weird flip-flop thing as I began scouring the donated clothes.

Okay, maybe I wouldn't mind Grayson losing his shit and allowing the stick to drop out of his ass.

Within a few minutes, I was dressed in new underwear, dark-blue jeans, black boots, and a charcoal tee that fit a little snugger than I was used to.

I headed back to the bathroom, leaving the door open so I could listen for Lia returning, but by the time I was done braiding my hair, since I didn't have a blow dryer, she still wasn't back.

My eyes glanced toward the living room then the closed door I knew Grayson was behind. Feeling a little adventurous, I went in his direction, down the short hallway.

I tapped my knuckles on the door and let myself in, only to find him standing at the window with his head pressed against the fogging glass and no shirt on.

The black and grey tattoos that I'd noticed on his arms extended over his shoulder blades. There was a cross there, along with images of various flowers, skulls, and trees with a moon near his neck.

I took a step forward, not saying anything, and he didn't move when I inched closer. The nearer I got, the more faint scars I could see on his back. My fingers twitched to reach up and soothe the bumpy lines.

When I was close enough to touch him, he finally spoke. "What are you doing in here, Kinsley?"

I swallowed thickly. "I don't know."

He turned on one heel, and my eyes were suddenly level with his sculpted chest. *Fuck.* I couldn't *not* touch him.

My hand raised and my fingers lightly trailed over his skin where it was puckered from past battles. "What happened to you?"

His thumb lifted my chin while the rest of his hand cupped my cheek. "Nothing you want to know about."

"I wouldn't have asked if I didn't want the answer," I countered breathily.

This was the closest we'd been and not fighting, and I wasn't prepared for the onslaught of feelings and *need* that coursed through me.

My legs quivered, barely keeping me upright, and my heart hammered in my chest as I kept my gaze locked with his.

Oh, this was either going to be really fucking good or absolutely terrible.

I was shamelessly voting for the former.

My mouth felt as dry as the Sahara. I licked my lips, trying to find some relief, but that only made my core explode with want when Grayson's chest rumbled.

He drew me closer. "You really shouldn't have come in here," he murmured, and then his mouth crashed down onto mine.

His touch was hard and demanding while his tongue pushed into my mouth. I gripped his sides with my hands since he didn't have a shirt on, and I tried to ease the heaving in my chest.

The hand holding my cheek moved behind my neck and gripped the middle of my braid, tugging my head back. His eyes burned into mine when he pulled away just an inch or two. "You're…"

His lack of words made me grin. "Not what you expected," I finished for him.

He gave me a slight shake. "Not what I was thinking, but that too."

Grayson picked me up, and I wrapped my legs around his waist, suddenly wishing I hadn't requested jeans for my change of clothes.

He walked us backward, but the mattress in here was also on the ground, so getting to the bed wasn't an easy feat. Instead, he pressed my back against the wall, and his lips nipped at the skin around my collarbone.

I tilted my head to the side, giving him easier access while dying a little on the inside over the fact that I'd waited twenty-eight years to feel something this good.

His continued reverberations pulsated my skin, sending jolts straight to my center unlike anything my own hands had ever been able to conjure.

I moaned in response and ground myself over the hard cock I could feel rising between my legs. "Fuck," I muttered when I could already feel myself building up just from him kissing and biting my over-sensitized skin.

Grayson's mouth traveled back up my neck, and his fingers lightly held me in a choke when he paused just before my lips. "Are you really a virgin?"

I was tempted to lie to him, but something told me it wouldn't help my situation if I did. My chin nodded ever-so-slightly.

"Has no one even touched you before?" he asked, and I shook my head only slightly.

He kissed my mouth, searing his lips to mine. "Not even here?"

"No," I whispered. "Not until today." My nails dug into his shoulders, praying he wasn't going to stop now.

I could hardly breathe from just his touch. I needed to know what more would feel like. More in any capacity.

I just needed him to release the pent-up energy that was warring inside me.

Shamelessly, I rubbed against him, hoping he'd get the point without me having to feel like I was begging, but I wasn't opposed to that if it was the only way to get what I needed.

He was frozen for a few seconds after I'd answered his questions, but then he came at me with a ferocity that hadn't been there before.

The grip around my neck got tighter, the pressure of his hard lips on mine increased, and I swore my back was going to leave an indent in the drywall if we stayed where we were.

I reached my hands between us, trying to get at the button on his pants, but he moved us so quickly that I had to suck in a breath from the swift movements.

Before I knew it, we were on the mattress with a sheet and a thin blanket underneath my back. He boxed me in just like he'd done earlier when I'd been lying down, and the flames returned to his eyes.

"*Mine*," he growled.

I'd thought the green flickers were part of his demon side, but with the animalistic way his stare was boring into me, there was no doubt that singular word was all wolf.

His hand slid over my chest and down my stomach, then slipped under the waistband of the jeans that were being total cockblockers.

My hips flinched as soon as his finger moved over my slit, rubbing in slow circles.

"Oh, fuck," I moaned, lifting my head up and reaching between us to undo the button and zipper.

As soon as he had more room, he slipped a finger inside me. I nearly came right on the spot.

My inner muscles convulsed around him while he pumped faster and faster between my legs.

I wanted to postpone the inevitable, but that wasn't going to happen.

Spots appeared in my vision, and the warmth that had been growing at my core exploded through my insides. I screamed without giving a flying fuck who might have heard me.

His mouth landed on mine, capturing the noises I'd been making, and his tongue became well-acquainted with mine while I battled through the tremors storming inside my body.

Grayson removed his hand from my pants and tried to roll away, but I wasn't done with him. Not when he had finally stopped being a grumpy mother fucker.

He pushed me farther away and got to his feet. "That shouldn't have happened."

Or maybe I was wrong.

"You've got to be fucking kidding me right now." I scowled. "And what's that supposed to mean?"

He went back to standing in front of the window with his back to me. "It means that just because we're mates doesn't mean we're going to be together."

I was already off the bed and fixing my pants when he'd finished speaking. I stomped forward and punched him in the kidney, making him grunt from the impact. "You're a fucking asshole, and I'm pretty sure I hate you right now."

The only reason I didn't reject him right then and there was because I knew he was being a chicken shit. Moods didn't just flip that quickly.

That bastard felt something, and it scared him, which was also why he refused to turn around, even when I'd hit him.

I threw my hands in the air and stormed out of the room.

Fuck this guy.

Unfortunately, not literally, though.

CHAPTER ELEVEN

GRAYSON

Mother fucking hell. What had I done? There'd been a reason I'd gone into the bedroom. I'd known I needed to stay away from Kinsley or I was going to do something that one of us—likely her—would later regret.

Yet I was a selfish bastard, and I hadn't sent her away when she'd come looking for me. Instead, I'd done what I knew I didn't have the right to, given how I'd treated her so far.

I'd touched her where nobody else ever had, because I had to be the fucking first and, possibly worse, I wanted to be the only.

Fuck. The bond had warped my ability to think rationally, something I'd hardly been able to do since finding Kinsley.

Sure, she was my mate. I believed that now. But that didn't mean I could just take what I wanted from her.

I was an asshole on my best day, but that didn't make me a monster on my worst. At least, I didn't want to be.

When she'd left the room, completely fed up with me, I didn't blame her. I felt the same way.

For now, it was best if she didn't want me. There were too many questions we didn't have answers to. The more time that passed, the more questions I seemed to have.

The most important one at the moment: Had it just been a coincidence that I'd been hired to track Kinsley down, or had that been intentional?

If someone else knew she was my mate, that made her a weakness to me and, likely, me to her. I didn't do weaknesses.

Kinsley might not understand how things worked in this new world, considering she'd never left the coven, but she was about to get an abrupt awakening.

Once I heard Lia return, I finally came out of the bedroom with the rest of my clothes on. "It's time to see if Kinsley can shift," I said, trying yet failing to keep the gruffness out of my voice.

Lia narrowed bright eyes at me. "Clearly. So she can kick your ass."

Kinsley smirked. "I already did that once, but I wouldn't mind doing it again with claws."

I was tempted to dispute that statement, considering I'd ended up kidnapping her, but Kinsley could have this win.

"Right," I said. "Let's go, then."

My eyes were forced forward so as not to stare too closely at Kinsley's still-flushed cheeks and chest. I made it out the door without making eye contact and headed toward the forest, giving the carnival area a wide berth to avoid the people milling about.

I saw Kinsley point at some of the rides and signs, but we weren't here to have fun. We were here to see if she was going to have a problem shifting, and then it was time for us to move on. That was it.

When all three of us made it into the small forest, I led the way to a spot past some of the denser trees that would allow us some privacy but still would offer plenty of moonlight.

We didn't need the moon to shift into our wolf forms, but that didn't mean its rays didn't give us more strength when we needed it.

When I stopped, Kinsley surprised me by standing within a few feet of me. "How do I do this?"

I glanced at Lia, expecting her to have some input since she was a shifter as well, but the unicorn stayed quiet.

"You need to relax your body and mind," I said. "Picture your inner animal and focus on the feeling within you that wasn't there before. That's your wolf."

Her lashes fluttered closed, and she took a deep inhale. My eyes flicked down to her chest as her tits rose briefly.

I was so fucked.

Kinsley reopened her eyes, a frown deepening on her face. "I don't feel anything right now like I did before. There had been heaviness in my chest after Lia did whatever she did. That's gone now."

"Maybe you shouldn't have gone in the bedroom," Lia snickered.

I cut her a sharp glare. "If you're not going to help, then you can leave."

She shrugged, then did just that.

So much for the two of them becoming fast friends.

So much for me not being alone with Kinsley again.

So fucking much.

Kinsley watched Lia walk further into the forest with just as much shock as I felt.

"It's okay," I promised. "We'll figure this out. You just need to relax more."

She sneered. "Then maybe you shouldn't be such a prick."

Ignoring the snide comment, I grabbed her shoulders and spun her around until she was facing away from me. "Close your eyes again."

"Ask me instead of ordering me to," she quickly countered.

She had to be fucking kidding me with the need for pleasantries. I ignored her again.

Kinsley broke free of the hold I had on her shoulders and turned back around. "You might not have expected a mate or this shitshow when you came to kill me, but I didn't fucking ask for any of this, either. I didn't ask to be kept hidden and lied to my whole life. I certainly didn't wish for some giant asshole to show up and reject me at first sight. So, maybe if you showed me a modicum of respect, this might be easier."

There was plenty of truth in her words. All of it I was already well aware of, but keeping her at a distance seemed easier.

Maybe I was wrong. Again.

I didn't like that. Not one fucking bit.

I stared straight into her eyes, trying and failing to hate the connection I felt as I did. "I'll try harder not to piss you off."

A heavy sigh escaped from between her lips. "You're... Never mind. Let's just figure this out."

With more gentleness than before, I moved Kinsley again until her back was to me. My hands cupped her shoulders, and I leaned forward. "You need to clear your mind and relax."

She shuddered all the way from where I held her to her feet. "Not fucking likely right now."

Instead of backing away like I should have, I pressed forward. If things were as fucked as they seemed, Kinsley needed to know how to shift under duress. Babying her wasn't going to help.

Though, what I had in mind had nothing to do with real *duress*.

My front pressed against her back, and her ass fit snuggly against me, right below my dick. Her breathing sputtered, and I lowered my head until my mouth was next to her ear.

"You have to know your body," I whispered. "You need to be able to command it to do what you want, no matter what's happening around you. That's the only way you're going to control your shift and subsequently, your wolf."

Kinsley's head tilted to the side, exposing her neck to me. I hardened behind her, appreciating that while she had a mouth on her and was expectedly still furious with me, her instinct was to still be submissive. At least with me.

"Good girl," I murmured, moving my hands slowly down her arms until they cupped her elbows. "Now, breathe deeply and call your wolf."

She did as I'd asked, and energy sizzled along her skin, reminding me to back away before she actually did hurt me.

Except when I moved, she stiffened and gasped before turning to face me. "What was that?"

"Your shifter energy," I answered, still staying back.

She rubbed her palms over her arms. "I've never felt magic like that."

The innocence she exuded was too fucking sexy for her own good.

"We're going to fix that," I said, trying to ignore the irritation I felt over the fact that the coven hadn't prepared her for life outside of their

House, regardless of whether or not they'd hoped to keep her locked up.

Kinsley nodded and closed her eyes again. This time, I had a front-row view of the process, and it wasn't just shifter energy that crackled over her lightly bronzed skin.

There was something else there that didn't belong.

White magic softly pulsed over her arms and hands, so faint that I almost couldn't see it. Then she bent forward and let out an impressive roar that had me backing up further.

I could hear the breaking of her bones as they reshaped into her wolf, but besides the initial shout, she stayed quiet. Considering it was her first shift, I was more than impressed.

When her wolf appeared, she was around four-and-a-half feet tall—larger than most females—and a dark charcoal color.

The faint white I'd seen before seemed to flicker around her, but then it fizzled out. I didn't know what that meant, but the fact that she could shift on her first try was what I focused on.

Until I had the sudden desire to bow before her.

What the fuck? I thought.

I kept her wolf's gaze and stepped forward with my hand out.

She eyed me suspiciously, not nearly as submissive as her human half. A low growl rumbled from her chest, and I paused my movements.

"Kinsley," I warned.

If she couldn't keep control of her wolf, we were going to have an even bigger problem on our hands. I hadn't considered the ramifications of forcing her first shift when she didn't have an alpha, but as the minutes ticked by, the beast settled.

"Do you want to run?" I asked, making sure to remain bigger and more in control than the she-wolf, even though a part of me still wanted to avert my eyes when I looked at her.

Things were getting more and more interesting. Or fucked.

The wolf wagged her tail, and her ass went up in the air before she darted farther into the trees.

I quickly shifted and caught her scent. She smelled like the forest after a storm, crisp and alluring.

With a forced shake, I pushed away the building attraction and continued our chase.

Kinsley's wolf was faster than I'd expected for her first shift. She was agile and strong, which allowed for her to jump over fallen trees and a creek that I would have expected a new wolf to be afraid of.

After circling around a boulder, I lost sight of the wolf, but I could still smell her sweet aroma. Just as I was about to let out a sharp howl, a hard form landed on top of me.

Claws lightly scraped down my side, and a playful yip sounded next to my wolf's head.

We rolled out from underneath her, and my head pushed into her side.

The she-wolf was quick on her feet and wasn't fazed by my nudge. I tried not to be impressed, but the more she moved, the harder that became.

Suddenly, I found myself fascinated by this creature, who was unlike anything I'd yet to encounter.

She was resilient and fearless and, if I were being honest, addictive.

The longer I was around her, the more I wanted her.

I knew that there would only be so long that I could fight the bond and my growing attraction—not that I'd done a great job of that thus far—but I tried to tell myself that didn't change anything.

Kinsley had access to her wolf now. She was clearly comfortable with the beast, who was surprisingly powerful.

I assumed that had a lot to do with why I'd been sent to find and capture her.

Someone wanted to use Kinsley, but I wasn't going to let that happen.

I'd kill every fucker who thought to come for her, starting with Johnathon if I could find him first.

Kinsley was mine, even if I wasn't ready to have her yet.

CHAPTER TWELVE

There might have been a small part of me that had thought turning into a wolf was a little overrated. Like, who would want to change into a massive dog? Though, after having shifted, I knew I was an idiot for thinking the transformation would be anything less than spectacular.

Sure, there was pain that rushed through my body when my bones broke and reshaped, but nothing compared to the surge of energy that blasted through me once I was on all fours, racing through trees.

The wind whipped around me, tousling my charcoal-colored fur and encouraging me to go faster than should have been possible.

Grayson took us around the small forest, zigzagging through the trees and over the creek, and when we started heading back, I'd even had fun leaping over a ridiculously tall boulder.

Not being able to talk to him was weird, but at the same time better. This man…shifter…demon… He was infuriating.

When he'd touched me in his bedroom, I'd wanted to know what other euphoric feelings he could elicit from me, but then…he'd kicked me out.

I was more furious with how badly his rejection had hurt than I was at the situation, because really, I shouldn't have been surprised by his actions. More importantly, I wanted to be stronger than my growing feelings toward him.

Fuck, I'd only known him a day—or maybe it was technically two now—and I already knew, if he wasn't such a dick, that I could have quickly fallen for him.

Though maybe that was the case, regardless of his attitude.

My wolf form shivered just remembering the way he'd held me before I'd shifted and how much I'd wanted him to claim me right then and there. I did my best to shove those thoughts aside when our run was over.

We'd stopped in the clearing we'd left from, and I was at a loss as to how to get back to two legs.

Grayson shifted first and walked toward me. As he did, I was reminded about the desire to challenge him that had come over me before.

My head rose higher, and I stared intently at him. Not because I was furious, but because I was stronger.

At least, that was the feeling my wolf was giving off.

Grayson's eyes narrowed briefly. "The process of changing back is nearly the same as before. You need to envision your human form, remove all other distractions from your thoughts, and demand the energy to do as you command."

That seemed easy enough.

I did as he said, but nothing happened. My wolf huffed, and I growled quietly. This was not like before.

The wolf magic I could sense along my skin before I'd shifted wasn't there any longer. The crackling power had guided me the first time, and no matter how deep I searched for it again, I came up empty.

Grayson walked slowly toward me, holding his hand out, palm up. "May I?"

His question shocked me, but I managed to nod my wolf head.

My eyes watched his every movement, questioning his motives but also desperately wishing for his touch.

He kneeled before me, putting his eyes level with mine. Without realizing what I was doing, my head nudged against his and a rumble vibrated from deep within me.

"I'm not going to hurt you," Grayson whispered. "Not again."

Power and desire shot through me. The bond flared, and my wolf nearly panted right in front of him, knowing that nothing could ease the ache inside other than this man.

The man currently on his knees and bowing his head ever-so-slightly for us.

Seeing him submit to me triggered something feral inside me. I looked up at the moon, and a howl tore through me, echoing into the starry night.

As the sounds faded, the energy I'd been looking for reappeared. I latched tightly on to the shimmering power and pictured my human form. My long white hair, the clothes I'd been wearing before, and my bright eyes.

The world around me got fuzzy, and then I was back to regular height. This time, I was looking down on Grayson.

His chin slowly raised until our eyes locked. Neither of us said anything, but one look was all I needed to know that this man, and everything that he was… He was mine.

Whatever had happened when he'd found me made no difference. I needed him, and he needed me, even if he wouldn't admit that with words.

I'd wear him down.

My years of being an outcast and doing my best not to let that solitary life crush me had prepared me for Grayson.

I would break him before he could break me. Or maybe we'd both shatter together.

He reached up and grabbed my hip. My skin rippled, and I suddenly realized I had no fucking clothes on.

With a glance, I confirmed I was naked as the day I'd been born. Grayson's cognac eyes had those flames back within them as he slowly stood, keeping his gaze averted toward the ground.

With one hand, he pulled his shirt over his head and then carefully slid the cotton material over my head.

My chest was heaving, but I gathered my wits enough to push my own arms through the holes and tugged the material down as far as it would go.

Good thing Grayson was tall. At least my ass cheeks were covered. Mostly.

He finally looked up and met my eyes. "I forgot you'd lose your clothes. We'll get you something like this to wear so that doesn't happen."

He held up his wrist to show me a thin, tan, braided bracelet around his left wrist that held a deep purple stone about the size of my pinky nail.

I pointed to it. "An amulet stone? I remember seeing witches prepare those around the coven for different things, but nobody ever told me where they went once they were made."

Grayson took a step closer to me. "They were likely used for trades. That's how I got one and how we'll get you another." His hand raised as if he were going to stroke my arm, but then lowered it back to his side. "How was shifting and running as your wolf for the first time?"

"Magnificent," I said with a grin. "I felt like I could bust through a wall."

Grayson's lips thinned, and his eyes pinched at the sides.

"What?" I asked, a sliver of rage rising within me that I wasn't used to.

He shook his head. "Nothing. This is just different for me."

"Different how?" I brushed the back of my hand over his chest, but he captured my wrist.

"Just different." His voice was distant, but not cold like it had been before.

I smirked. "Right. So, what now?"

A branch snapped behind us and I turned to see Lia's unicorn waltzing forward before she changed back to her human form.

"All done?" she asked while taming her indigo hair with her hands.

I glanced back at Grayson, who nodded. "We can stay here for the rest of the night and then drive to Fire and Fluorite in the morning. Unless you know something else that you haven't shared yet."

Lia glanced between the two of us and frowned. "No, nothing else. Fire and Fluorite is still where we need to be. We should leave before sunrise, though."

"Why?" I asked.

Her shoulders shrugged. "Just a suggestion." Then, she turned and started heading back toward the apartments.

Lia had been distant all evening. I'd thought that maybe she was going to be different than the others I'd tried to befriend growing up, but maybe I was destined not to have any friends. It was a shitty thing to realize, but I wasn't a fan of pretending things weren't what they were.

Grayson's hand gripped my forearm when I took a step forward. "Are you okay?"

What? Was he really asking me that?

"Of course." I forced my mouth into a smile. "Why wouldn't I be?"

He didn't answer. Instead, we went back to the apartment silently, entering to find Lia already on the couch with her eyes closed. With a sigh, I headed toward the room I'd already slept in and watched Grayson enter the other without uttering another word to me.

Well, fuck.

Lia's singing from the other room woke me while it was still dark out. Not because she sounded offkey, but because she was so damn good.

I tried to enjoy the softly sung words that were sending shivers down my spine, but then my skin began to itch and the need to move overwhelmed me.

I was out of bed in the next second and opening my bedroom door without really thinking things through. Moving down the hallway, I found Lia in the living room. She was already dressed in leather pants that melded to her skin but looked soft and pliable. She had on a white tank top, and her midnight hair was pulled back into a ponytail.

Basically, she looked like a badass biker chick. I was in awe.

She turned her smile on me, acting friendlier than she had the day before. "How'd you sleep?"

"Not as well as usual, but good enough for the few hours I got," I answered, scratching at my skin.

Her eyes watched my movements. "Shifter jitters. I forgot about those. They'll go away eventually."

Right, I thought. Would have been nice to be warned about this, given I'd been feeling it since the day before.

"Oh, and I got this for you." Lia threw a small bag my way. "Might make shifting more comfortable for you."

I pulled the drawstring open at the top of the black velvet pouch and saw a silver chain inside with a yellow stone attached to it.

"Is this an amulet?" I asked, trying not to tear up at the gift. I didn't think anyone had ever given me anything before. Necessities, yes, but not something more meaningful like this.

She nodded, leaning against the counter. "I figured not having to worry about always being naked if you shifted would calm any lingering nerves. Plus, we don't need *someone* ripping men's eyes out if others see you unclothed."

I snorted, because she was probably right. "Thank you. Like, seriously. This means a lot to me."

I took a step forward to… I didn't know. Maybe hug her? But she waved me back. "Go get dressed so we can get on the road. I'll get you a snack."

As if she'd known it was coming, my stomach growled, but the sound was overshadowed by a deep rumble.

Unhurriedly, I turned around and found Grayson standing in the hallway. His flaming eyes were focused on my bare legs.

Oops. I wasn't used to living with other people, so my style of pajamas wasn't usually an issue. Though I could see how my lack of pants, thin, probably see-through shirt that I'd changed into after I'd thrown his into the corner of my room, and barely-there underwear could be a problem for…my mate. Then again, he'd seen me completely naked the day before—twice—and had already stuck his hand down my pants.

Fuck. This bond thing was complicated.

"I'm just going to get ready to go," I said cautiously with a glance back at Lia.

She chuckled. "I'll just be in here gathering snacks for the road."

Grayson had already retreated to his room by the time I'd started walking down the hallway again. I smirked. He could be cold all he wanted. I had plenty of heat to go around.

Swiftly, I gathered the donated clothes and got dressed, channeling Lia's style. Except my dark-wash jeans were more like jeggings and my tank top was charcoal, much like my wolf.

Then I secured the necklace around my neck, centering the stone over my chest. The skin beneath warmed and the itchiness I'd been feeling previously subsided immediately. I pressed my palm over the gift and smiled before moving out of the bedroom with my newly acquired things.

I stopped by the bathroom next, took care of business, put my hair in a ponytail, then double-checked that everything was cleaned up. I didn't want to disrespect D's hospitality by leaving a mess in our wake.

Once everything was cleaner than it had been when we'd arrived, I found Lia whistling in the kitchen and Grayson brooding in the corner, staring out the window.

"Oh, good," Lia said. "You're ready. We need to get going or we're going to be late."

Grayson whipped his head around. "Late for what?"

"Don't know," she quipped, then she grabbed the couple of bags from the counter and headed out the door.

He snarled. "I really don't like her."

"Then why is she here with us?" I asked, because something told me that Lia would have been left on the side of the road where we'd found her if he truly minded her company.

His lip lifted, and he said nothing in reply.

Instead, I followed him outside, taking up Lia's whistling as we got into the jeep.

The car ride was tense as Grayson headed away from the apartments, seeming to be avoiding the city buildings I could see behind us.

"I want to come back here when we're not hiding," I said with a sigh. "I've only ever read about a circus in books, and that carnival section looked like it would be fun."

Lia cringed. "I doubt D's place is anything like what you've read about."

"No, it's not," Grayson agreed stiffly.

Of course it wasn't. Not in the new not-so-new supernatural world.

Hell, I'd probably never even get the chance to see an elephant in my lifetime. I'd have to amend my bucket list to remove "ride an elephant."

We drove in the dark toward Fire and Fluorite, not seeing any other cars on the road for the first hour. When we finally did, there was a dark-colored van pulled over with two men standing on the outside of it.

My skin began to crawl, and not in the itchy way it had been before, but in the "my stomach was churning and something wasn't right" way.

"Pull over," I told Grayson when we'd already passed the vehicle.

"No," he retorted.

Fine. I didn't need his permission before when I'd jumped out the window, and I didn't need it now.

Though I hadn't considered that last time the jeep had been stopped before I'd leapt onto the road…

I heard Lia's shocked gasp and Grayson snarl my name, but there was nothing I could do once I'd committed to exiting the jeep one way or another.

To my surprise, I didn't fall into a heap of arms and legs, knocking the shit out of my body like I'd expected. I somehow managed to land gracefully on my feet, then kneeled quietly in the tall grass at the side of the road.

Grayson hit the brakes, but I wasn't paying attention to the jeep. No, my sights were set on the van still on the side of the road. I could faintly hear a child crying and two men arguing.

"You fucking moron!" one shouted. "Do you know what this fuckup is going to cost you? Go back to Fire and Fluorite and fix this."

The sound of metal bending came next. "This is on you, man. You gave me the picture with three kids. I took the one you pointed to."

There was a low growl. "Shit. This is why Johnathon only trusts the witch. We had one shot to move up. One fucking shot."

Grayson's heat pressed against my side as he and Lia joined me.

"Did he just say 'Johnathon'?" Grayson hissed, and I nodded. "We need to get them alive."

I glanced around. "Are we still in No Man's Land, or are we in Fire and Fluorite yet?"

Learning the boundaries was something I needed to figure out sooner rather than later.

"No Man's Land," Lia answered with a whisper. "The border is only another mile up, though. We need to be careful."

The child wailed again, and I tensed. We had to save the kid. I wasn't leaving here until that happened. No matter what.

"You two stay here," Grayson demanded, and I rolled my eyes.

He was such a man. More than that, I was a stubborn woman.

I let him go ahead a few yards, and then I stood, taking soft steps forward.

Lia's hand rested on my shoulder. "You're going to be such a badass."

Her words were quiet but sure and warmed my heart. A complete contrast to how I'd been feeling the night before.

I needed to ask her what had been happening yesterday, because I didn't do well with not knowing exactly where I stood with people. A life of being politely shunned had a way of fucking with one's head like that.

We followed Grayson to the van, but he was so singularly focused that he had no clue we were behind him until he'd paused at the rear. By then, it was too late to say anything or he'd have given away our current advantage.

I winked at him and peeked my head up to try to see through the window. There was a little boy bound with what I was pretty sure to be duct tape. He was lying on his side on the floor.

Fucking bastards hadn't even put him in a proper seat.

Without any idea as to what Grayson had planned, I at least wanted to let him lead. I might not have been afraid of these guys, but I also wasn't an idiot.

I had zero life skills when it came to this shit. I could fight alongside the best of them, but I wasn't about to act first without thinking and get the child hurt.

"What was that?" the man in the worn, black leather jacket asked.

The bald guy glanced around, then sniffed. "We're not alone."

Grayson casually strolled out from behind the van. "No, you're not, and if you want to live, then you're going to tell me who Johnathon is and where I can find him."

His stance was loose, but there was nothing calm about the man standing between us and the two sick assholes.

Grayson was pulsing with rage and sexy as fuck as he growled. "Don't make me ask twice. I won't be as kind the second time."

Leather jacket guy laughed. "Who the fuck do you think you are?"

I barely saw Grayson move before the idiot's head was removed from his body. "I'm the guy you don't want to fuck with when he's already pissed off."

Baldy tried to run away, but Lia and I were ready to snatch him. We each grabbed an arm and slammed him face-first into the van until I remembered the boy. Then we pinned him to the ground.

Grayson stalked forward, and the green flames in his irises that I was beginning to really enjoy made another appearance. He bent forward and grabbed the guy by the collar but kept him low.

"Where is Johnathon?" he snarled.

The smell of urine filled the air.

I gagged. "Seriously? That's fucking disgusting."

My knee pressed into the guy's shoulder blade so that I could keep my nose as far from his stench as possible.

"I-I-I don't know, man," Baldy stammered. "I'm just getting started with this crew. They hardly tell me shit. I swear."

I bent forward and gripped the collar of his shirt. "Where were you supposed to take the kid?"

"R-Right here and then Pete was going to take over next."

I glanced at Grayson, who nodded, as if to confirm he believed the blubbering shifter.

"What do we do with him now?" Lia asked, looking between me and Grayson.

Since I wasn't the professional kidnapper or killer here, I let him answer.

"If he doesn't know anything, we have to kill him," he muttered with annoyance.

Baldy wailed beneath us. "Please, don't. I swear I won't tell anyone what happened here today. I'll say I gave Pete the kid and went on my way."

With how easily Grayson had killed the other dude, I wasn't sure he was in the "letting kidnappers go" kind of mood, but I previously hadn't expected him to kiss me and stick his hand down my pants, either. Crazier things had happened in the last few days.

Grayson picked the guy up from the ground and held him in the air with one hand. "You're coming with us."

Baldy's muddy eyes widened. "Why? Just kill me now if you're not going to let me go."

I scoffed. This asshole wanted mercy after he'd stolen a kid? Not fucking likely, but cool of him to think it was possible.

"You're going with us to Fire and Fluorite," Grayson said. "I want this kid's parents to know who stole their son and let them decide what to do with you."

"Watch out," I shouted, but Grayson was already paying attention and he threw the dude back on the ground as Baldy vomited all over himself.

Apparently, fear took away the guy's ability to control his bodily functions.

He used the bottom of his navy shirt to wipe his snot away while pulling his knees to his chest. "Please just kill me. I'm begging you."

It seemed as if Grayson was tempted, but Lia stepped between them. "No, you were right. We need to take him with us."

"I know that," he muttered, bending down and grabbing the guy by the foot. "Take the kid in the jeep. I'll tie this asshole up."

Without needing to be told twice, I moved to the back doors and opened them slowly, hoping not to startle the poor boy after everything he'd just overheard.

He whimpered when the rising sun shone down on his dirtied face and blond hair that fell to his ears. Hell, he couldn't be more than six. He had to be terrified.

I lowered myself to his height and smiled as I reached for the duct tape over his mouth. "Hi, there. I'm Kinsley. What's your name?" I asked, trying to distract him a little while I jerked the covering from his face.

He winced, and a single tear formed in his soft blue eyes, but then he tilted his head up like a brave little boy and whispered, "Sammy."

"Well, Sammy. My friends and I would like to take you back to your family," I said softly. "Would you be okay if I took the rest of the tape off you and carried you to that car over there?"

He glanced over my shoulder with shiny eyes, then nodded, raising his bound hands. "It hurts."

I reached for his wrists. "I know, buddy. I'm really sorry this happened to you, but we're going to get you home soon. I promise."

Using my new shifter strength, I ripped the tape from his skin as gently yet quickly as I could, and the brave little boy didn't even shed a tear.

As soon as I had the restraints off his ankles, he shocked me by throwing his arms around my neck, clinging to me so tightly that it was a little hard to breathe.

My arms circled around him, and I rubbed a hand over his spine before turning around.

Lia was grinning. "I'll drive." She headed to the jeep.

I glanced at Grayson. "Do you need help?"

He was staring at me oddly. Given he'd just murdered someone, I didn't expect to see something soft within the depths of dark eyes, but there it was, nonetheless.

"Just keep him safe," Grayson said gruffly, then he resumed throwing the kidnapper into the back of the van.

Before I could analyze anything else, Sammy shuddered in my arms, and I decided walking away before he could see Grayson not-so-kindly tie up the kidnapper was probably a good idea.

CHAPTER THIRTEEN

GRAYSON

Kinsley continued to take me by surprise with everything that she did. She hadn't even blinked an eye when I'd taken a head off the first guy, and she'd been ready to kill the other if I'd wanted. And even though I knew she hadn't done the things I'd first accused her of, seeing her with that little boy changed something in me.

She was gentle and kind and patient with him, asking for permission to do what needed to be done instead of scaring him more by just removing him from the van without explaining that he was safe now.

It wasn't as if I was a family man with dreams of settling down one day, but my baby sister had been the brightest light in my life for the ten years that she'd been alive. She'd been everything to me. When she was taken from me, I'd lost a piece of myself that I knew I would never get back.

Yet watching Kinsley walk away with Sammy, as I'd heard her call the boy, reminded me that the world wasn't always a cesspool of shit. On top of that, the bond was clawing at my chest, begging me to claim the woman I wasn't sure I wanted.

Well, that was a lie. I knew I wanted her, but I didn't deserve her.

She was strong, sure, but she was innocent. Being with me would take that away from her, and while I was a selfish bastard at times, I wasn't sure I could take away the life she could have without me if we didn't complete our bond.

But now wasn't the time to think about those things. We needed to get Sammy back to his family, and I needed to get the reeking piece of shit I had tied up in the back away from my sense of smell.

Lia drove the jeep the rest of the way to Fire and Fluorite with Kinsley, who kept Sammy in her lap the whole time. I followed behind in the van, staying right on their ass. I didn't want to be any farther from them than I already was.

The structures we passed had broken windows, no lights on, and some of them looked like they'd been on fire a time or two. Based on the stories I'd heard, I expected to see people in the streets with weapons, but that wasn't the case.

Instead, it was eerily quiet this time of morning, which had the muscles in my back tensing as we continued through the streets.

I could see the boy giggling in Kinsley's arms as she seemed to keep talking to him until he pointed up ahead.

Lia turned down a street and he pointed again.

Houses began popping up, and I saw a few curtains flutter, but nobody came out to see who was creeping through their neighborhood. Interesting.

Thanks to not having a top on the jeep, I caught Sammy frown at Kinsley, then shake his head. He must have gotten lost. Not surprising, considering he was maybe six years old.

Kinsley looked back at me, and I could see the frustration in her eyes, but when she turned back to Sammy, she was smiling again as if everything was okay.

How could anyone have thought this woman would pass for a murdering witch? That had been Johnathon's first mistake. His second had been trying to trick me into doing his dirty work.

I glanced back at the guy I had tied to the metal floor of the van. "Where did you take the kid from?"

"I'll tell you if you promise to kill me quickly," he pleaded, snot and tears covering his face.

Fucking hell. Johnathon clearly wasn't as powerful as he'd

portrayed through that well-crafted message if he was hiring pathetic men like this.

I nodded. "Sure. We can work that out, but first, we want to get the boy back where he belongs."

His sigh of relief was like nails on a chalkboard for my ears.

"I found him playing at a park near Seventh and Peach," he answered, then he closed his eyes. "I'm ready."

I chuckled darkly. "You're fucking out of your mind if you think I'm going to show you any mercy."

I got out of the van, leaving him bound to the floor while I went to tell Kinsley and Lia what he'd shared.

My head shook. Peach Street. Humans and the things they named. I never understood why they used food names for roads. It was fucking weird.

"He isn't sure which way to go from here," Kinsley said when I approached her side of the jeep.

I patted Sammy's shoulders. "It's okay, little man. I figured out where the park is. Does that help?"

He brushed his tears away. "I think."

His big lips still trembled, so I offered him a smile. "I'm sure your family is there looking for you right now."

Sammy frowned. "My daddy is going to be so mad at that bad man."

Kinsley's stare met mine, and I was certain we were both thinking that was an interesting thing for a kid to say. Maybe we'd stumbled on to something more than we'd yet realized.

"Follow me," I said to Lia before getting back in the van.

The street we were currently parked on was Second Ave, so we didn't have much farther to go. Though when we got to Seventh, I wasn't sure if we should turn left or right, given I couldn't see a park from the intersection.

I glanced back at the jeep, and Kinsley was pointing left, so that was where I went. Sure enough, within five blocks, there was a park and a nicer neighborhood that was surrounded by fences with barbed wire circling the top.

Up ahead was a group of about twenty shifters, all dressed in black combat clothing. Their eyes locked on me in the van when I stopped, and I held my hands up as I got out of the driver's seat.

"Are you looking for someone?" I asked calmly, and a man pushed through the center of them. He wasn't dressed for combat, but instead, was wearing a crisp, charcoal-colored suit with a white shirt and black tie.

His hazel eyes narrowed on me, and his blond hair was nearly identical to that of the boy behind me.

"Daddy!" Sammy called out.

The approaching man stared behind me briefly, and then he pointed at me. "You're going to fucking wish you'd never touched my son."

His voice was menacing, but I didn't try to reason with him. There was no point until he had hands on his child. I might not have been a parent, but I'd still loved Addie fiercely. I could understand the fury he was undoubtedly feeling.

After he stomped past me, Kinsley was helping Sammy from the jeep and the boy ran right into his father's arms. "I'm sorry, Daddy. The bad man tricked me. I didn't mean to leave the swings."

"It's okay, Sammy," he said softly. "I've got you now and Daddy's going to take care of the bad man."

Sammy pointed to the van. "He's in there."

The man's brow furrowed. "What do you mean?"

"That nice man over there put the bad man into the back of the van I was in," Sammy said. "Then the pretty ladies let me ride with them. I got to sit in the front seat!"

Any fear that the child had been feeling seemed to be gone, and he went on and on about how there was no roof and how silly that was, but it was also really fun, so maybe not so silly.

The man gave his son another tight squeeze, then set him down. "Why don't you go see Uncle Tuck while I talk to these *nice* people?"

Sammy frowned. "Is he mad at me?"

His hand rubbed over Sammy's messy hair. "Not at all. We're just glad you're okay."

The boy nodded, then ran for the group of men who had moved a little closer but still were about twenty feet away from us.

"I'm Ryder," the dad said, walking toward me. This time, without a murderous glare.

I shook his offered hand. "Grayson." I nodded behind him. "That's Kinsley in grey and Lia in white."

"What happened to my son?" Ryder demanded, glancing behind me, likely at Sammy.

Kinsley stepped forward and moved to my side. My arm twitched to pull her against me and mark my territory, but I refrained as she began to speak.

"Sammy told me that he was swinging with his friends while the adults talked. The 'bad man' as he called the asshole we have tied up in the van, apparently had balloons and, from the sounds of it, was hiding behind some bushes. His friends told him not to go, but Sammy wanted to be brave like his daddy, so he went anyway."

"Fuck," Ryder snarled. "How did you get him?"

Lia answered this time. "Just the right time, right place."

I went with that answer, even though I knew rescuing Sammy must have been the reason Lia had insisted we leave No Man's Circus before sunrise. The unicorn could keep her secrets. They weren't mine to tell when they didn't affect me or Kinsley.

"Did you kill him?" Ryder asked, turning his stare to me.

I shook my head. "I took the head off the guy he was meeting up with, but I thought you might want to speak with the kidnapper your-self. He'll probably tell you anything if you don't torture him, but from what I gathered, he doesn't know much. Do you know someone named Johnathon who runs a crew in No Man's Land?"

Ryder's lips thinned. "No, but I will soon if he had anything to do with this."

"Are you the House leader here?" Kinsley asked, one of her hands rubbing over her chest as she took a deep breath.

Something was clearly bothering her, but I hadn't the slightest clue what. I tried to halt the rising annoyance that was causing me while Ryder responded.

"Fire and Fluorite doesn't technically have a leader right now," he answered. "There are three factions fighting for supremacy in this area, and I lead one of them. While I have stepped up when needed as our

House representative when the other leaders have met, nobody rules over our House like Shade and Mathis did. Though I wouldn't call what Mathis did here ruling."

"What happened—" Kinsley started to ask more questions, but I cut her off.

"Later might be better for questions," I said.

Ryder nodded and stuck his hands in his pockets. "Yes. I'd like to know more about where the three of you came from and what you were doing when you stumbled across my son, but for now, I need to tend to Sammy and then meet his captor."

The leader whistled, and another man with a thin scar down the left side of face quickly appeared at his side. "Drake, take these three to one of our guest houses until I decide what to do with them."

The dark-haired warrior nodded. "Of course, Alpha."

Drake reached for my arm, but I snarled at him. "Touching me isn't necessary."

He shared a look with Ryder, who merely nodded curtly, then began walking. The three of us followed Drake, heading in the opposite direction of the faction leader.

Kinsley was fidgeting, and her breathing was heavy as we continued walking down the nearest street within the fenced neighborhood.

"Are you okay?" I asked.

She didn't answer right away, a crease deepening between her brows. "I don't know."

I didn't continue with any other questions. Ryder's men didn't need to know anything more about us than they had to. All that mattered was that they were offering us refuge in a House that was as volatile as a homemade bomb.

For now, that was good enough.

CHAPTER FOURTEEN

We were taken to a small house with dark-green siding and cream trim. There was a small porch out front that looked like a nice place to relax until I noticed the scorch marks and bullet holes in the chairs that were sitting next to the door.

Right. We were in somewhat of a warzone. Just because we'd made it inside Fire and Fluorite safely didn't mean that we would stay that way.

More importantly, something within me was off. I was freaking out at first, but the longer we were within the House, the more the stirring inside me seemed familiar.

I had no idea why since I'd been trapped at my coven for nearly three decades, never even venturing through Earth and Emerald, because I didn't have a House ring.

Nowhere should have been familiar to me. Yet…this desolate place was. Like the home I'd always hoped for. Somewhere I could truly belong.

Drake opened the front door and stayed outside as we passed by him. "Ryder will come see you whenever he has time. There's food inside, along with three bedrooms. If you leave this house, you leave behind the protection you've been temporarily offered."

The unspoken threat was clear. They'd possibly be the ones to kill us if we did anything besides what we'd been told.

I expected Grayson to disagree with that, but he stayed quiet and shut the door.

Given how off-kilter I was feeling, I headed for the kitchen and opened the fridge. There wasn't much there besides condiments and drinks. Inside the freezer were icy-looking corndogs. *Fuck.*

I checked the cabinets and groaned. "So much for the food he mentioned."

"You won't die from whatever's there," Lia said from the couch.

I raised a brow and peeked around the corner at her. "How do you know?"

"I can still sense your future," she said nonchalantly.

Super. So I could maybe get sick, but I would still live.

Whatever. I was fucking ravenous and needed more than the snacks we'd had in the jeep during the drive here.

I grabbed two of the corndogs and popped them into the microwave. I pressed a few buttons and was thankful the house was at least magically charged with electricity. We didn't have to worry about not being able to use things like lights and water since power companies weren't a thing anymore.

Grayson came into the kitchen. His eyes were on me, and I shivered from the depths of their darkness. I should have been afraid of what I saw there, but instead, I wanted nothing more than to lose myself with him.

Insane, I knew, but it was the truth, and I wasn't going to bother denying it.

I walked toward him, fully expecting him to move away or stop me somehow, but he didn't. I pressed my palms over his chest, and his heart was hammering beneath my touch.

Yeah. The fucker could tell me all he wanted that he didn't want me, but I knew that was utter bullshit.

If only I knew more about what I was doing besides what I'd read in books.

"What's wrong with you?" he asked through gritted teeth as I stared up at him.

Being near him had taken away my previous unease, but his question had the foreign feeling rising to the surface again.

I pointed to my chest. "Something feels off here. Not like wrong or bad, just different. Is that a wolf thing?"

His hand raised, and he hesitated to touch me, but then he finally caved as he pushed aside my new necklace without commenting on the gift. His heated skin felt like it was burning through my tank top and scorching my chest.

I shivered from equal parts pain and pleasure. "Do you feel anything?"

"Do you ever stop talking?" he countered.

He had a point. I tended to ramble when I was nervous, because silence only made me more uncomfortable, but whatever he was doing was drawing out the weirdness I'd been feeling, so I tried to keep my mouth shut.

"It's your wolf, but this isn't a normal 'wolf thing,' as you put it," Grayson answered another minute later.

My mouth turned down. "Am I still broken?"

He moved until he was cupping my cheek. "There isn't, and never has been, anything broken about you, Kinsley."

Fuck me. Why did those words make me want to strip our clothes off?

"Will you shut that stupid thing off?" Lia yelled from the living room. "I can only pretend I don't hear everything for so long."

Oops. Though I wasn't sorry. I reached back and opened the microwave that had apparently been beeping for who-knew-how-long while I'd been enraptured by Grayson.

The corndogs looked even worse cooked, and suddenly, I didn't have an appetite.

Grayson made a noise I'd yet to hear from him. "I'll be back with something proper to eat."

Before I could object or remind him of Drake's unspoken warning, Grayson was halfway out the door.

I threw the corndogs away and tossed myself onto the couch opposite Lia. "This fucking sucks. Why did we come here again?"

She peeked her eyes back open and grinned. "You're just hangry for your man and a proper meal. Once you get at least one of those things, I'm sure you won't be so frustrated."

The unicorn wasn't wrong about that.

Considering I didn't expect to get much alone time with Lia, I sat up and tucked my feet under me. "Are you trying to sleep?"

She turned her head, which was resting on a flat throw pillow. "Meh. More just trying not to be a third wheel."

I glanced down at my twisting hands. "You got us to Fire and Fluorite. You don't have to stay any longer if you don't want to."

Lia was up and out of her seat in the next second. She sat beside me and lifted my chin. "Where is that confident woman I met before who was putting Grayson in his place?"

I shrugged. "That was survival instinct."

She grabbed my hand and held it between both of hers. The frostiness of her skin cooled my own, something I hadn't noticed before.

"Listen," she said. "Unicorns aren't all-knowing. If I've offended you, please don't be afraid to say something."

I choked on a laugh. "If you've done something? I thought *I'd* done something. You weren't around much yesterday when I expected you to be, and I don't know. I just… Well, I've never had a friend, so I don't know. Just ignore me. It's dumb."

Her bright eyes stared directly into mine, and she glared. "Kinsley Ash. Don't you ever say your feelings are dumb. I won't tolerate that kind of bullshit. Not in our friendship. Even if you're not seeing the situation fully, what you *feel* matters. You matter. Never be afraid to speak your piece. That's the only way to build a true friendship. Something I hope you and I will have one day."

Emotions burned at the back of my throat. "Seriously? I thought you were only here because you felt like you had to be and that you'd probably be gone just as soon as your obligations from the visions were met."

She waved a flippant hand. "Hell no. Not unless I need to be for reasons beyond my control. I haven't had a vision in years. Learning about you in the weird ways I did was the highlight of my decade. I only disappeared yesterday because you and Grayson need to work out your shit sooner rather than later. You won't do that with me hovering around all the time."

My hands covered my face. I felt so stupid. Maybe the reason I'd never had friends wasn't only because I was supposed to be in hiding without knowing it, but also because I was just terrible at this whole thing.

Lia pried my fingers apart until she could see my eyes again. "Talk to me."

I shook my head and dropped my arms back to my sides. "No. Just forget I said anything. Everything is fine. I swear."

She huffed and rolled her eyes. "Seriously, woman. You've got a vagina. Use it. Don't be afraid to say how you feel. Anyone who shames you for that isn't worthy of your time, and you should consider yourself thankful to get rid of them if they can't handle who you are."

I was pretty sure I was falling a little in love with Lia as she continued to build me up. Nobody in my life had ever done that.

Again, it wasn't like I'd been treated as a slave in my coven, but that almost would have been preferable. At least then it would have seemed as if people *saw* me.

I threw my arms around her neck. "Thank you."

"Don't thank me yet." She chuckled and the action vibrated through my chest. "You still haven't told me what you're really thinking about. Even if we're good, you still need to talk through that shit. It's the only way to grow, and I'm really good at making people uncomfortable in the name of growth."

My stomach churned, and I backed away from her. "No, thanks. I think there's been enough uncomfortableness over the last few days to last me a lifetime."

Lia flicked me in the boob and glared. "Don't tell me *no*. You have no idea what I'm capable of."

"You're right, I don't know much about you, but you seem to know tons about me," I said sincerely. "How about you tell me a few things?

Like maybe how old you are, where you lived before we found you, or even about your hopes and dreams?"

She sighed at my antics. "I'm old enough, and in case nobody ever told you, it's impolite to ask a woman about her age. Also, to ask if she's pregnant, even if it's blatantly obvious, or to ask how many sexual partners she's chosen to have. Everything else should be pretty much free game, but you might also not get the answers you're hoping for. Especially from me."

Lia paused, and while her tone was completely sweet, I was once again feeling uncomfortable with not knowing how to properly do this friendship thing.

She nudged me then continued, "That's not to say I don't want to tell you in particular, but I just don't talk about my personal life a lot. I've lived a long time, I've lost all of my family, and I had to keep who I am a secret for many years. This is just the way I'm wired, and it's all on me. Hopefully, you can understand that."

My heart ached for her. I hated that she'd been alone for any period of time, but I could at least understand that. Well, sort of, since my past seemed to be riddled with secrets I'd yet to uncover.

"Thank you for sharing what you have," I said sincerely. "I can't relate to what you've been through, but maybe we can figure all this out together. It also helps to know you didn't disappear yesterday because you were already tired of me."

I laughed at my own words, but deep down, my anxiety still twisted at my core. That was going to take some serious pep talks to work through.

Lia waggled her brows at me and grinned. "Are you going to tell me what happened between the two of you? There's no way you avoided each other the whole time you were alone."

Heat crept up in my cheeks, and I shook my head. I wasn't even sure I could say the words out loud. Hell, I'd just had my first kiss the day before. Going from that to gossiping about how hot Grayson made me was quite the leap.

"I think that's a secret I'll keep to myself for now," I said, "but I can tell you things went from okay to really great to horrible, then to weird over the course of yesterday. I'm not sure how much of my attraction is the bond pulling us together and how much is because Grayson is too sexy for his own good, but I know he's also feeling something. So that helps."

"If the horrible moment is something you need me to help you get revenge for, just know, I have no boundaries when it comes to giving people their comeuppance."

The laugh that bubbled out of me felt so freeing. Like shedding a layer of my prior life and finding something new and exciting that offered a bright spot in my future.

It was…unexpected, yet something I wouldn't soon forget.

"Thank you," I said. "I don't think that will be necessary, but I'll keep your offer in mind."

She closed her eyes and leaned back against the couch. Her eyelids fluttered, and she took several breaths, then sat straight up. "I need to go."

"What? Why?" Panic rose as I glanced back at the door.

Sure, I could kick some serious ass in hand-to-hand combat, but being alone in a house owned by a bunch of wolf shifters who looked like they murdered people for breakfast didn't seem all that appealing.

"Grayson is almost back," Lia answered as she got up and tightened her ponytail. "I promise, you'll be okay. I wouldn't leave otherwise, but this is important enough to ignore Drake's threat."

I got to my feet and followed her a short distance. "Can you share anything?"

"Not yet, but something about this nudge is powerful. I'll tell you more when I'm back." She went to the door and cracked it open, winking at me. "Don't worry. I know how to blend in when I have to."

Yeah, that wasn't helpful in easing my worries, considering all the shit that had been going down around us.

Lia walked out, and I heard the door lock on its own.

Great. What the hell was I supposed to do now?

I got up and noticed one short hallway on the right and a longer one on my left. I went right first since there was only one door and it was closer.

Opening it, I found there was a small bedroom with a glass door leading out into a backyard with dead grass. The mattress was covered with a white comforter that I was pretty sure was filled with feathers that were suddenly calling to me.

Glancing around, I also noticed a bathroom and small wardrobe area, but my eyes kept going back to the bed. They even started to burn with weariness.

Maybe a nap wouldn't be so bad…

That was my last thought before my face met the soft pillows.

CHAPTER FIFTEEN

GRAYSON

Getting proper food shouldn't have been so fucking difficult, but apparently, the guards were under strict orders to ignore us until Ryder had further vetted us. Something I got out of a teenager who nearly pissed himself when I cornered him behind a building.

After only managing to find a store that had already been looted, I at least found some canned food. It wasn't much better than a freezer-burnt corndog, but it would be good enough for the time being.

When I got back to the house, the door was locked. I knocked, but I couldn't hear any voices inside.

I swore to the gods if those two women had left of their own accord, I was going to tie them both up next time I had to leave.

And if they'd been taken… Well, that made my inner demon perk up, considering my last hunting expedition had ended with me finding a mate and not someone who needed to have their still-beating heart removed from their chest.

I was tempted to bust the door down, but since I didn't want to make things more tense with our stay than they already seemed, I headed around the side of the house, checking for windows and other doors.

None of the windows were unlocked, but I found a door at the back of the house. I tried the handle, but it didn't budge. Blocking the glare of the rising sun with my hand, I looked through the glass of the door and I saw Kinsley lying face-first on the mattress.

She wasn't moving and, if she was alive, I was pretty sure she couldn't sleep like that and still breathe properly.

Rage overpowered my rationale, and I yanked the door from its hinges, shattering the glass window as I did.

With the noise, Kinsley screamed and scrambled to her feet, arms out and ready for a fight.

"Fucking hell," I snarled, dropping the paper bag I had in my hand. "I thought you were dead."

She let out a shuddering breath. "It's called a nap, you psycho. Maybe you need one, too."

I stalked toward her, fury born from so many things rising inside me. Impressively, she didn't even flinch when I got in her face and grabbed her arms.

"Don't call me a 'psycho,'" I growled. Kinsley had never met a true psychopath like my father and his demon followers had been. Regardless of my rage, I would never be like them. I could control who and what I was.

She cocked her head to the side. "Would you prefer I used 'demented'? 'Crazy'? 'Manic'?"

Her mouth needed to be taught a lesson.

My right hand moved further up until it was cupping her chin. "Enough."

"Or what?" she countered.

I sat on the bed behind us and laid her over my lap. "Or my hand is going to become acquainted with your ass."

She stiffened. "You wouldn't dare."

My hand came down firmly over her right cheek, but not enough to leave a bruise. The sound was drowned out by Kinsley's gasp. Though, if I was reading the situation right, it wasn't because of pain. Nowhere near that.

"You bastard," she hissed, but there was a slight moan lacing her words.

I spanked her again. "Keep it up. I can do this all day."

"Fuck you," she spat, moving out of my grasp, and then she was shoving me until I was lying on the bed and her knees pinned my arms down.

Her move wasn't anything that I couldn't get out of, but given her ass was settled over my hardening cock, I decided to see what this innocent, mouthy woman was going to do next.

"Fuck me?" I challenged. "I didn't think you were being literal."

She took in our compromising position, then raised her hand, but I blocked her attempt to punch me in the jaw.

"Uh-uh. I don't think so," I said, then I flipped our positions. Violence wasn't what I was in the mood for.

Regardless of the voice in my head telling me that I didn't deserve to touch this woman, I couldn't help myself when her cheeks were flushed and her tits were pushed together, begging me to devour them, thanks to the way I had her hands locked over her stomach.

Without any resistance from Kinsley, I moved her hands above her head and lowered myself until our heads were even. "What do you want from me, Kinsley?"

"I want you to go fuck yourself," she snarled.

Someone clearly wasn't happy about her abrupt wake up, but I could sense the lie in her words.

I trailed a single finger over her chest and the swell of her cleavage. "You see, I'd believe you if I didn't know better."

She glared hard at me, her breathing becoming ragged. "What makes you think you know better?"

D was the only person still alive who knew that I could tell truth from lie, but as Kinsley lay underneath me, squirming from my touch with a fire in her eyes that reminded me much of my own, I didn't want to keep this from her.

"You haven't asked about my demon side," I pointed out. "Something I'm sure you know very little about, but something you should be aware of, is that I can tell if someone is lying to me. That gift has never failed me and it's not now."

"Maybe you're wrong." She heaved.

I shook my head lightly. "No, my little temptress, I'm not. You don't want me to fuck myself, you want me to fuck *you*. To make you feel more of what you felt back at the circus. To know what it's like to have my dick pounding inside you, owning you, body and soul."

It was easy to forget that I'd overheard she was a virgin when the pull of the bond was pulsing between us, and she was licking her lips hungrily while digging her nails into my hands.

"And what would you do if that was what I really wanted?" she countered, her words still sounding choppy.

My nose brushed against her cheek, and I scraped my teeth over her neck before whispering in her ear. "Then I'd give you what you needed, but only if you asked nicely."

Her responding moan was combined with a growl that no doubt meant I'd pushed another one of her buttons, but then…

She broke free of the hold I'd had on her hands and grabbed my shirt before smashing her lips against mine.

The kiss was rough and angry, but it was filled with so much fucking passion.

My tongue sank into her mouth, tasting her sweetness and battling for dominance against her.

She was hardly submissive in this state, and I would have thought I'd hate that, but she was too fucking sexy to hate anything about her.

"I'm not asking for shit," she muttered against my lips, then she shoved me off her.

I wasn't in the business of taking anything from a woman, so I let her movements push me onto the mattress.

When I thought she was going to leave the room, she surprised me by undoing the top button of her pants. "Fuck me."

Her demand was hot as fuck, and my dick twitched painfully in the jeans that were currently keeping it restricted.

Still, as much as I wanted to, I wasn't going to fuck Kinsley. Not yet.

She might have thought she was ready for more, but I needed to make sure she understood what having sex with me meant, given how sheltered her upbringing had been.

It wasn't just going to be the best fuck she could ever have or about losing her virginity. Having sex meant tying us together in a magical sense. Completing a bond she may or may not want when she was thinking clearly.

That was a decision she wasn't going to make while her libido—and our connection—was driving her mad with need.

I stood up and yanked on her ponytail until her chin pointed upward. "Get on the bed."

She shivered and reached for her pants again, but I batted her hand away.

"I *said*, get on the bed."

"I don't want to be dressed when I get back on that bed," she said, keeping her eyes locked on mine. "And if you fucking treat me like you did last time, my wolf's teeth are going to leave a mark or two on your body."

"Do as I say and there won't be any need for threats," I said evenly.

Fucking hell. It was going to be hard not to fuck her the way I wanted, but my mouth on her wetting pussy would have to be good enough for now.

Her eyes heated as I helped her undress, but the small creases around her eyes told me the heat wasn't just from the building hunger between us.

As soon as her pants and underwear came off, I finally saw the flash of uncertainty in her face. She nibbled at her lip and slowed her movements, but before the nerves could completely unravel her, I bent forward and captured her mouth with my own.

I normally wasn't one to give a shit about a woman's feelings, but this wasn't just any woman. This was Kinsley. My mate, even though I hadn't been looking for her. I had to be what she needed, even if she didn't know what that was.

She kissed me back, and her hands began tugging at my shirt, but I pushed them to her sides. "No."

Her brows furrowed as she settled down onto the mattress. "No?"

"I won't leave you how I did back at the circus," I promised, "but we're not having sex until I know you understand what that means."

And given I didn't want to have that conversation with my cock aching and her writhing beneath me, I dropped to my knees before she could respond.

My hands pushed her thighs farther apart, meeting no resistance from my little temptress. When I traced a finger between her folds, she bucked from my touch and moaned loudly.

I pressed my thumb over her clit before bringing my face forward and trailing my tongue over the path my finger had just taken.

"Holy fuck," Kinsley cried out. "Don't you fucking stop."

It was hard to believe she was as innocent as the previously overheard conversation made her seem, but I couldn't forget that Kinsley wasn't a child. She was nearly thirty years old and didn't need to be coddled.

I lapped at her folds, devouring her sweet taste, and grew harder by the second. My thumb circled around her clit as my tongue did the rest of the work. All too soon, her thighs were squeezing around my ears, and she was panting heavily.

"So c-close," she stuttered.

Using my other hand, I slipped a finger inside her, enjoying how responsive she was. Her inner muscles clamped down, and her back arched before another moan ripped from deep within.

I pressed my finger up and must have hit her detonate button, because she screamed and shuddered around me.

"Grayson," she moaned, and the sound of my name coming passionately from her lips was like throwing gasoline on an already raging fire.

My face lifted and I saw her head still tilted back on the bed with her glorious tits raised into the air, ready to be feasted upon.

Her body convulsed several times before she reopened her eyes to find me watching her. A blush covered her cheeks and her lashes fluttered. "That was... I've never felt..."

I stood up and closed her legs before I got any other ideas, grinning proudly. "I know."

She raised a brow. "Oh, you do, huh?"

"I can smell my triumph, and there's nothing wrong with that." I wasn't in the mood to banter with her when I could also still taste her pleasure in my mouth.

Her eyes cast down to my bulging pants. "There's something wrong with that, though."

"And that's not your problem." I turned to head into the bathroom, but she grabbed my hand, halting my movements.

Without waiting for me to turn around, she said, "Just because I haven't had sex yet doesn't mean you need to treat me any differently than you would any other woman."

I moved slowly, taking a breath before speaking. "I'm 'treating you differently' as you say, because you're *not* just 'any other woman,' Kinsley. You're my mate."

She sucked in a breath and lifted her knees up to cover herself. "Oh."

Yeah. *Oh*.

I hadn't expected those words to leave my mouth, but it was the truth, and I didn't want to lie to her.

Shit. If I were being honest, I didn't even want to keep her at a distance. Everything about her called to me. Bond or not, there was something powerful about Kinsley. She was confident in herself. She wasn't afraid to say what was on her mind. She had a strength inside her very few others did. One that I couldn't wait to see flourish.

I walked back to her and gripped her chin. "I'll be right back, and then we're going to talk."

She nodded, and my inner wolf hummed in approval.

This woman was ours.

CHAPTER SIXTEEN

KINSLEY

Well, fuck. I hadn't expected to wake up to a raging Grayson or to be ravaged by him in the next second. Though, neither of those things was bad.

I might have enjoyed pissing him off, but that didn't mean my feelings for him weren't growing. The attraction had been instant, but the deeper emotions—those weren't something I'd be able to ignore forever.

More importantly, I didn't think they'd been fabricated merely because of the bond I knew we shared. Grayson was slowly showing me that he was more than a hunter of people. That he cared more than he liked to admit. That he would do anything to protect those he deemed innocent.

Hell, even his demon side didn't deter me. I knew there was something darker festering inside him, but Grayson was in control. That much, I felt confident about.

And the way he made me feel? I removed my already loose ponytail and let my head drop back onto the mattress. There were so many emotions filtering through me that I didn't yet understand, but more than what Grayson elicited from me, there was something about this place that was different.

Something about Fire and Fluorite felt familiar, as if I should have known more about the House than I did.

A stirring moved through me, and I got up from the bed to get dressed before Grayson came back. Presumably, he was in the bathroom taking care of *his* business. I would have done that for him, but I'd seen the fire in his eyes and known there'd been no point in arguing with him.

As much as I enjoyed our banter, I couldn't deny I was eager for him to come back so we could talk. We'd only been around each other a few days, but we were due for some open communication.

That was at least one thing I didn't normally have a problem with outside of trying to make friends. Then again, I'd never had a boyfriend…or mate. Hopefully, I wasn't about to freeze up on him.

I got dressed and waited for him on the bed. Within ten minutes, Grayson was back in the bedroom, and the dark-green flames I enjoyed in those cognac eyes of his were no longer present.

His hair was wet and falling over his forehead, making me want to run my fingers through the ebony strands.

"Good shower?" I asked.

"Could have been better." He sat next to me on the bed, leaving about a foot of space between us. "How are you feeling?"

Chuckling, I twisted until I was facing him. "That's a bit of a loaded question, don't you think?"

He shrugged. "Not really."

"How about we start with you?" I countered since he rarely opened up. "How are *you*?"

Grayson surprised me by reaching for my hand, his eyes staring down at our intertwining fingers. "I'm glad I couldn't kill you."

I wasn't sure how I was supposed to feel about that statement, so I stayed quiet, thankful when he continued.

"You know that I was murderous when I thought you'd taken the lives of children, but you don't know why." He paused to take a deep breath. "I had a little sister. Her name was Addie, and she was ten when her life was pointlessly taken by demons from my past."

Fuck. I'd just thought he had a soft spot in his heart like any normal being would for kids. I didn't consider the situation had been personal for him.

"I'm so sorry, Grayson," I said softly, squeezing his hand tighter.

His head shook gruffly. "Don't apologize. It wasn't your fault, and I got my revenge. A few demons at a time. Including my father."

"Did it make you feel better?" I asked genuinely.

Grayson shrugged. "In some ways, yes. None of the demons I killed would be able to hurt anyone else. Knowing that helped, but it took years to process the real grief that I'd temporarily been able to push down while I hunted them."

My other hand reached up and briefly stroked his cheek. "Thank you for sharing that with me."

One side of his lip lifted slightly. "I figured you deserved that and probably more, but enough about me for now. Are you doing okay?"

"All things considered, yeah. I've wanted to find a life beyond Earth and Emerald for years. Sure, I could have gone without being kidnapped, but the end result is going to be the same." I added a wink, trying to lighten the heaviness around us.

"How do you know things will be the same?" he asked with a tilt of his head.

"I just do. Something about all of this feels right." I paused. "Not like Lia's intuition or anything, but being here doesn't make me nervous like I'd expected it to after everything I'd heard about this House."

Grayson's eyes darkened. "What do you know about your parents?"

That was a swift change in conversation.

"Nothing," I answered. "Well, besides the fact that there was a woman I assume was my mother who left me at the coven when I was a baby."

He looked away and nodded before turning back to me with a softer look. "About earlier. Do you know much about mates?"

I knew enough. Or at least, I had thought so before he'd asked me. Once I'd learned what I'd considered to be the basics, I'd decided I hadn't needed to know anymore.

Well, assumed instead of decided. When I'd accepted that romance wasn't going to be in the cards for me unless I found a way to escape my coven, my attention had shifted to fictional love stories. Fantasy and supernatural romance that I had lived vicariously through and that had helped me get through the darkest of my lonely days.

"A little bit," I answered honestly. "It was easy to know who you were to me when I saw you. The energy that connected us didn't seem like it would accept being ignored. I also knew about the rejection, but that was more because Sally Jones had been rejected and the whole coven felt her wrath and it was gossiped about in length."

Grayson didn't say anything for a long moment. "You still have the opportunity to reject me until we have sex."

That I hadn't been aware of. I mean, I should have known there was an expiration date on kicking him to the curb, but I didn't realize there was an action associated with that.

"Oh."

He smirked. "You say that a lot when you're surprised."

"Well, it's better than *mother fucking hell,* don't you think?" I countered with a raised brow.

"No, I don't actually." He licked his lips, and I badly wanted to kiss him again, but this was the first time we'd actually talked without fighting. I wasn't ready for that to be over yet.

"So that's why you didn't want to have sex with me?" I asked, feeling slightly better than before.

His chest rumbled. "I absolutely want to have sex with you. I just knew better than to let you do something before you were fully aware of the consequences."

I was pretty sure I was supposed to be happy about his reply, but I wasn't sure how I felt.

Maybe I was still on a high from leaving my coven and experiencing so much in such a short time. Maybe it was the bond or possibly even being in this House. Or maybe this was just how things were supposed to be and a part of me already knew that.

The part that was feeling extra connected to the things and people around me. That wasn't afraid of whatever was coming next.

His eyes darkened and stared up at me. "There's one other thing."

He paused. "When the full moon comes this weekend, you'll have a deadline to decide about the bond. For shifter women, you go into heat after meeting your mate two weeks after the lunar cycle completes. It lasts two-to-three days, and resisting sex is rather difficult. Or so I've been told."

Another "oh" was at the tip of my tongue, but honestly, the timeline wasn't an issue. Not when I took a moment to think about how I felt and what I wanted.

I might not have known Grayson intimately, but he'd shown me enough and, as long as we could keep from fighting daily over the next three weeks, a deadline wasn't an issue.

Though, I would have to ask Lia about what to expect from a heat. I was pretty sure witches didn't go through something like that since I'd never heard of it. I wanted to have an idea of what to expect.

"I'm sure we'll manage to get our shit together by then," I finally said with a wink, hoping to lighten the mood.

Grayson nodded, then reached toward me and lightly pressed his palm over my chest. "Not to change the subject, but the power inside you is distracting at times." His eyes squinted at the sides. "Are you sure you don't know any details about your parents?"

I chuckled. "You know, it's not great for a woman's confidence when you bring up her life-givers while we're supposed to be having a conversation about sex."

His face remained unemotional. "Well, then maybe you should stop pulsing with power and I wouldn't bring them up."

"Power?" I tilted my head. "I'm not a witch, though." At least that was what I had thought I understood before.

"Witches aren't the only ones with power," Grayson answered. "Every supernatural has some form of it. Especially ones who rank higher on the food chain. You have a strong wolf inside you and that had to come from someone. Like an alpha people would think twice about fucking with."

My chest tightened and stomach churned. It was easy to pretend my past didn't exist—that I hadn't been abandoned as a child—but when something so specific was pointed out, there was no ignoring that fact.

"How do you know?" I asked cautiously.

Instead of answering, Grayson leaned closer and our eyes locked. A strength rose up inside of me, and I felt the need to sit up taller.

"That right there," he said without breaking eye contact.

I wanted to blink, but something inside me wouldn't let me.

"What is this?" I wasn't sure if I liked the dominant feeling that was growing inside me or not.

Grayson gave nothing away as he replied, "Alpha power."

"And that would mean…" I was pretty sure I could guess, but I really didn't want to.

He finally broke our stare, the action causing my shoulders to drop. "It means that your father or mother was an alpha. Knowing that and seeing what I have since deciding not to kill you, I think I—"

"Don't be naked, please!" Lia's voice called from the front door. "I'm back with a guest."

Grayson was on his feet before she'd finished speaking, and he moved to stand in front of me.

Sweet, but not necessary. Lia wouldn't have brought anyone she didn't trust into the house.

Well, as long as she'd had a choice.

Okay, maybe Grayson had every reason to be overly cautious.

"Come on out here when you're ready," Lia said chipperly, and I stood up.

Grayson glanced back at me, and I remembered he'd been mid-sentence, saying something that sounded like it had been about to change what I knew about myself.

"What were you saying?" I asked, standing in front of him and running a hand over my long, white strands so I didn't look a mess when we went out to see Lia and her "guest."

He shook his head. "We'll finish that conversation later."

I was tempted to argue with him, but I was equally curious about what was waiting for us outside the bedroom, so I let the conversation drop.

When I moved to head down the hallway first, Grayson grabbed my arm. "I'm going first."

An objection to his macho statement sat at the tip of my tongue, but

I managed to keep the words to myself. We'd just had our first conversation without fighting. I didn't want to be the reason it ended in one.

He went ahead, and I followed close behind for the maybe twenty feet it took to get to the living room.

My eyes widened when I spotted Lia, who was sitting in the lap of a man I'd yet to meet. Her arm was draped over his shoulder, and her other hand was drawing circles over his chest with her finger.

"Hey, guys," she said with a wide grin when she looked up at us. "Meet Markus. He's my mate."

Grayson's chest expanded and growled. "Is that why you said we had to come here? So you could find your mate? Un-fucking-believable."

Before I could say anything to defuse the situation, Markus settled Lia onto the chair they'd just been occupying and was moving toward Grayson. "Don't fucking talk to her like that."

"I'll do whatever I—" Grayson snarled in return, but I stepped between them before punches could be thrown.

"How about we let Lia explain why she brought us here?" I suggested, feeling confident that she wouldn't have been so selfish as to bring us to a warzone without a good reason that concerned us all.

When Markus finally looked down at me, I sucked in a breath. There was something about him…

His similar blue eyes. The curve of his nose. The straight, strong jawline. The only thing overtly different, besides the fact that he was a man, was that his hair was more of a dirty blond opposed to my nearly white strands.

All features I saw in myself every time I glanced in the mirror, but not only that. The energy I felt inside myself… I wasn't the only one with it.

Lia was suddenly by my side. "You sense it, don't you? I knew two things when I saw him driving down the street: He was mine and he was your family."

"What the fuck does that mean?" Grayson growled.

Markus and I were still staring at each other, so Lia answered. "It means that Markus here is Kinsley's half-brother. They share the same father and *that* is why we're here. Not because I knew I would find my mate."

Holy fucking shit.

I didn't know if I wanted to cry, scream, or run.

Out of all the things I'd learned over the last few days, this was… This was a lot. I had family. Someone who hadn't been given away and hidden.

If he was here, why hadn't I been? What was wrong with *me*?

I glanced at Grayson. "What were you going to tell me before? What do you think I am?"

My hands clenched at my sides as I waited for him to answer. I tried desperately to get my shit together, but I was losing at a fast pace.

"I was going to say I think you're the previous Alpha Supreme's daughter if you feel such a pull to this place and have the power that you do," Grayson answered with a tightness in his voice. "And it appears as if I was right. Markus here was the last one's eldest son."

"'Was'?" The word sent a fire down my throat while I turned back to Markus…my brother.

Fuck.

"He died a few months ago," he answered with a tightness around his eyes. "If it helps, you probably had a better life than I did, and you didn't miss anything by not knowing him."

I needed a minute to process this. Hell, I needed hours or even days to wrap my head around all of this. My muscles began to ache from the tension rising within me, and I didn't know who to turn to.

Grayson, the man who was supposed to be my mate.

Lia, the new friend I didn't really know yet.

Markus, the half-brother I hadn't known existed before two minutes ago.

All of this was nearly worse than my mate trying to kill me.

CHAPTER SEVENTEEN

GRAYSON

Seeing Kinsley come so unraveled for the first time since knowing her made my insides burn with fury. Watching her walk back to the bedroom without saying a word and closing the door behind her, made me want to bury Markus, regardless of whether this was his fault or not. Him being here was what upset my mate.

Instead, I considered Kinsley—a new thing for me—and gave Lia my attention. "Tell me how this happened."

"Well, two people had sex and then—" she started, but the growing rumble in my chest cut her off.

"Not fucking funny, Unicorn," I muttered.

She rolled her eyes at me, then moved with Markus back to the chair they'd been sitting in, resuming the same seating arrangement before she continued.

"Like I told you previously, I had an intuition to find Kinsley, then once I did, I knew we had to come here," she said. "I didn't know why or I would have told her. I care about Kinsley, too, but I wasn't going to keep Markus from her once I knew who he was."

My eyes glared at him, and I crossed my arms, suspicion rising inside me. "And how do you know he's really her brother?"

She snuggled further into his lap and sighed. "Because I do. It's my gift, and I can't explain that to someone who doesn't have the same ability. It's just like breathing. My eyes see images and I sense feelings. Then my mind translates them into thoughts that guide my decisions."

Lia glanced at Markus, stroking his cheek right under his eye. "Look at him and tell me you don't see the similarities."

She wasn't wrong, exactly. I could see they had the same nose and eyes, maybe even facial structure, but nothing else felt the same. Not the hair color or skin tone, and he didn't have the same wolf strength that Kinsley did.

He was weaker, yet he seemed oddly okay with that as I stared hard, judging him.

"Your father was a monster," I said, my tone leaving no room for argument. "How do we know you aren't the same?"

The shifter straightened his shoulders and met my dark gaze. "If you know of my father, then you should also know that anything you might have heard about me was done because I felt like I had no choice until I realized I did."

"And when was that?" I asked, annoyed that his words were ringing true.

He shared a constricted look with Lia, then answered. "When he told me to kill my first mate because she rightfully rejected me. I wouldn't do it and he banished me from the House. I'm a member of Blood and Beryl now."

I didn't really care about his past or how that might affect Lia, considering it sounded like she was his second-chance mate, but I was curious why he'd returned to Fire and Fluorite, so I asked as much.

"I came back to check on my younger brother," he answered. "Given the current state of this place, I've been trying to convince him and my mother to flee, but he's afraid of leaving the boundary line and getting denied entry to Blood and Beryl."

Again, he spoke the truth, which meant Kinsley didn't just have one half-brother…

"Do you have any other siblings?" I asked cautiously.

He shook his head. "Not that I'm aware of, but it wasn't a well-kept secret that my father slept around on our mother. Him casting me out was probably the only good thing he'd ever done in his life, even if it took me a while to see that. Though he'd clearly meant it as a punishment."

"And what are you going to do now that you know about Kinsley and have found a second-chance mate?" I asked, because if they thought they were going to leave Kinsley behind and cause her further hurt, that was going to be their last thought.

More importantly, I hoped she was at least listening in on this conversation, even if she didn't want to be directly part of it at the moment.

Markus glanced longingly at Lia. "I don't know. I need to contact Blood and Beryl to let them know of my circumstances. They'll be expecting me back today, otherwise."

"You'll tell them nothing of Kinsley," I demanded. We didn't need more Houses coming around and wondering what it meant that one of Mathis's heirs had surfaced. One who had been hidden away for nearly three decades.

I could assume now the reason she'd been abandoned had been just to keep her away from Mathis, which would be valid enough on its own, but if there was something else—something that had made Johnathon send me after her—I didn't want anyone else to know before us.

Lia leveled her bright gaze on me. "We can trust him, and I know you know that already. Are you done with the interrogation?"

I opened my mouth to tell her I'd be done when I was damn well good and ready, but I heard the bedroom door open, and I stood up to find Kinsley coming back down the hallway.

Her face was still tense, but she was breathing evenly. My first instinct was to go to her and pull her into my arms, but I refrained, letting her handle this however she needed to.

"I heard what you guys were talking about," Kinsley started. "What do you think your mom and brother would say if they knew about me?" she asked Markus, staring him down with the alpha power I'd already been feeling from her.

"My brother—his name is Triton, by the way—would probably be pretty excited for a sister, and my mother…" Markus grimaced. "Well, she's pretty broken after everything that's happened. She doesn't talk much anymore and hasn't left the house in months. No offense, but I probably won't tell her until I think she's mentally capable of knowing that there's physical proof walking around this House of her mate's infidelity. Considering how much worse things are getting here, that might not ever happen. Unless you've come to change that."

Fuck. I had a feeling someone was going to ask that once I'd figured out who Kinsley was. She was strong, but I wasn't sure she was ready for what he was suggesting.

"What do you mean?" Kinsley asked, proving my point.

My mate was smart, and she'd catch on quickly, but she'd been sheltered for too long to understand.

Markus shared another look with Lia, who nodded, seemingly encouraging him to continue. "You're the eldest heir of the previous Alpha Supreme. Since nobody has taken the House Leader's seat, you're technically the next in line to rule over Fire and Fluorite, should you want the position and be capable of claiming it."

She chuckled darkly. "You've got to be fucking joking."

Markus shook his head and remained unsmiling. "I'm not. This House has been a nightmare for far too long. Maybe you're exactly what it's been waiting for."

Kinsley stood rigidly next to me. "You're serious."

"As the plague," he quipped. "Talk to Ryder. I have a feeling he'd back you on this. If you can get the factions to stop fighting, there's a chance this House might be able to claim its previous glory that it had before my father caused the war that allowed him to take over."

Fuck. Mathis had been worse than even I'd heard.

I glanced up at Kinsley, who was just learning that the man whose blood ran through her veins was a monster. She remained devoid of outward emotion, but the light pressure I could see around her jaw and the way she kept moving her hands told me she was barely managing to process all of this.

She finally took a seat next to me, relaxing her shoulders some. "Tell me about the fighting within the House."

Or maybe she was going to handle this better than I'd assumed.

"It started when my father kicked me out and said things publicly that he couldn't take back," Markus said. "Though it probably started more secretly before that. Mathis pissed off a lot of people and did shady shit not everyone was okay with. I think even if he hadn't died, a House war was coming. He banished a lot of people just because he could, and that led to families being separated. People do crazy shit when they're backed into a corner, just trying to survive."

He spoke as if he knew that from experience, but this wasn't about him, and I hoped he didn't elaborate.

Markus continued. "I know there are people trying to get back in from No Man's Land and that there are two other groups within Fire and Fluorite that want to rule, but Ryder stepped up and made that much harder. He's been keeping as many people safe as he can, including my brother and mother, but I know he's exhausted."

Kinsley frowned. "His son was just kidnapped, and we brought him back. That's how we ended up here."

Markus and Lia shared a look that wasn't as understanding as their previously shared gazes. "You could have shared that with me," he said sternly.

She shrugged and grinned, taking nothing overly seriously, like usual. "Didn't seem relevant once I knew you were Kinsley's brother."

Markus turned back to meet my darkening gaze. "It's very relevant. I'm not going to force anyone to do something they don't want to, but if there's any hope of saving this House and the good people still left here, this is the time to do something. I don't imagine, after having his son taken, that Ryder will continue with his mission for much longer unless he has any reason to hope this mess is almost over."

"If Ryder doesn't want to lead, then why has he been doing this?" I asked. Though I'd also be asking Ryder, regardless of how Markus answered.

"From what I know, he was just doing his best to protect his family," he answered. "Not many of the Houses are allowing any of Fire and Fluorite members refuge in case there's backlash from whoever becomes the new leader. Ryder had no choice but to stay here, hiding or fighting back. Clearly, we all know which he chose."

Clearly.

A decision I could respect, but what did that mean for Kinsley, and what did she think about everything Markus had just said?

This wasn't something I expected her to decide on right away, but we also didn't have time on our hands. We still had Johnathon to consider. He'd sent me to find Kinsley for a reason, and if I didn't return with her, then he'd send someone else.

Not that I was afraid of someone coming after us, but there was suddenly a lot more happening than we'd gone into this knowing about. I didn't want to be focused on the wrong thing at the wrong time.

Now that I'd gotten the idea into my head that claiming Kinsley might not be such a bad idea, the thought of losing her made me see red.

Fiery, burning, and all-consuming *red*.

It wasn't just my wolf half that had already accepted Kinsley, but I knew then that it was also my demon half, and that meant no one other than Kinsley would be safe from my potential wrath if anything went wrong.

Not even the others in this room would be spared if it meant keeping my mate safe from whatever was headed our way.

CHAPTER EIGHTEEN

KINSLEY

One breath in, one breath out. That was what I kept telling myself after I forced my way back into the living room. Hearing everyone talk about a family I apparently belonged to but never knew existed had been difficult at best. Though, there were a few things that I couldn't deny.

The wolf stirring inside me was helping keep me calm-ish. The familial connection with Markus had been immediate, which also eased some of the anxiety, along with how much this place felt like home. Like this was somewhere I could figure out who I was meant to be.

There was something in the air. I didn't know how to describe it, but after hearing Markus talk about Fire and Fluorite needing someone to come in and make things better again, I knew I needed to be that person.

I'd never been a leader in my life—not in any form—but I was confident enough in myself to know I was strong. Not just in the physical sense, either. I'd spent years living amongst witches I hadn't belonged with. Deep down, I'd known I hadn't. I just hadn't known how true that had been.

My nights spent under the moon and in the forest should have been my first clue, but then again, I'd been sheltered and kept ignorant. It was as if the coven had known I'd figure things out if given the opportunity.

I briefly wondered if the witches would come for me, if there was some sort of deal that had been made when I'd been dropped off. But then I realized none of that mattered. I couldn't change the past. There was no reason to be angry about things that had already happened.

There was only moving forward in the best way possible, because if I wanted the life of freedom I'd always dreamed of, then living in the past was the last thing I needed to be doing.

"So, how does one become the new Alpha Supreme of Fire and Fluorite?" I asked. Since nobody had been appointed, I assumed there was a process we needed to be aware of before deciding our next moves.

I felt Grayson's eyes burning into me, but I didn't meet his gaze. He might have been my mate, but it was my life. Hell, technically, it was my family.

This was something I needed to decide on my own, though I already knew my choice. In a way, I felt like I'd been preparing for this moment all my life. My body wasn't weak, and neither was my mind. Not after the way I'd grown up. Not unless you counted my hesitancy in making friends.

Markus blinked at me several times before answering. "Sorry. Being around you and recognizing you as my sibling is going to take time to get used to."

I smiled, and a flutter of emotions moved through me. "Same."

"Anyway." Markus shook his head. "An Alpha Supreme can be passed down generationally should the current Alpha produce a strong enough heir. Our father was trying to prepare me, and I let him dictate my life and my actions for a long time, but once I saw how easily he turned on me, I knew this wasn't the life I wanted."

That was admirable to hear. He could have taken Mathis's betrayal and decided to best him, becoming an even worse version, but the fact Markus had chosen to walk away made me want to know him more.

He continued. "The other way is to fight for the role. I believe that's why nobody has been elected yet. Ryder doesn't truly want the spot and the others who are leading the opposing factions aren't strong enough to consistently win fights that will garner the support they'll need to rule over a House that has been savagely led for decades."

"You're saying Kinsley will need to fight these other wolves in order to garner their respect?" Grayson asked, his voice husky.

I finally looked at him. His eyes were nearly black, and his fingers dug into the arm of the couch. Yeah, this was going over really well.

"You can check with Ryder since he's been here more than I have lately, but I would say yes, that's correct since a current Alpha Supreme isn't here to pass down the title," Markus answered.

Lia grinned widely at me. "That won't be a problem. We'll prepare her."

Grayson slowly turned his head toward me. His eyes appraised every inch of me, burning my skin as he openly judged me. "Do you want to do this? More importantly, do you believe you *can* do this?"

The directness of his questions made my head flinch back. I took a deep breath, carefully considering what he was asking.

Finally, I straightened and placed my hands in my lap. "I know I can do this. The heaviness in me, the power you were explaining to me...I can't ignore that even if I wanted to—which I don't. I might have needed a moment to process everything, but I know this is where I'm supposed to be, helping this House."

He nodded stiffly. "I figured as much." Then he muttered almost inaudibly under his breath. "Damn woman."

I had a feeling he was only annoyed because this information changed everything, but he'd come around eventually. At least, I hoped.

Lia clapped her hands and moved from Markus's lap. "Great. So, we know why we're here and we know what we need to do. Let's get started with a plan."

Grayson growled. "We're not rushing into any of this. There's still Johnathon to consider. I don't believe the groups inside Fire and Fluorite are the only ones we need to worry about."

The unicorn frowned and closed her eyes, but her lips turned down further when she looked at Grayson again. "I can't get a read on this Johnathon guy. Maybe he doesn't have anything to do with this."

"He sent me to kidnap or kill Kinsley," Grayson answered brashly. "I doubt when I don't deliver that he will let that go. He likely knows who she is somehow and is hoping to use her to get into Fire and Fluorite himself."

"If he's from No Man's Land, why would me being Mathis's heir be of any use to him?" I asked, considering it hadn't sounded as if Mathis was missed or revered.

Lia sighed. "Maybe it's not as complicated as we're trying to make it. What are the things men typically want most? Power, sex…"

"Vengeance," Grayson cut, voice gravelly, making me think he knew a thing or two about being vengeful. "Maybe Johnathon didn't always live in No Man's Land."

"He could have been a member here." Markus raised a finger. "That would link all of this together. I might even be able to get more info on him if so. We have archives of past and current members. I could search for Johnathon in the past member archives. It might be pointless, but it's all electronic, so it shouldn't take me long if I can get access."

I leaned forward in my seat, intrigued about how all of that worked. "How would you get access?"

"Assuming my father's home office hasn't been ransacked, I should be able to find something there," Markus said, but then he frowned. "I'd have to go by myself. I won't cause my mother further harm by bringing all of you."

Lia grabbed his hand and squeezed. "But you could bring me and maybe introducing your new mate would help her heart a little and give you a reason to be visiting again so soon."

His eyes glistened, and he smiled softly at my new friend. "Of course. I don't know why I didn't think of that."

With how mushy and lovey they were being, I was glad that Grayson and I hadn't gotten along immediately. Hell, I wasn't sure we were really getting along just yet, but at least we'd found common ground and the rejection threats seemed to be over. For now.

The front door opened without anyone knocking and in strode Ryder. His face was less twisted than before, but the faint pink scars there still put off plenty of "don't fuck with me" vibes. Though, energy inside me didn't feel the need to challenge him like I had experienced a few times with Grayson.

"Markus Del Reyes," he said with an air of annoyance. "What are you doing in my faction without permission?"

Markus walked toward Ryder and held his hand out. "I'm not here to cause trouble. In fact, if you'll let me stay, I'd like to help."

Ryder snorted. "You'd like to help after your father was suspiciously killed and you never returned to take his place? Why the fuck should I believe you?"

"Because it wasn't my place to return to," he said, then he pointed at me. "But it is hers. Kinsley is my father's oldest known living heir. She was drawn here, and she'd like to know more about what's going on."

Ryder raised a brow, then narrowed his gaze on me. "I thought there was something familiar about you. What could a princess like you want with Fire and Fluorite?"

I had no idea what came over me, but I was up and out of my seat within a half-second, then I was in Ryder's personal space in the next half. My hand grabbed hold of his wrist, twisted his arm, and I used the leverage to put him on his ass. "I'm not a fucking princess."

So much for not feeling the need to challenge him.

He stared up at me and chuckled. "Noted."

I reached a hand down to help him back up, thankful he hadn't taken my impulsive move the wrong way, but I was tired of people thinking of me as something that I wasn't.

Ryder dusted himself off and shook his head. "All this time and nobody knew you existed. How is that possible?"

I shrugged. This guy didn't need to know anything about me that didn't pertain to this House. My past was my own and nothing more.

"I can only guess, but what good would that do?" I asked. "I'd rather know why nobody has stopped the chaos that has been going on in a House that, from what I'd grown up learning, was the most savage of the bunch?"

Ryder glowered and leaned against the wall in the living room we were all still gathered in. "That's the problem. We're wolf shifters. We've been taught from an early age that around here, it's the strongest at the top and you never want to be at the bottom. Most of us who wish to see change—whether that be bad or good—are equal to each other. A wolf might win a fight today and then lose tomorrow when he's challenged again. None of the factions that have been created with the House over the last few months have faced someone they fear enough to back down."

"Why does it have to be fear?" I asked. "Can't the people here just be happy if someone they can respect, and who wants to make a positive difference, shows up?"

"The last person who tried that ended up dead," Ryder deadpanned. "And that's the reason I haven't stepped up more officially. I love my House and I will do whatever it takes to keep as many safe as I can, but I won't lead only to end up like others. I have a son to consider. One that needs me more than ever."

Well, fuckity fuck.

I hadn't expected to hear that the last person who tried to make a difference had died. I also would have thought Markus might have shared that tidbit, but I guessed that was a story for another time.

"So, you're saying if I decide to announce who I am in an attempt to lead, that unless I want to be a ruthless killer, I'll likely end up dead sooner rather than later?" I asked, cutting to the chase because there was no other option I could see.

"Not exactly." Ryder glanced at Grayson and then back at me. "Based on the aggression I can sense from him, you two are mated. Something this House hasn't had in a long time is a leader who has a strong mate. The both of you together could probably make people piss their pants depending on the looks on your faces."

I was going to take that as a compliment.

Grayson moved to stand next to me. "And what if we walked away right now?"

"Then I'd pretend I never saw you," Ryder answered swiftly. "I don't have time for games. While I'm thankful you brought my son back to me, you either want to be here, making a difference, or you can fuck right off to where you came from. The most important thing to me is keeping my family safe. Anything else is just white noise unless I decide otherwise."

I glanced up at Grayson, and the tension in his jaw released. "Very well." Then he met my gaze. "What do you want to do now?"

The thought of walking away made my chest feel as if it were being torn in two. On the other hand, potentially facing off with a bunch of pissed-the-fuck-off wolf shifters… Well, that actually didn't sound like the worst thing I'd ever done.

I'd been drawn to the coven forest nearly every night back in Earth and Emerald. Lia had found me and led us here. Grayson hadn't walked away from me when I knew he could have, despite our bond. A bond he hadn't been seeking out before he'd met me.

All of these things had happened for a reason.

Either way, I faced what was happening here or I left and stayed hidden for the rest of my life.

The latter made me want to vomit, and I felt confident in my next words.

"I want to stay and fight," I said in response to Grayson's previous question. "I'm not afraid of a bunch of cocky wolf shifters who don't know that fear isn't the right way to lead people."

Grayson glowered but nodded. "Then that's what we'll do."

Ryder let out a heavy sigh. "This is going to get messy. Like really fucking messy. In the form of bloodshed. Are you all prepared for that?"

I might not have killed anyone before, but I knew right from wrong. I knew that the people here didn't deserve to live in fear, worrying if their children or mates were going to come home at the end of the day.

So if I had to get comfortable with a bunch of fucked-up shit really quickly, then that was what I'd do, because walking away wasn't an option.

"We're more than prepared," I answered with my chin held high.

"Yeah, I'm beginning to see that." Ryder glanced at the four of us and then back at me. "Let's figure out where we want to begin."

CHAPTER NINETEEN

The four of us followed Ryder to a warehouse-type building. The outside was sided in ribbed metal with rust stains running down intermittently from exposed nail heads. White doors without windows were at the side we approached, and I was hesitant to follow this particular leader inside, but I knew that had nothing to do with him and everything to do with Kinsley.

The more I was around her, the more she talked about being okay with putting herself in danger, the more my need to mark and protect her rose.

Kinsley was mine, but she wasn't a woman to be claimed easily. Even if I knew she wanted me in return.

No, if I was going to make her my mate officially, then I needed to show her that I was more than what she'd seen so far. I needed to show her that I could stand by her side and be the partner she needed to fight the battles to come.

I hadn't been sure that was what I wanted, but seeing how unafraid she was to face other wolves in a battle for a House she didn't know? That made me realize I needed to quit hiding behind my own strength.

Ever since my baby sister Addie had been murdered, I'd used my aggression to destroy any soft emotion I dared to feel. I didn't want to ever let anyone get close to me, because losing them wasn't worth whatever happiness they might have brought me.

Except Kinsley wasn't just anyone. She was the one created for me. The one the fates deemed my perfect balance.

Even if I wanted to deny her again, I knew I couldn't.

I was done for, and I wasn't going to pretend otherwise. Not when time wasn't on our side.

We entered the warehouse, and I could see stairs immediately to our right that led to two other floors, but Ryder kept left, leading us farther into the first floor.

There were rooms made from plywood with curtains for doors that prevented us from seeing inside. The concrete ground was cracked with grotesque stains, ones I didn't need to know the origins of.

There was a chill in the air as we continued, but given wolf shifters ran hot, I wasn't surprised they kept the place cooler.

Kinsley glanced up at me when we went through another door and entered a dark hallway. Her eyes were bright, and her body remained relaxed with her breathing even. I shouldn't have been surprised about that, considering how she'd responded to being kidnapped, but still, I thought at some point, this whole shitshow might start to weigh down on her.

"We'll start out here," Ryder said before opening one last door that brought us back outside. The light from the sun was bright, and I squinted a bit before taking in the area.

It was a small alleyway between two warehouses, the one we'd just left and another I hadn't seen before entering.

Connecting both buildings were brick fence-like structures at least twenty feet in height. There was no way out from this space unless someone could scale walls.

I heard the door creak behind us, and Ryder was back inside the warehouse. "Here's your first test."

He closed the door, and I noticed there wasn't a handle on the outside of the door to get back in.

"That fucker," I muttered, then grabbed Kinsley's hand. "You better be acquainted enough with your wolf."

Her body stiffened, but she nodded and turned away from me, watching our surroundings.

Shadows shone down on the weed-filled ground, then I caught the first wave of attackers coming from over one of the brick walls.

They all charged for Kinsley, but what surprised me more was that I wasn't the only one to move into their path. Markus was next to me, helping protect her.

Maybe he really wasn't anything like his father.

Kinsley shifted into her wolf behind us and snarled loudly when two other wolves leapt for her on the opposite side.

There was no way to protect her back while combatting with the new attackers, forcing me to be okay with her fighting on her own while I took care of as many wolves as I could.

I charged forward and grabbed the nearest one by the neck, then slammed him down onto the hard ground, cracking the earth from the impact.

His eyes fluttered, then closed when his head lolled to the side as he passed out.

I was up and reaching for the next, but Markus was already trading blows with the quick bastard.

I went to Kinsley's side, tempted to shift myself, but I didn't want to flame out just yet and wasn't sure how well I could control my demon if we had reason to believe that Kinsley was truly in trouble.

Control was something I'd long ago mastered, but I wasn't stupid enough to believe that the bond wouldn't mess with that.

My fist met the snapping jowls of a wolf and broke his jaw with one hit as I stepped forward. Kinsley was battling two men. One in human form and the other in his wolf. The black beast was foaming at the mouth while the man was trying to keep her distracted by continuously circling around them both.

His speed was impressive, but Kinsley's wolf was smarter than that.

She went for the wolf's throat, finally ignoring the second guy, and tore at his skin there. His sharp claws dug into her side, and she yelped, but the noise ended in a growl. She seemed to recover enough to keep control of the opposing wolf, forcing him onto his back.

Blood coated her muzzle, and he whimpered beneath her.

I thought she was done, but the other man finally shifted and landed on her back.

Ire rose within me, and I couldn't stop my next movements.

My body heated, dark-green energy coating my skin as I shifted into my wolf. My body became a blur as I raced toward my mate.

Using my wolf's head, I shoved the second attacker off her and he went flying into the metal side of the building, leaving an indent in the shape of his body before he dropped to the ground.

Markus was just finishing with his two men, and I turned to find Lia standing in the corner with her hands out.

I hadn't realized she wasn't in the fight, but now I could see that she was in her own way.

She stood with each of her hands directed toward the brick walls. A barely visible shimmering energy projected from her palms.

My eyes followed the trails of power and they each created a shield, likely keeping more wolf shifters from joining the impromptu attack.

It was nice to see she was capable of being something other than an annoyance to me.

In the seconds it had taken me to see what was going on around us, Kinsley had shifted back to two feet, fully dressed, and her chest was heaving while her eyes were wide and wild. "That was a fucking rush."

Hell. She was possibly more insane than I'd realized.

"It's...not over...yet," Lia said with a strained voice. "Need to let go."

Without needing to be told, Kinsley shifted again, and this time, Markus did as well, revealing brown fur that had hints of red filtered in. As soon as Lia dropped her shield, four or five wolves jumped over each brick wall, foaming at the mouth.

Lia disappeared from sight, and the second round began.

I stayed as close to Kinsley as I could, but a wolf slammed into her side, pushing her farther from me, and I couldn't get to her again without leaving my back exposed.

My claws tore the skin of the nearest wolf's neck. He howled in pain, but he didn't back down.

The distraction of needing to know Kinsley was safe had my eyes constantly darting to the left to make sure she was okay. That likely wasn't necessary, given what I'd already seen, but I couldn't help myself, especially after just admitting that I wasn't going to fight the bond.

The wolf I'd hit sank his teeth into my front leg while I was otherwise occupied, and I instantly felt my demon power surge forward.

I did my best to keep the flames at bay, but that energy was harder to hide when another wolf jumped onto Kinsley's back, biting deeply into her shoulder.

She cried out, but the sound rang more furiously than painfully.

I tried to keep my eyes on her, but the wolf on me wasn't relenting. It was time to show these pups what a real shifter was capable of.

Just as the first lick of flames began to come forward again, Ryder threw the door open. "Enough."

His voice bellowed over us, holding no alpha power, which surprised me, given he was leading his own faction.

His wolves immediately backed up against the wall, but there was too much rage pumping through my blood. This man had put my mate in harm's way without proper warning. For that, he needed to pay.

Ryder held his hands up and stayed by the door. "This is only a preview of what you'll face out there. Would you have rather I took your mate to face this in real life, where the wolves may have been even more ruthless? I needed to see what she was capable of. All of you did."

Fuck. He wasn't wrong, but still, this hadn't been the right way. Not in my eyes.

I continued to move forward and shifted back to my human form. When I approached Ryder, I wrapped my fingers around his neck, squeezing hard enough to lift him a couple of inches off the ground. "If you ever fucking *test* her again without giving us a heads-up first, I will rip your heart from your chest."

It didn't matter that he'd given us a place to stay. We could have found that anywhere. We owed him nothing and, from what I could tell, he should have been fucking kissing our toes in gratefulness that Kinsley saved his son and wanted to help this House.

Ryder held my sneer for a few seconds before his eyes cast toward the left. "I was only—"

I cut him off with a growl. "You were acting as if you were in charge of us. Which I want to make very fucking clear right now, you are not. We are not a part of your faction, but we are willing to help keep your people safe if you don't piss me the fuck off again."

Kinsley joined me at my side and placed her hand on my shoulder. "Let him down."

Only because I wanted to support the fact that she was the future Alpha Supreme here did I loosen my hold on Ryder.

"I understand why you did what you did," Kinsley said, "but you didn't know what Lia could do and that could have gone very differently. I would have never willingly put myself into a situation to be attacked until I felt more comfortable with my wolf, and you had no right to put me in one, either. I assume you realize your mistake now?"

He nodded and rubbed a hand over his bruising throat. "They were under strict orders not to hurt you any more than you might have been during a training session, but I can see now that surprises won't work well for this situation."

"No, they won't," Kinsley replied. "I'm glad we're all on the same page now.

Ryder didn't seem to agree as his stare moved between me and Kinsley. "Are you going to tell me more about Lia? She's the only reason your group wasn't overtaken within minutes."

Kinsley moved to stand in front of the unicorn, who wasn't recovering as quickly as I'd expected her to. "That's not for us to share. If she'd like to tell you more, then she will. When she wants to."

I could sense Kinsley's alpha power rising to the surface, and I wondered if she realized when she did that. Her wolf didn't seem to like to stand down to anyone. Not even her mate.

It was going to be interesting to see how that worked moving forward.

Hell, all of this was going to be more than *interesting*.

CHAPTER TWENTY

KINSLEY

I'd thought Bruno back at the coven in Earth and Emerald was a savage beast when it came to training in the gym, but between Ryder and Grayson, I felt as if I knew nothing about my body.

Well, I'd at least felt that way when we'd first started training.

A week later, I was growing muscles in places where muscles didn't normally belong, and the charge from my wolf energy made me feel like I was on crack at times. She was ready to claim this land. To take what my sperm donor had destroyed. To make Fire and Fluorite a House the people here could be proud of again.

Not that my wolf spoke to me with words, but her feelings were loud enough—and mostly matched my own—that it made it easy to decipher how she felt.

The only thing we didn't agree on was Grayson.

Every time I thought about him and the connection between us, her emotions were more hesitant. I didn't understand why, but I also didn't let that reluctance stop me from getting closer to him.

My body and hormones *more* than wanted our demon-wolf mate, but I wasn't being a complete fool. We still hadn't had sex and, while our timeline to decide what we wanted before the heat was lessening by the day, I wasn't trying to rush anything.

Ten days weren't that long to get to know someone, but at the same time, it had felt more like a month had already passed, given we'd spent nearly every waking moment together.

I'd also really enjoyed learning who I was, something Grayson had been overly supportive of. I thought he'd have more issue with me fighting or being put into danger, but he'd pushed me hard, something I wouldn't soon forget and very much appreciated.

While our beginning wasn't something that should have been easily dismissed, after getting to know Grayson better, learning about his values and the integrity he had, I knew now that Grayson hadn't been acting cruelly when he'd come after me.

Not only had he been under a magical influence, but he'd also thought I murdered children, for fuck's sake. A soft spot for him considering his own sister had been ruthlessly killed. I couldn't, and wouldn't, hold those first couple of days against him.

Maybe that was why my wolf was still prickly over our mate, and if so, she'd better come to the same realizations I already had, because Grayson was ours, whether she liked it or not.

Her presence lightly bristled in my mind, then eased off when my thoughts changed from Grayson to Markus and Lia. It wasn't that I wanted to have exactly what my brother and friend had, but I'd begun to find myself wishing that my mate bond with Grayson could have been at least half as easy as theirs seemed.

I wasn't sure if Markus and Lia had already made things official since that was a subject I'd rather not talk about, but they were almost a little too comfortable with each other, especially around other people, making me think it was more likely they'd already solidified things.

There wasn't a time that I'd seen them this week without witnessing soft touches, passionate kisses, and longing gazes.

But I wasn't jealous. Not when I'd had Grayson's brooding, flamed-filled eyes on me constantly, demanding my best when we were training.

The passion between us hadn't come from kisses. It had come from punches thrown during workout sessions, our sweaty bodies pressed together, and it had ended with dark nights, sharing the same bed.

Even my wolf couldn't be mad when Grayson touched me and lit my body on fire with just a stroke of his tongue or the caress of his hand.

Though those weren't thoughts I needed to be thinking about when he wasn't around. Well, not unless I wanted to take care of business myself.

Except time wasn't really on my side at the moment. I was just getting cleaned up from the day's training session, and I could smell the dinner that Lia and Markus were cooking.

By the time I was dressed in loose, black pants and a green tank top, I tossed my hair into a messy bun and headed for the kitchen, hoping Grayson was almost back from the conversation he'd gone to have with Ryder.

"Shit," I moaned when I exited the bedroom and rubbed a hand over my growling stomach. "That smells divine."

The scent of garlic, some sort of red meat, and potatoes wafted through the air.

Lia glanced up at me, grinning as she chopped carrots. "Of course it does. I'm an excellent cook."

Markus kissed the side of her head as he walked by with a sizzling pan. "You're excellent at *everything*."

I almost gagged from their sweetness. So fucking close, but I didn't want to hurt Lia's feelings. She was a badass, but I'd learned she was rather sensitive, especially when it came to Markus.

She'd been alone a long time. Finding me, then him, felt like her family was starting anew. I wanted to say I felt the same way, especially since I was blood-related to Markus, but...I just couldn't.

Not yet, anyway.

He was at least trying to connect with me, which I appreciated.

"You did really good today, Kins," Markus said once he'd put the food back on the stove. "You made taking out four of those wolves on your own seem easy."

My chest spluttered oddly at his use of a nickname for me. Nobody had ever called me that. I quickly decided I liked it and went to the table next to the kitchen, pulling a chair out before sitting. "Thanks. Though my wolf should get most of the credit. It's like the world's best drug letting her fight for her place at the top."

He chuckled. "Spoken like a true Alpha Supreme."

The way those words made my heart soar had a smile growing on my face. I'd never pictured this life for myself, but damn if I didn't want it with a fierceness now.

I just wish I could know what, exactly, "this life" included.

Was it asking Markus and Lia to stay here with me even after all this was over? Was it keeping this bond with Grayson like my initial thoughts wanted? Or was it rejecting him like I thought my wolf wanted?

I hadn't completely shut down the idea that I was possibly meant to do this on my own. Alone for the time being, showing the world who Kinsley Ash was.

Of course, I wouldn't truly be alone finally belonging to a pack, but without a mate... Picturing that made my stomach churn, and, for the first time, there was a sense of longing from my wolf.

Maybe she was finally seeing things from my perspective.

Grayson chose that moment to walk inside the house. His dark eyes landed on me first while he closed the door with a soft click.

His chest expanded, then settled slowly. He took tentative steps toward me that had my heart pounding in my chest.

It was that look and slight hesitation in his movements that had me wanting him more.

He never took from me. He was continuously waiting for me to give him permission to touch me...to make me feel so fucking much.

A complete contrast to the man I'd first met, but that didn't make him any less intimidating, given what I knew he was capable of.

The best part was he was starting to learn what I was capable of as well.

"How was your chat with Ryder?" I asked as he sat across from me, staring more at my chest than my face.

He made a grunting noise, then finally met my eyes. "I wanted to talk to him about something I overheard the other wolves speaking about today."

I raised a brow and leaned forward with my hands folded on the table. "And what would that be?"

"There was another fight between the other two factions today,"

Grayson answered. "The leader of the North group challenged the East for the second time. He's won both times."

I glanced back at Markus. "Didn't you say there hadn't been an Alpha Supreme selected yet because none of them could win continuously?"

My half-brother wiped his hands on a towel and nodded. "I wonder if the fight was staged. Someone could have told them that I was still here or even about you. If word is getting around, that could make the others desperate, but I didn't want to say anything in case I was wrong."

Lia moved to Markus's side and wrapped a hand around his arm. "You just said how well Kinsley is doing in training. Why doesn't *she* challenge the leader of the North faction?"

"She could," Markus replied. "With how strong her wolf is, I don't think there's anyone here she couldn't beat."

Grayson stood abruptly, hands clenched into fists at his sides. "I'll fight him first, so we can better prepare Kinsley to begin going against these other wolves."

I shook my head. "We're getting ahead of ourselves. What did Ryder say when you brought this up *without me*?" I spoke that last bit pointedly.

Grayson at least had the decency to lower his chin. "He said that you were ready and tomorrow we could do one last test fight just to be sure."

Well, at least my mate wasn't in the business of lying right to my face, even when I knew the words were hard for him to say.

I took a deep inhale as I saw Lia and Markus finishing up with the dinner they'd been cooking. "Then we'll worry about the rest later. For now, I'm going to enjoy a good fucking meal and then we're not going to talk about tomorrow, because there's no sense in anyone getting worked up about anything tonight."

Grayson took a steady breath and rubbed a hand over his jaw. I expected him to say something to contradict me, but instead, he stepped around the table and reached a hand out, helping me from my chair before we entered the kitchen to grab our dinner.

After the first day, Ryder had given us access to proper food.

Normally, our protein came from chicken, but tonight's steak smelled like heaven and had my mouth watering.

I piled potatoes, steamed veggies, and a slab of meat onto my plate before heading back to the table.

This was my favorite part of the day, because we never talked about training or anything to do with the shit going on around us. Lia had made that rule the first time she'd cooked, and I'd easily agreed to it.

Instead, we asked a mix of stupid questions and interesting ones, and everyone had to answer.

Well, everyone was supposed to. Some things Grayson wouldn't acknowledge, like if he preferred the toilet paper roll to be put on the holder one way or the other, stating "stupid questions don't deserve responses."

"So..." Lia started first. "I was thinking: If you could teleport anywhere to either live or just visit, where would you go?"

Markus quickly chewed the bite he'd already shoved into his mouth. "That's easy. Arcadia."

I cocked my head to the side. "Where is that?"

Every face at the table stared incredulously at me.

"Seriously?" Markus asked.

I nodded and frowned. "Is that another House I don't know about?"

This time, it was Grayson who answered. "It's the shifter realm. A place that has been closed off to this world for over two decades."

"Why?" I'd never heard of a portal being closed, but there had certainly been talks of ones being opened and even created, especially recently.

Grayson poked at his food. "Nobody knows, and those who try to find out don't ever come back."

Interesting, but also not our problem. Hopefully not.

I glanced at Markus. "Is that why you want to go there? Because nobody knows why it was closed?"

"Not really," he answered. "I'd just like to know where my family originated from. Plus, I've yet to go to another realm. Really any of them would be interesting to visit."

I doubted that. I'd heard some hellish stories about the other realms and the conflicts within them. At least according to some of the gossiping witches. I was good staying right where I was.

Lia smiled widely. "I'd want to go back in time. To the world pre-supernaturals. Maybe back in the 1800s without technology."

I shuddered at that thought. "You're insane."

"Tell me something I don't already know." Her chuckle had my smile growing, then she nodded at me. "What about you?"

"Uhhh." I paused. "I never thought I'd leave Earth and Emerald, so I don't really know."

"What's the first thing that comes to mind, even if it makes absolutely no sense?" Markus asked.

"Home." The word left my lips so quickly that I didn't even realize I'd said it until Lia frowned at me and Grayson cracked his knuckles under the table.

Markus reached across the table and squeezed my forearm. "You'll get there one day. Sooner than you think, hopefully."

Yeah, I hoped he was right, and even though we weren't supposed to talk about the shit happening around us, the thought of fighting one of the factions soon hadn't left my mind, even while eating the delicious meal.

I might not ever have a home if I couldn't win these fights.

That thought was nearly paralyzing when I considered it too deeply.

"I'd want to go to the islands west of here. I think they were called 'Hawaii' before," Grayson said, shocking the hell out of myself and probably the others that he'd answered without prodding from one of us.

I cocked my head to the side. "Why?"

He shrugged, closing off just as quickly as he'd opened up. "Why not?"

Though he wasn't wrong.

Sometimes we didn't need a reason to do the things we did. We just did them because they felt right, and that was enough.

At least it was for me, especially when it came to Grayson or anything to do with Fire and Fluorite.

CHAPTER TWENTY-ONE

My head thudded against the hard ground for the umpteenth time that morning. Grayson stood over me and glowered. "Again."

"Fuck you," was at the tip of my tongue, but I knew he was pushing me for good reason and a part of me—a very fucking small part at the moment—appreciated that he wasn't treating me like a fragile woman.

I was supposed to be fighting a group of wolves in preparation for challenging the North faction leader named Dylan, but apparently, he'd disappeared. None of Ryder's wolves could find him, which had disappointed me more than I'd expected it to.

I was never too sad about private trainings with Grayson, though.

After pushing myself up from the ground that was covered in dying grass, I dusted myself off as well as I could. When I'd taken a deep breath, I held my hands up, ready for him to charge at me again.

Except this time, he didn't.

Instead, Grayson snapped his fingers, and a ball of flames came racing toward my head.

Every muscle in my body might have been screaming at me, but the idea of getting my face burned off sent a wave of adrenaline pulsing through me.

I was on the ground in less than a half second with one leg out straight behind me, the other bent at the knee and my hands keeping me in place while my forehead nearly touched the dirt.

Instinct kicked in, and instead of asking him what kind of fuckery that was, I launched myself up and managed to quickly close the distance between Grayson and me.

My fist met the underside of his chin and sent him back a few feet. Energy raced through me, and I didn't deny my wolf what she wanted.

I shifted into my more powerful form, my paws coming within inches of Grayson when I finished out on all fours.

My wolf stalked forward, the air crackling around our form and sending shivers down our spine.

She bared her teeth and took a swipe at the mate she hadn't quite accepted.

Grayson was swift on his feet and was out of the way before any claws could cut him, but my wolf was prepared for that. I was curious as to her intentions, so I sat back, letting her take charge.

She leapt forward, ramming her head into his side, and he stumbled toward the ground, only managing to stay up on his feet because he was so close to a rock he used as leverage.

"Kinsley," he said with a warning growl.

My wolf bared her teeth and continued forward.

The wave of hype flowing through the animalistic part of me had my focus changing from curiosity to skillful intent.

Grayson needed to go down.

He must have seen the determination in our eyes, because he shifted in the next second and his wolf tried circling us, but there was no backing down for my beast.

She shadowed his movements, keeping the distance even until we were ready to strike, but that moment didn't come for several beats.

Grayson's silver wolf lowered his head, a tell I'd learned over the last week meant he was preparing for something. Though it was usually something different each time he attacked, I at least knew to be prepared to move.

When he feigned right, then leapt left, I thought my wolf would dart out of the way. Instead, she rolled to the ground, lying on her side, then lightly clawed the underbelly of Grayson's beast.

The ferocious snarl that left his wolf gave me pause.

Shit. Had we really hurt him?

Once we were back up on our feet, I noticed Grayson was covered in green flames, but the freaky demon energy didn't deter my wolf.

She charged forward, going for a direct hit. Our head slammed right into his chest, and while the flames coming from him were hot, they weren't overwhelmingly so.

Even still, it must have scared the hell out of Grayson, because he was shifting back to two feet faster than I'd yet to see.

His hands were on my wolf, patting her back and chest while he scanned every inch of us with his eyes.

"Are you okay?" he demanded.

I nodded my wolf head and he let out a strangled breath. "Fucking hell, Kinsley. You can't do that. Those flames are derived from dark magic straight from Soleil. Your wolf... You could have been turned to ash."

I wasn't sure what he was panicking about, because nothing had happened, but still, I stepped away from him and transformed back to two legs so that we could have a proper conversation.

My fingers brushed over the necklace that Lia had given me, grateful I didn't have to be naked every time I changed forms, then my attention fully focused back to Grayson.

"What are you talking about?" I asked. "Your flames didn't hurt at all."

He cocked his head to the side and furrowed his brow while his hands moved lightly over my arms, inspecting every inch of skin that was visible.

"How?" His voice was filled with equal parts awe and confusion.

I shrugged and waited for him to look back up at my face. "Maybe it's the bond."

His nod seemed almost absentminded. "Maybe." He stiffened and positioned himself in front of me, but the instinct to protect wasn't necessary.

It was only Lia and Markus joining us.

They were holding hands while they walked across the park, coming toward us. Markus had a folder in his grasp, and his eyes—so similar to mine—sparked with a happiness I'd never known, but I thought maybe I could with my grumpy demon wolf.

"What's going on?" I asked them when I moved around Grayson.

Markus answered first. "I finally got my mom to give up the passwords for my dad's personal computers."

The house where the last acting Alpha Supreme had been staying had been destroyed, and the only access to House records had been on Mathis's private devices, but getting into them had been difficult. I wasn't sure Markus would be able to do it after the first couple of failed attempts, but I couldn't deny I was eager to know what he'd learned.

"Did you find Johnathon?" Grayson asked first.

Markus handed him the file. "I found *a* Johnathon who meets the profile of someone who would want vengeance on Fire and Fluorite, but I can't be positive yet that he's the one you're looking for. This guy is a mangy, older wolf shifter who was banished by Mathis about two years ago. From what I read in there, this Johnathon was trying to gather a group of people to overthrow Mathis, but nobody joined him. They instead told my father and Johnathon managed to escape before he was killed."

Just because this guy had been unsuccessful the first time didn't mean this wasn't our Johnathon. He could have learned from his failure and found new friends in No Man's Land.

Grayson flipped open the folder, and I pressed up onto my tiptoes to peek at the pages as well. There was a fuzzy black-and-white photo of a man who appeared to be in his forties but could be much older thanks to magical genes.

He had dark hair but bright eyes that seemed almost silver, and there was a deep scar on the right side of his forehead.

Grayson glanced up, something feral in his voice as he spoke. "Do you think he's still in No Man's Land?"

"I'm up for heading there to find out," Markus replied with a bit of glee in his voice. I hadn't heard that emotion from him before and was curious about it. Was he excited to be fighting for this House or just fighting in general?

I glanced at Lia, and she was frowning, which was very unusual for her.

"What's wrong?" I asked.

She shifted her feet and met my worried stare. "I've never not been able to help once I was this involved in a situation. Yet I haven't sensed anything on this Johnathon guy."

Markus wrapped an arm around her shoulders, but before he could say something to console her, I spoke. "What if he doesn't exist?"

All three sets of eyes swiveled toward me. "What do you mean?" Grayson asked first.

"I mean, what if his name isn't Johnathon or he's not even from Fire and Fluorite?" I clarified. "You might be trying to force something to come to you that your magic can't grasp because we don't have the right facts."

Grayson smacked the papers over his open palm. "This right here proves he exists, and I already knew he was working with a witch based on the delivery of his message, so he could just be shielded."

Markus's jaw tightened while he held onto Lia. "There's only one way to find out for sure, and that's to find this fucker who wanted to kill my sister. We need to check this guy out."

A flicker of something ignited in my chest when he so easily called me his sister—just like when he'd used the nickname for me.

"I agree with you," I said once I'd recovered from the unexpected emotions. "Let's see if Ryder knows anything about what you found and then head out."

"What might I know?" the shifter in question asked from behind us.

I turned around to find him standing only about ten feet away, dressed in a suit with his arms crossed.

Before Grayson could be extra stubborn, I snatched the folder from his grip and handed it to the faction leader. "Have you ever heard of this guy?"

I felt irritated eyes glaring holes into the side of my head, but we'd already proven our point with Ryder the day he'd thought surprising us with an attack was okay. Ever since, the respect Ryder had shown us made him deserving of this information being openly shared with him.

Ryder shook his head and gave the papers back. "Can't say that I do. There are thousands of shifters in this House, and it's not like Johnathon is an unusual name."

"We're going to go after him," Grayson said in a tone that told us this wasn't up for debate.

The faction leader met my mate's dark sneer, seemingly unfazed. "Do you want some of my men to go with you?"

Grayson glanced down at me, his gaze softening just slightly. "Do you?"

Something unfamiliar spread through my chest and I stood a little straighter while I nodded. "I don't think that's a bad idea."

Ryder nodded. "I'll call for Tuck and his team. There are six of them in total and they're the shifters I trust most in this pack."

"Thank you," I said as he started to turn away, presumably to find Tuck, then my attention went to Lia.

She wasn't a fighter. Her powers only lasted for so long, and then she was too vulnerable unless she decided to shift, and even then, she had her limits. Though she didn't often shift, given she liked people assuming unicorns were extinct.

"You should stay here," I said to her without pulling any punches.

Her fiery gaze shot up and she glared at me. "No."

"Yes." I could feel power growing inside me, pushing up from my core and filtering through my words. "Unless you've changed your mind about shifting."

She crossed her arms, and a line formed between her eyes as she tried to fight against my innate abilities. "I liked you better before you started embracing your alpha side." Then she looked up at Markus, who nodded and smiled encouragingly at her. "I'll change if I need to, so I'm going with you."

I raised a brow and tilted my head. "Are you sure?"

Last I'd heard her say, she was trying to stay hidden and since she hadn't had any visions, I wouldn't have thought anything would have changed in that regard.

"I think denying who I am might be why I haven't been able to see what I want," she admitted sheepishly. "Something cracked inside me on our first day here when you were attacked. Instead of shifting to help protect you, I used my magic to put up the shield, which was helpful in the moment, but if Ryder hadn't called his wolves off, I would have soon been useless to you. I would have failed at protecting you all, because I was trying to keep my secret."

There was too much self-loathing in her tone, and I couldn't stop myself from moving forward. I wrapped my arms around Lia, pulling her away from Markus and into a tight hug. "It's not your job to keep me alive. You got me to Fire and Fluorite. You did exactly as the vision suggested you do."

She shook her head against my shoulder. "Vision or not, my job here isn't done. I know that."

The surety of her tone felt so familiar—like how I'd just known staying here and fighting for this House had been the right thing to do. So I didn't argue the point with her any further.

"Then you do whatever you feel is necessary," I said while stepping back and offering her a genuine smile.

When I turned back around, Grayson's attention was on a group of four men and two women who were walking toward us. Five of them stopped far enough back that I couldn't really make out their faces, but they were all wearing matching tan cargo pants and black T-shirts and boots.

The leader, whom I recognized as the "Uncle Tuck" Sammy had run to when we'd first arrived, came toward us.

He surprised me by shaking my hand first. "Tuck Castor."

I kept my grip firm and nodded. "Kinsley Ash. This is Grayson Barrett, Lia, and I'm sure you know Markus." I pointed at each of them once I'd released his hand.

Tuck's hazel eyes appraised each person in our group. His long, blond hair fell over his ears, and his sun-kissed skin was puckered with scars along his arms.

"Ryder told me we were heading to the smaller portion of No Man's Land up north," Tuck said, his gaze bouncing between myself and Grayson.

Since I wasn't familiar with the areas around here yet, I let Grayson give that confirmation. "Seems the Johnathon we want to check out is holed up at a warehouse just a few blocks from the bar out there."

Tuck smirked. "I know where that is."

I didn't care enough to know what had him smiling, but it seemed as if he was going to tell us anyway.

"There's a mermaid server there who nearly cut my head off last time I went for a drink," Tuck said. "Fun place."

"Right," I said, my tone flat. "We'll take your word for it. Is your team ready?"

The shifter seemed to finally remember that we weren't there to chitchat. His face lost the grin, and he nodded. "We'll follow and remain slightly spread out, staying in the shadows so as not to draw too much attention." He reached into his pocket and handed a small device to me. "If you put that into your ear, we'll be able to communicate."

I rolled the small, plastic earpiece between my fingers before putting it in place. "Follow us, then."

Grayson's hand rested at the base of my spine when I turned around to head in the direction of No Man's Land. "You're going to make one hell of an Alpha Supreme," he whispered into my ear.

Compliments from my mate had been far and few between during our training, and this one went straight to my heart.

Partially because I enjoyed seeing the softer side of Grayson, and also because when he'd said that...I couldn't help but hope he was right.

CHAPTER TWENTY-TWO

GRAYSON

Tuck's team did just as he'd said they would. They stayed in the shadows, keeping things from looking out of the ordinary. We decided to walk, because my jeep might have been recognized in No Man's Land and Lia could teleport us out if needed.

I wasn't sure the unicorn had any limits when it came to what she was capable of. I also didn't know if that was a good thing or not.

Kinsley seemed to trust Lia explicitly, but power had a way of twisting a person into something they never thought they'd be. If Lia was willing to reveal who she was in order to tap into the greater depths of her energy…

Well, I'd be keeping an eye on her.

We were only a few blocks from Ryder's territory, which we learned was marked by blue paint on the street signs, and when we began seeing green in places, that meant we'd crossed into Ethan's faction.

He hadn't won as many fights as the other two, but according to Ryder, the shifter was still someone to be leery of.

Kinsley took that seriously, and her focus seemed sharp as we traveled the cracked streets under the ruse that we were headed to the bar.

The Riff-Raff was apparently run by rejected supernaturals and attracted an interesting crowd. I had no desire to step foot in there, but Markus mentioned it was near where we were headed. If anyone was suspicious of Ryder's guests moving through Fire and Fluorite, talking about where we were going might help us avoid any unnecessary fights.

Though, I'd been itching to really beat the shit out of someone. Especially since I'd had to spend several days watching others lay hands on my mate and even beat on her myself.

That, I wasn't a fan of.

Sure, I'd had no problems punching Kinsley and plotting her death when I'd thought she'd been a power-stealing, child-murdering witch, but the thought of truly hurting her or letting anyone else do so now… made every facet of me boil with the darkness I worked to keep tightly bound.

"I'm going to get so drunk when we get to Riff-Raff." Lia giggled, hanging on to Markus.

I couldn't tell whether or not she was putting on an act with the way she draped herself over the wolf shifter, pawing at his chest. Regardless, I looked away.

Kinsley seemed to be ignoring them as well, which made me want her even more.

She had no expectations about who I was supposed to be as her mate. She didn't ask me to fawn over her or be someone I wasn't. She accepted my gruffness as equally as she accepted my need to touch her when we were together at night.

There wasn't an inch of her body that I hadn't worshiped with my mouth or fingers yet, but since I'd told her about sex solidifying our bond, she hadn't asked for more.

She also hadn't pushed me away. I was okay with her need to wait, but I could already smell the heat coming. Subtle hints of arousal wafted from her during the day, and I knew there was no way I was going to be able to keep from claiming her fully when she hit the peak in just a week. The inner frenzy would be too much for me or my wolf to ignore.

Not unless someone chained me inside a cell, or worse…Kinsley rejected me.

I grimaced and rubbed a fist over my chest. *Fuck.* Just thinking about the fact that she could choose to reject me felt terrible. It had my insides constricting, making it hard to breathe.

My own issues were swiftly shoved away when I caught Kinsley flinching next to me.

I brushed my lips casually against her ear and tucked her closer to my side, whispering, "What is it?"

She pressed her face closer to me and fluttered bright eyes at me. "Maybe twenty or so wolves, coming in fast."

My wolf senses had already been searching for threats, but somehow, it had taken me seconds longer to detect them coming than it had Kinsley.

Another sign that told me this was the right path for my mate, even if I'd have rather kept her to myself in No Man's Land after killing Johnathon and the threat I knew he might be to her.

"Will you two…chill?" I said to Lia and Markus, trying to say something out of character so they'd be more alert but not sound fucking awkward, either.

Lia giggled and turned toward me and Kinsley. There was tightness around her eyes as they searched around us. "Oh, come on. We're just having a little fun."

Well, we were about to.

The pack of shifters was closing in. I couldn't sense where Tuck had gone, but I could hear murmurs in Kinsley's ear, which hopefully meant they'd be here as backup if needed.

"No," I heard Kinsley mutter, but before I could ask what she was replying to, a strangled howl cut through the quiet afternoon heat.

Wolves leapt from their corners, coming at us in groups of two and three.

Kinsley shifted, and I quickly followed her movements, except she was faster than me—something I'd had a hard time admitting to myself this week—and was already engaged with two wolves before I'd landed on four paws.

Two more were headed for my mate, but they weren't going to fucking touch her. I sped forward, cutting off their path. My teeth ripped into the neck of the nearest one before throwing him to the side while I kept eyes on the second.

He came at me with teeth bared, but I wasn't scared—not in the fucking slightest—of these pathetic wolves.

My claws extended and slammed into the side of the wolf's tan head like a counterbalance that sent the ragged beast right into the ground with little effort. His body thudded against the pavement so hard that I was sure the cracks beneath him grew longer.

He continued to fight back, trying to get up, but that wasn't happening.

With a warning snarl, I ripped into his front flank, taking away his ability to walk right, then shoved him away with my head and a dark, pointed look. I hoped the young wolf took it as the only warning I was going to give and stayed down. Otherwise, my canine teeth were going to be the last thing he ever saw.

Kinsley was already battling another group of wolves while Markus and Lia stayed together on her other side. Nearly a dozen wolves were already on the ground, and Kinsley was covered in blood I could scent wasn't hers.

I leapt back into the fight without missing a beat until a man exited one of the alleyways with three wolves flanking his sides. Between clawing and snapping at our attackers, I did my best to keep an eye on him, assuming he was Ethan, the leader Ryder had mentioned.

His long, ebony hair was tied at the base of his head, and he had a fresh scar that started behind his ear and disappeared beneath his black T-shirt.

He kept his arms crossed, watching his wolves die, or at least go down, without doing a fucking thing about it.

There was no way the asshole would have ever had a chance leading a territory like Fire and Fluorite. Even if Kinsley hadn't shown up.

One wolf bit my tail and scratched down my side, but it was only a surface hit that hardly made me flinch before I raked my paw across his face, taking out an eye.

The whimper and moan that sounded from him grew quieter as he limped away, something I soon noticed the rest of the wolves were doing as well, except for the three who still flanked their leader.

"Markus Del Reyes," Ethan said first. "You're trespassing in a House that banished you."

Markus shifted back to his human form, and I noticed that Lia had never transformed into her unicorn. So much for her no longer hiding.

"I was banished by an Alpha Supreme who no longer lives, not by this House," Markus replied confidently. "Unless you're here to tell me you've successfully filled the Alpha Supreme position, there's not a fucking thing you can do about my presence, Ethan."

The dark-haired leader stepped forward. "Are you here to fight for that role?"

"No, but you still won't ever have it," Markus spat.

Ethan chuckled and waved back the three russet-colored, snarling wolves. "And why do you think that?"

I turned to Kinsley, already thinking she better not fucking do what I thought she was about to do, but I was too late to stop her.

She'd finished shifting back to her fully dressed human form and stepped forward. "Because this House belongs to me."

Ethan hissed and seemed to lose control of his wolf, judging by the claws I watched his fingers turn into. "Who the fuck do you think you are?"

His voice was raspy and thick with fear.

"I'm the woman who will gladly remove your head from your body if you don't back the fuck down," Kinsley said with an eerie calmness that impressed even me.

"Attack!" Ethan shouted, but it seemed as if one of us was already prepared for that.

Lia finally shifted, and a shimmering silver glow emanated from around her soft, white coat, highlighting the midnight blue in her mane and tail.

Kinsley changed back to her wolf as well, but before she could do anything, Lia had already skewered two of the three wolves, and the third had run off like the fucking coward I believed their leader to be.

"Take one step toward my sister, and it will be your last," Markus threatened Ethan when his eyes didn't leave Kinsley's charcoal wolf, which was pulsing with energy even I knew better than to fuck with.

Ethan glanced at each of us, but instead of taking a step back, his back arched forward and his clothes exploded around him.

Fucking idiot. So much for her not fighting one of the faction leaders today.

His off-white wolf stalked toward Kinsley, snapping his teeth and foaming at the mouth. My eyes paid more attention to Kinsley, but there wasn't the slightest ounce of fear coming from her.

She was ready. She'd been made for this.

I didn't know how—after the sheltered way she'd been raised—she'd settled so easily into this more gruesome lifestyle, but when Ethan swiped at her wolf, she was more than prepared for the hit.

CHAPTER TWENTY-THREE

KINSLEY

I hadn't been certain if I'd killed any of the wolves I'd been fighting so far, but I knew as soon as Ethan took his first step toward me that he wasn't going to bow down to me.

There was a darkness in his eyes. A rage there that told me he had nothing left to lose.

Completely different than what I saw in Grayson's.

Ethan was desperate.

I ducked and rolled in my wolf form when he tried clawing at my eyes with his first hit. He must have been expecting the move, because before I was on my feet again, the mangy wolf sank his teeth into my back.

My wolf snarled, and energy from deep inside us swelled through our body.

It wasn't the normal wolf magic that I felt, but something that was still vaguely familiar. The burning in my matted fur began to lessen and I whipped around, digging my claws into his back leg and tearing through the muscles there.

Fury filled me, and I let instinct take over. Instinct I hadn't known existed before I'd first shifted, but one I trusted with my whole being after all the time I'd spent in my wolf form this last week.

I assumed that was what had helped me bond with my wolf more seamlessly and would serve to keep us alive much longer than anyone suspected at first glance.

With Ethan's back leg busted, he hobbled himself a few steps back, but I wasn't relenting. Not when he was still snapping razor-sharp teeth at me.

He began running on three legs toward me, but when I thought he was going for a direct hit, the fucker surprised me by crouching low and swiping at my front legs.

Ethan cut through my fur, drawing blood, but not enough to keep me down or prevent me from moving fluidly.

My wolf's teeth snapped again, missing his back, but that wasn't our intended mark. While he was busy fending off my intentionally flawed attack, we were simultaneously pushing him into the corner of a building.

I didn't actually want to kill this wolf shifter. I'd have much preferred for him to stand down, but that didn't seem to be happening.

The moment Ethan realized what I'd done, he turned even more feral. Saliva dripped from his jowls, and his chest heaved with unnecessary force. He lowered himself, then leapt for me with canines and claws extended.

Instead of moving out of the way like I easily could have done, I decided to quit playing with him. This wolf couldn't beat me. I knew that the moment he'd lost control of his emotions.

This was my House, and he wasn't going to take it from me.

I let his claws scrape down the length of my spine—the worst injury I'd yet to receive—and when he landed on the other side of me, giving me his back, I used my larger wolf size to jump on top of him.

My right front paw tore out one of his eyes while the other cut clean through his throat just before my jaws locked around the back of his neck, keeping him somewhat still.

The bubbling gurgle that sounded soon after made my stomach churn, but I didn't release the hold I had on the stubborn bastard. This was the fate he'd chosen, and I wasn't going to turn my back too soon and get my ass bit. Possibly literally.

When Ethan had finally gone limp beneath my wolf, I released his neck and spit what blood of his that I could onto the ground. That was when I noticed that none of the attacking wolves were still present. At least the ones that had been alive, last I'd checked.

Grayson was standing in front of me in his human form. His eyes were filled with flames, and veins pulsed in his neck and along his forearms.

I moved away from the dead faction leader and shifted. The transition was painful as fuck, considering my injuries, but I ignored the agony in my back and focused on Grayson.

He seemed frozen in his rage, and when my palm pressed over his chest, the heat scorched my skin—worse than when I'd touched his demon flames—forcing me to pull away.

"Grayson," I said in a stern whisper.

He still didn't move.

I stepped closer, exhaustion seeping in as my inner muscles attempted to heal from the fight. "Look at me," I demanded.

He finally blinked, but only his eyes moved, and the flames there hadn't lessened.

"I'm fine," I said, hoping that was the only reason he was pissed the fuck off.

His head cocked to the side, then he looked in my ear, where the comm no longer sat. "Where were Tuck and the others?" he asked with a tortured voice.

"They were likely where I told them to stay," I answered confidently. "He asked if I wanted their help, and I said *no*."

"Why?" He growled.

My shoulders straightened, and I looked him dead in the eyes. "Because I had a fucking point to prove, and I believed I could handle the situation."

Hunter and killer for hire. Scary-as-fuck wolf. And my mate.

Grayson was all of those things, but the last ten days with him had shown me something inside myself.

I wasn't the orphaned, powerless witch I'd thought I'd been.

I wasn't a member of a coven or Earth and Emerald.

I wasn't unlovable.

I was Kinsley Ash.

An alpha wolf shifter who belonged right where she was.

This was my House, and nobody was going to take my home away from me again.

The more I thought the words, the more they became ingrained in me. It wasn't just because Lia had brought me to Fire and Fluorite thanks to a vision or because Markus had shown up, revealing I had half-brothers.

No, I'd felt something deeper the moment we'd arrived here, and while I hadn't understood those feelings in the beginning, I grew more attached to them by the day.

More attached to this House and the people I was meeting and the people I knew needed saving, so they no longer had to live in fear.

I might not have had the same terrors growing up, but I understood what it meant to never feel safe. Nobody deserved to live that way.

Grayson finally broke from his frozen state, and the heat from his skin died down enough that when he touched me, I no longer burned. At least not in the painful sense.

"You're okay," he said, his voice still hoarse but softer this time.

I nodded and held his gaze with my own. "I am."

A rock crunched behind us, and I glanced behind Grayson to see Tuck walking toward us with his hands in his pockets and his head high.

"Per Ryder's call, we let the wolves you didn't kill escape," Tuck said. "Ryder assumes they'll head back to the faction and tell them about you."

I knew it was only a matter of time before I publicly had to acknowledge what I'd already mentally accepted, so this news didn't bother me. "We're still going to search for Johnathon."

Grayson's hand tightened around my palm. "We should rest for the day and try again tomorrow."

Given the aches in my back that I assumed would take a couple hours or so to heal, I wanted to agree with him, but still, I shook my head. "We had a plan, and we're not going to deviate from that just because some asshole decided it was his day to die."

Tuck glanced at the asshole in question. "We'll clean this up while you figure out what you're going to do."

Without looking at Grayson again, I saw Markus being held up by Lia. He had a bruise along his neck, and I wondered if his wolf had been bit there. My friend, however, seemed fine at least.

Grayson's lowered voice sounded in my ear. "I'm not saying you can't handle looking for Johnathon, but you've made a very loud statement here today. Do you want to risk searching for Johnathon, finding another few supernaturals to fight, and possibly coming back here beat to shit?"

Fuck. He made a good point. Markus was hurt. I was...not one hundred percent.

Unless I was going to rely on Tuck and his team, which I didn't want to do, then Grayson was right.

It wasn't that I didn't trust Ryder's people, but just as I'd said before, I wanted to prove a point.

I'd shown up here with a rejected House member, a supernatural who was supposed to be extinct, and a mate with powers most wolf shifters had no access to.

We had something to prove as a whole, just as much as I did as the future Alpha Supreme to Fire and Fluorite.

There wouldn't be a point, at any time, that we could appear weak. Even after multiple fights.

"Fine, but we leave again first thing in the morning." I took a step closer to Markus. "Are you okay?"

He grimaced just looking up at me. "Nothing that won't heal overnight."

"I'll take good care of him." Lia grinned widely. "Don't worry."

I hadn't been *that* concerned, but now I was a little grossed out.

"I'll get us home," Lia added when she reached for me. "Keep a tight hold on Grayson's hand."

As soon as my fingers squeezed harder around his, the air was pulled from my lungs and my vision went dark, but only for a couple seconds. Then, I was wobbling next to the couch in our living room.

"Impressive," I said with a bit of a groan.

She winked while helping Markus to their shared room. "Convenient."

As they disappeared, I looked back at Grayson. "Are you okay?"

He nodded and slowly pulled me closer to him, wrapping his arms gently around me. "Are *you* okay?"

Even his light touch had an adverse effect on my throbbing skin, but I wasn't dying, so I didn't want to say anything. "Of course."

He squeezed just the tiniest bit tighter. "Liar."

I couldn't hold in the hiss that escaped through my lips. Then, before I knew what was happening, Grayson picked me up and carried me down the hallway.

There wasn't a single part of me that wanted to object to his caveman ways, so I put an arm around his neck and just enjoyed the lift.

When we entered the bedroom, he kicked the door closed behind us, then gently laid me on the bed with my head on the pillows.

His dark eyes burned a fiery trail down my body before they landed at my feet. He began removing my boots. I considered objecting finally, but beneath all of Grayson's gruff and tough exterior, he seemed to enjoy taking care of others.

Well, at least me.

Plus, now that we were back in the house and the adrenaline was wearing off, the slivers of pain I'd been ignoring were becoming slightly louder.

Grayson was working on my pants when I let my eyes flutter closed and took a deep breath. His fingers lightly touched my stomach, sending shivers through me that somehow began easing the agony that had been building.

I heard my zipper being tugged downward and nearly melted when Grayson's hands lightly pulled my pants down my sore legs.

"I've got you now," he murmured over my stomach, pressing his lips to my belly button.

Fuck. Me.

It wasn't like he hadn't already touched every part of me in some form or another, but still…

Grayson wasn't always gentle. Respectful? Absolutely. But "softness" was a rare sight, one that had me forgetting all about the battle I'd just been in and feeling needy as fuck as he continued touching me.

He stripped me down to only my underwear and bra before he moved to kneel over me, one knee placed beside each of my hips. Then his fists pushed in until they touched my shoulders and he lowered himself, making the air between us so thick that I could hardly breathe.

"When that fucker hurt you, I wanted to burn the world to ash," he said huskily. "I wanted to rip him off of you and pluck each of the hairs from his hide while he slowly bled out from where I intended to lightly slit his throat."

That was quite the haunting image, but my mate wasn't done.

"Then I saw how you knew it was better to get hurt and have the upper hand than to drag out an unnecessary fight," he added. "I forced my wolf and demon desires for blood down and waited, watching in fascination as you did what needed doing. You showed this House that you're not a weak woman trying to claim something you have no right to just because of who your father was. You showed them that you're the alpha we can all sense inside you."

I reached up and cupped his cheek. "I only did what I had to. Nothing more, nothing less."

His mouth pressed against mine, and he scraped my lower lip before pulling back. "There is nothing 'less' about you or what you did, Kinsley Ash."

Fuck, I wanted him so damn badly when he spoke like that.

For once, my thoughts didn't seem muddled. The murkiness that had been there after he'd rejected me had been washed away, and all I could see was the light around him that he'd fought to diminish. I held tightly to the euphoric sensations my heart was blooming with as our stares remained locked together.

This man, wolf, and demon… Every part of him. They were all mine.

I'd known that since the moment I'd seen him. I'd only tried to push those thoughts away for a short time because he'd denied me, but I'd learned long ago that one wrong should never be canceled out with another. If Grayson was what I wanted, and he accepted he wanted me in return, then what was the point in denying fate?

I couldn't see one and, honestly, didn't want to. Not any longer.

He was trailing kisses over my chest when I'd come to that realization, and his slow, tender movements suddenly weren't enough for me.

My heart raced and hands shook with the need I was consumed with. The need to touch him...to claim him...to make him mine. Officially.

Hell, even my wolf seemed to be in agreement.

I grabbed onto his face and kissed him with ferocity. My legs wrapped around his thighs, and I held him to me while our mouths became a tangle of tongues and teeth.

When he pulled back, there were slits in his dark eyes and only a faint appearance of the flames I so often saw there.

"Kinsley." He spoke the word as a warning, but a warning wasn't necessary.

"I want you, Grayson," I said confidently. "All of you."

He appraised my face, sweeping his eyes over every inch, then his chest rumbled. "Fucking finally."

His hand wrapped around my neck, tilting my head back as he kissed me again. His tongue owned my mouth while I blindly pulled at his clothes that needed to disappear.

The last week of getting to know each other's bodies made the idea of sex seem considerably less daunting, but that didn't mean I wasn't aware of the significance of this moment.

It wasn't only having sex for the first time, but I was tying myself to this man for the rest of my life.

Taking a moment, I searched internally one last time for any leeriness inside me, but there was none.

I wanted Grayson. All of him.

His hand traveled over what should have been a familiar trail down my sides before they paused where I was still wearing my underwear.

His pants were barely unbuttoned, but he seemed to be inpatient about getting me naked, because the next thing I knew, the fabric around my hips began to tear from his tight grip.

I started shoving at his jeans, and he took mercy on me, helping until all barriers between us were removed.

Heat seeped into me, branding my skin and taking away my breath, along with any prior pain I'd been feeling.

His cock thrummed over my wet pussy, and I tilted my hips up, needing to feel Grayson in ways I'd yet to experience.

His fingers brushed strands of my haphazard hair away from my eyes. "After this, you're mine, Kinsley. There's no turning back, and I will be yours in the same way. Nothing and no one will ever tear us apart, because I will turn them to dust if they try."

My thumb stroked over his cheek. "I think your flames are my favorite part about you."

Something darker flashed over his eyes, but it was gone before I could really tell what difference I was seeing.

Then, like the expert he'd become with my body, he slid his hand between us and rubbed circles over my clit.

My back arched until my tits pressed against his chest. I closed my eyes, trying to soak in every ounce of the pleasure he was offering.

Grayson's thumb and forefinger pinched my jaw. "Look at me, Kinsley. I want to see into your soul when I make you mine."

He could glue my eyes open for all I cared, as long as he kept talking to me like that.

I nodded and licked my dry lips. "But just know that I don't need to see you to know it's only your touch that makes me feel this way."

I swore thunder erupted inside his chest just before his mouth claimed mine again. The hand he had between us must have gripped his cock because the head replaced the movements his fingers had just been making and I swore I was going to explode just from the anticipation.

His teasing was going to be the death of me. We'd spent all week preparing for this moment. I didn't need him to take things slow.

My hand covered his as I leaned sideways—ignoring the tinge of pain in my back from the movement—to reach down and guide his hard cock right where I needed it.

Grayson growled when I attempted to take charge, a battle of alphas that I was happy to let him win if he did what I wanted.

The thick head of his cock pressed into me. My breath hitched, and I did what I probably shouldn't have. My hips jerked up and shoved him several inches inside without warning.

"Fuck," I muttered, slowly adjusting to the feeling of him stretching the walls of my pussy and hoping nothing had ripped. At least, nothing that wasn't supposed to.

His eyes never strayed from mine, and his jaw was so tight, I thought there might be a possibility for some of his teeth to shatter. "Be careful."

I took the warning in his sharply spoken words to mean I wasn't even allowed to self-inflict harm without risking his wrath.

Something I found hot as fuck while he continued to rock back and forth, easing his dick into me.

The gentleness Grayson was showing me wasn't the man I knew beyond these doors, but in a way, that made me want him more. This part of him was mine and mine alone.

Nobody else would know this dangerous yet caring man the way I did, and I was more than okay with that.

"Halfway there," he muttered over our combined mouths.

I nipped at his lower lip. "You better hope I last long enough to take all of you."

He smirked and grunted. "Oh, you will."

I wanted to argue with him that what I did was up to me, but he surged forward just a bit faster than he'd been going, and I swore I saw stars.

"Fucking hell," I heaved, trembling beneath this beast of a man and wondering how in the world this had become my life.

It might not have been conventional in any sense, but staring into his eyes, seeing beyond the darkness and into the layers I knew he kept from everyone else, I knew this was right.

We were right.

My hands slid over the tense muscles in his back, then my fingers gripped his ass cheeks. "Now, Grayson."

I was officially done with the slow and careful movements. I couldn't wait any longer for him to be mine in every way.

Thankfully, he seemed to be on the same page and thrusted

forward, gently holding my head with one hand while the other gripped my hip.

His stare seared my soul, and we never once broke eye contact while he began moving more fluidly above me.

My inner walls burned from being stretched, but that ache was easily overshadowed by the bond between us growing like a bright light within my chest.

Energy swirled inside me, pounding against my ribs and begging to detonate, branding myself to Grayson.

Even his normally dark-brown eyes were briefly turning a light, tan color while he peppered light kisses all over my face.

As euphoric tensions rose, sending shivers from my chest all the way to the tips of my toes, I held tightly to Grayson and moved my hips in time with his. Every thrust came easier and more passionately than the one before.

Tremors shook Grayson's arms where I held him, and his eyes began to pinch at the sides, presumably from the power growing within each of us.

I brought a hand up and rubbed my thumb over the creases, and he lowered his forehead to mine, sealing our lips together.

Fuck, nothing had ever felt so branding. Not when I'd shifted for the first time. Not when I'd entered Fire and Fluorite. Hell, not even when I'd first laid eyes on Grayson.

Emotions clawed at my throat, and the swirling energy inside me moved from my chest, where I assumed the source of the bond to be, then down to between my legs.

A throbbing pulse sent tingles along my skin, and my nails dug into Grayson's biceps. "The bond…"

"It's close," he whispered in reply as he increased the speed of his thrusts.

As much as I wanted to be an active participant in this moment, the second I began to let go, there was no controlling what was happening.

Heat unfurled from my core, blasting through me with an intensity I hadn't expected. White flickers of magic sparked between us, and Grayson's movements slowed yet deepened at the same time.

The assault on my senses was more than I could handle. Every shivering touch, branding look, and powerful stroke took me closer to the edge until there was no holding back.

I leapt right the fuck off the metaphorical cliff as I cried out his name, finally closing my eyes and allowing the moment to own me.

Grayson buried his face into the crook of my neck, breathing me in while I tightened my arms and legs around him, never wanting to let go.

"Mine," he murmured against my slick skin. "All fucking mine."

A smirk lifted on my lips. "Yes, you are."

His teeth scraped over my shoulder before he propped himself back up. "Are you okay?"

I was sore as fuck between this and the fight, but "okay" didn't even begin to describe the elation still running rampant through me.

I'd been alone and abandoned all my life.

Knowing Grayson was officially mine… It was indescribable.

"I want to stay in this bed with you for the next week," I replied.

The tension returned to his eyes and jaw. "I wish I could say that was possible."

I knew it wasn't, but that didn't mean we couldn't hope for things that needed to wait.

Those hopes and wants would be what got us through whatever was coming next. I was sure of that, because all my life I'd waited for something better, hoping for something more.

If I could survive twenty-eight years of rejection by a coven I'd never belonged in, I could wait a little bit longer to be selfish with my newly claimed mate.

Just a little, though.

CHAPTER TWENTY-FOUR

GRAYSON

Bonding with Kinsley hadn't been how I'd seen our day going, but I was more than okay with the change in plans.

After seeing her hurt in the fight, I'd thought I'd explode, but I knew that wasn't what Kinsley needed, so I'd used every ounce of my strength to keep my rage contained.

That had proved harder than it'd been in years, but the moment I'd had Kinsley alone, the fury storming within me had slowly begun to fade.

I'd have been content to just touch her as I'd done every day for the last week, but when she'd said she was ready, I wasn't going to hesitate to claim her.

Her innate magic now hummed through me, thanks to our connection, and while that was going to take some getting used to, I had no regrets.

Well, one.

I couldn't ravish her in bed for as long as I wanted and as long as she deserved.

We still needed to find out what it meant that Kinsley had killed a faction leader and figure out when we would be heading toward No Man's Land since we hadn't made it there the night before.

When I'd helped Kinsley to the shower and she'd moved in front of me, I'd nearly broken my own hand from clenching my fingers so tightly.

There was massive bruising where she'd been attacked, and I was glad I hadn't seen it until now. Otherwise, we might not have gone as far as we had in that bed.

I brushed a light touch over the edges of the injury while she rinsed herself off. She shivered but didn't wince, which I took to be a good sign. Her wolf healing was already taking care of the worst parts.

"What do you think is going to happen now?" she asked as she stepped out of the shower.

While she dried off, I stayed put and washed up while answering her. "The House is going to know that an heir to Mathis has returned. One who hasn't been cast out. They're also going to know that she isn't to be fucked with."

She peeked her head back around the curtain. "That doesn't mean nobody will fuck with us."

No, it didn't. Fire and Fluorite was known for its brutality, but that didn't mean they were all idiots like Ethan had been. I wasn't even sure how he'd become a leader of a faction, given he hadn't known when to walk away, but that didn't matter now.

What did matter was that his wolves would have already gone back to tell the others what had happened and we needed to know what was being said.

"We'll go see Ryder," I said as I turned off the water and reached for my towel on the hook.

Even if he didn't tell us what I hoped, it didn't make much of a difference. I just needed him to confirm what I already suspected: The third faction, led by Dylan, would be coming for us.

It would also be helpful if Ryder could fill in other details, but no matter what, once Kinsley was healed, there wasn't a fight I didn't think she could win.

Even if it enraged me to see her hurt, I'd known soon after meeting her that there was a superior wolf lying in wait inside her.

Soon, all of Fire and Fluorite would know that as well.

While being part of a House and stuck to one place wasn't

exactly what I'd had in mind for my future, I knew as I watched Kinsley get dressed again that I would do and be whatever she needed.

It might have taken me a few days to get there, but as soon as I'd quit being so fucking stubborn, everything else had clicked into place for me.

When we came out of the bedroom, Lia and Markus weren't in the house, but they were hanging out in the front yard. Seemed like an odd place until I realized they would have heard us having sex.

Markus was staring intently at his boots while Lia was grinning like she was the one who'd just gotten laid.

She jumped out of her seat and wrapped Kinsley into a tight hug. "I'm not going to say anything, but just know… Great things are happening!"

Kinsley blushed. "Right."

"No, seriously," Lia continued. "I finally had another vision. I think I was blocked because I was hiding who I was, but shifting back there seemed to have reignited my powers."

I hadn't faulted Lia for keeping her lineage a secret, given I had been doing the same thing. Though, we'd had different reasons and mine weren't something I had time to deal with at the moment. I'd use what abilities I needed to when the time came.

Kinsley hugged Lia again. "That's great. What did you see?"

Lia glanced back at me, then Kinsley. "Nothing that needs to be shared."

Markus groaned. "At least not ever again."

Lia reached back and grazed the back of her hand over his arm. "I didn't mean to tell you. I just got so excited."

His palms rubbed over his eyes, then he stood, still avoiding looking at Kinsley. I could guess what Lia might have spat out from her vision.

"We need to talk to Ryder," I said, deciding to help Markus out with a distraction. He'd fought to keep Kinsley safe, so I was going to attempt not to treat him as if he were nothing more than the unicorn's mate.

He glanced up at me. "Let's go, then."

Markus left the yard, then seemed to think twice about walking away from Lia since he stopped and glanced back at her.

She skipped ahead to join him, and I wrapped an arm around Kinsley's shoulders. She shivered, then looked up at me and whispered, "This is really fucking awkward."

"Only for Markus, but he'll get over it," I said.

"Maybe Ryder can spare another place for us to stay in," she suggested. It wasn't a terrible idea, but while I didn't mind staying with Ryder's faction, I knew sticking together was better, given Lia's talents.

She might have annoyed the fuck out of me, but I was finally accepting that the unicorn just might be willing to die for Kinsley and, until my mate was titled Alpha Supreme, she couldn't have too many people watching her back.

I wasn't too proud to admit that.

"Let's focus on the factions and Johnathon first," I said as we continued to walk down the sidewalk toward the park where we'd first arrived.

Someone had brought my jeep over to the house the day after we'd arrived, but driving the few blocks seemed pointless.

Ryder was just coming out of a building across the street, and his son Sammy was tugging on his hand until Kinsley caught his attention.

The little boy let out a squeal and then raced toward us. Kinsley paused and lowered herself to one knee, but she didn't stay that way for long.

Sammy leapt toward her, and if I hadn't been watching, they'd have tumbled right onto the concrete sidewalk. Instead, I hooked my hands under Kinsley's arms and managed to keep them mostly upright.

"You're still here," Sammy said.

Kinsley nodded. "Of course. Your dad is helping me with something."

Sammy looked around Kinsley's head and frowned. "I thought you'd have a crown."

She laughed and smiled. "And why's that?"

"Because Daddy said you were going to help him and that he wouldn't be in charge anymore. You would be," he said, his voice full of seriousness. "I thought that meant you were like a queen, especially since you save people instead of hurting them."

Kinsley seemed at a loss for words, so I bent down and tapped his chin. "She is a queen, but she likes to keep it secret."

His mouth formed an "O," then he glanced back at Kinsley. "I won't tell anyone else." He frowned again. "Neither will Jacob and Billy."

Kinsley squeezed his little hands. "I'm sure they won't."

I stood back up, helping Kinsley at the same time, when Ryder approached. "I didn't expect to see you so soon. Tuck told me what happened."

"Have you heard anything else since?" Kinsley asked as Sammy went back to his father's side.

Ryder shook his head. "But I expect by tonight, we will. If you're hoping to get back to No Man's Land with little issue, I'd recommend driving this time and going soon."

Lia shook her head. "He's right. Nighttime won't be our friend for a few days."

I wasn't sure what the unicorn meant by that, but nobody else seemed to question her statement, so I let it go.

"Will Tuck and his crew still follow spread out behind in case we run into more trouble?" I asked, glancing around and not seeing the man in question.

"They're already in place by the border," Ryder answered. "Go north on Tenth Street and you'll drive right past them. They'll follow behind."

Kinsley glanced over at Markus. "Are you sure you want to come?"

He glanced at Lia. "I'm all healed up."

Ryder gestured toward her as well. "Having a unicorn on my property would have been nice to know about beforehand."

"And what would it have changed?" Kinsley challenged. "Would you have given us nicer accommodations? Or maybe you wouldn't have helped us at all?"

The faction leader glowered. "That's not what I meant. I just don't like surprises."

"Right," Kinsley said flatly, seeming unconcerned with Ryder's annoyance. "We'll go back to get the jeep and be on our way."

She turned and walked away, but I didn't follow immediately. Instead, I gave Ryder my full attention, aware Sammy was still watching the whole interaction.

"We also don't like surprises, as we've already discussed," I said sternly. "If you hear anything about our fight earlier from the other House members, I expect to know about it just as soon as you do."

My demon pushed forward just slightly and, this time, I didn't fight him. I assumed there would be a hint of fire in my eyes, but Ryder didn't seem fazed if so.

"Understood," he said, then he tucked Sammy closer to him. "We'll see you when you're back, then."

I nodded, then turned to find Kinsley waiting for me just another ten feet ahead. She glanced between me and Ryder. "What was that about?"

"Just making sure he knows we expect to be kept in the loop," I answered. "Just because he took us in doesn't mean we can fully let our guard down with him."

Kinsley bit her lower lip like she so often did. "I think we can."

"What do you mean?" I asked when she didn't elaborate.

She glanced back briefly. "I sense something in him. Not like I do with Fire and Fluorite or Markus, but there's a flicker of confirmation there when we're around him."

I briefly wondered if that meant Ryder could be related to Kinsley's birth mother, but I didn't want to mention that to her if she hadn't already come to that conclusion herself. We could figure that out when there was less shit going on around us.

We quickly got back to the house and went right into the jeep. Kinsley sat in the passenger's seat but stared longingly at the steering wheel. "I want to learn to drive."

Another annoyance about her past that I kept to myself. Kinsley was already well aware of how shitty her coven had treated her, even if they'd been trying to protect her for reasons unknown. She didn't need me to comment on that, so instead, I nodded. "I'll give you your first lesson just as soon as we have some downtime."

She smiled and squeezed my thigh. "That would be perfect."

We headed toward No Man's Land, all four of us watching the streets as we went. There weren't any large groups out, but a few small ones were hanging out in the alleys at various points. None of them seemed to follow us until we got to Tenth Street, like Ryder had suggested.

A group in all black disappeared into the shadows as we passed by and I saw a flash of blue, which was the color of Ryder's faction.

Nobody in the jeep said anything as we continued. When we crossed over the border, leaving Fire and Fluorite behind, tension weighed down on my shoulders.

It was my job to protect Kinsley, and I was potentially bringing her closer to the man who wanted her dead or as his captive.

I'd been tempted to ask her to stay behind, but I'd already known her answer, so I hadn't bothered.

She reached across the center console and grabbed my hand without looking over at me. Her eyes stayed on the road, like mine should have been, which was how I missed the body being thrown right in front of our vehicle.

"Watch out!" Kinsley shouted.

My reflexes were at least still working as needed, and I slammed on the brakes, no longer able to see the body, but I hadn't felt a thud, either, so I didn't think we'd hit them.

I glanced right to see a young woman rubbing her hands over her jeans and wearing a dark smirk as she shrugged. "The dumpster was full."

She flicked ebony hair with an iridescent sheen to it behind her shoulder, then opened the door back into a bar that I then noticed was the one called The Riff-Raff that Tuck had mentioned previously.

The name seemed even more fitting after that little display.

The guy who'd just been thrown out finally got up. He was grumbling about something, but when I revved the engine, he at least had the decency to move the fuck out of my way.

"That was Myra," Markus said as we got going again. "The

mermaid shifter Tuck mentioned before. Her bite is known to be more severe than her bark."

"Why is she working in No Man's Land?" Kinsley glanced back at her half-brother.

He shrugged. "Not my business to know."

Kinsley started looking around now that we were surrounded by more buildings. "Isn't the circus over here?"

Lia pushed forward in her seat and pointed over Kinsley's shoulder. "It's that way. Just before those taller pines. We took the long way into Fire and Fluorite, so we didn't pass most of these buildings before."

Remembering the instructions Markus had given me previously, I knew that we were getting closer to the warehouse, so I parked in front of the least rundown building of the block.

"We're going to walk from here," I said once I'd turned off the engine.

Nobody argued with me, and after I got out, I waited for Kinsley at the front of the jeep. She took my hand and kept her head high while her eyes did all the scanning.

I glanced back at Lia, wondering if she would sense anything before the rest of us, but since she hadn't said anything, I switched into my normal tracking mode.

My wolf rose to the surface just enough for me to use his senses. Normally, I had something to go off of, but my memory was fuzzy from the day I'd received the letter. I could remember the words and what I was supposed to do, but the scent of the magic was gone.

That hadn't ever happened to me, and it pissed me the fuck off.

We kept walking while I searched for unusual power, except there was none. At least not on this street.

When the warehouse in question came into view, my grip on Kinsley's hand tightened, but she didn't try to pull away. We stopped before a window and listened quietly with Lia and Markus behind us.

I couldn't hear a fucking thing inside, which either meant that there was a silencing spell on the building or nobody was there.

Either way, we were about to find out.

CHAPTER TWENTY-FIVE

KINSLEY

Something about being in No Man's Land made my skin crawl. I hadn't ever been an official member of a House, but still. I didn't like being here, where people were apt to be more reckless. That didn't mean I was afraid, though.

Lia moved in next to me and pressed a hand to the exterior of the building. "It's empty."

I glanced over at her pinched expression. "Are you sure?"

She nodded but kept her hand on the wall. "Yeah, but they just recently left, and they could be back anytime."

Grayson didn't waste any time heading for the door, and I was right there by his side. If we only had one chance to look around, I didn't want to give that up.

We went around to the front of the building and Grayson opened the door with a quick tug. The metal of the lock snapped, clattering to the cement, but Markus kicked the broken pieces toward the street before we stepped inside.

The door closed nearly all of the way behind us, and the lights were still on in the area we'd entered. There were a few rooms with doors up ahead, but the main area seemed to be where most everything had been before whoever had up and bolted. If only we'd gotten here earlier like planned.

Tables with cords dangling from them that likely went to computers and other tech filled most of the space. Potion bottles I'd seen before were on a shelf against the far wall, and that was what drew my attention the most.

Not because I thought I knew a lot about magic, but because these were purple stained-glass bottles with an insignia on them that I had seen on occasion while growing up.

These were from Hazel's shop back at the coven.

My fingers touched the glass lightly as if I expected the material to do something grand, but there was nothing out of the ordinary about these potions except for the fact that I knew where they'd come from.

"What is it?" Grayson asked from next to me.

I glanced up at him, unsure if I was overthinking this or if I was on to something. "I know the witch who made these," I said. "Well, I more knew *of* her. She housed me for a few weeks when I was, like, seven. I never talked to her after that."

A rumble built in Grayson's chest. "He could have gone to your coven for magic trades and stumbled upon you, forcing her hand in some way."

"Or the witch turned on her coven and sought Johnathon out," Lia said from behind us, pointing at the bottles. "That magic is familiar."

She reached between us and took one, opened the corked lid, then sneered a second later, quickly closing it back up. "Yep. That's the same magic that was used on you, Grayson."

"Are you sure?" he asked with a strained voice.

"Positive." She nodded at the same time. "Honestly, it was an excellent plan now that I'm seeing all of this, one that would have worked except there was no way to know that you were Kinsley's mate or that I'd show up."

"I've got something over here," Markus said from across the room.

He was standing over one of the tables and sorting through some papers that had been scattered about. "What is it?" I asked when we joined him.

Markus handed me a sheet of paper with just a few confusing

sentences on it, then he pointed to certain words. "Shade. Heir. Factions. War. Throne. Spread out, those make no sense, but if you put them together, this Johnathon person knows exactly what he's doing, and I would assume he's been fucking with things longer than any of us realized if he's talking about Shade."

"Who is Shade?" I asked as I scanned over the paper again.

"He was Dad's second-in-command," Markus answered, but the hard set of tension in his face told me not to ask anything else about the guy.

I noticed Lia still moving around the room with her eyes closed and hands hanging loosely at her side. I watched her for several moments until she paused next to one of the doors.

"We need to go in here," she said, slowly looking at each of us.

Grayson was the first to move, and I quickly followed, with Markus right beside me. Lia waited for one of us to open the room, and my mate gladly took that job.

The heavy metal door groaned as it was shoved open, and the space was dark with no windows. While Grayson trudged forward, I skimmed the wall until I found a light switch.

Mother of fuckity fucks.

"What the hell is this?" Markus asked.

A stalker's lair.

They'd taken the computers, but they'd left plenty of photos behind. I wondered if this was a message. One meant just for us

There were pictures of Grayson, me, and Markus scattered through the room. Even Ryder and the other faction leaders were in the photos, along with a few others I didn't recognize.

"He's been following you all for months," Lia said with an edge to her voice. "Probably about the time I started having visions."

There was one of me alone in the forest back at the coven. Me sitting in my studio apartment with the curtains open. Me eating alone at a table. Me fucking sleeping.

My skin crawled, and my wolf itched to shift so we could search for this fucker, but the more I stared at these images, the more certain I was that these photos had been left behind as bait, not a message. It was a trap to get us to react emotionally, and I wouldn't fall for that. Not when we had a House of supernaturals to protect.

Grayson began ripping photos down and tearing them with his partially shifted hands. He was silent, but I still gestured for the others to leave the room.

Markus closed the door behind them once they were gone, and I placed my hand between Grayson's shoulder blades.

The shudder that moved through him at my touch broke my heart.

"It's okay, Grayson," I murmured, pressing my lips to his back.

His body tensed, and he looked back at me. "It's not fucking okay." There was a picture still in his hands and I took it from him.

There was a little girl in the image with long, ebony hair; bright, silver eyes; and the cutest dimples I'd ever seen.

"Who is this?" I asked, thinking we now had someone else to find and protect.

"That was my baby sister Addie." He growled through clenched teeth, snatching the photo back and putting it into his back pocket.

Fuck, he'd mentioned her death before, but it had been so long ago…I hadn't expected her to have anything to do with this.

Instead of saying anything else, I wrapped my arms around him and pushed my ever-growing feelings for him through our bond, hoping to ease whatever grief was storming through him.

"They used her death to trick me," Grayson finally said. "They know who I am. I've tried to hide who I was this whole time, thinking it could be an advantage later, but they've fucking known."

His whole body shook with unfiltered fury, and he wasn't hugging me back, but that didn't mean I was going to walk away. We might have only been mated for a couple of hours, and I hadn't even known him two weeks, but there was no abandoning him now.

Not when we needed to stick together most.

I pulled back and glanced up at my mate. "Then let's make sure everyone else knows who you are as well."

Grayson's skin was heating, and the fire in his eyes was back as he stared intently at me. "If I let go and express the rage boiling inside me, even you won't be able to stop me from the destruction I'll cause."

I gripped both of his hands with all my strength. "Turn them all into fucking ash if you need to."

He nodded, then cupped my cheeks and seared his lips to mine. Rough passion flowed between the two of us, and I knew then that as long as none of the innocent members of Fire and Fluorite were caught in the crossfire, I'd let Grayson burn this whole damn place down.

Hell, it might be better that way. A fresh start for everyone.

"We need to go," Grayson said when he finally pulled back, slightly calmer than he'd been before.

I glanced around. "Should we destroy any of this?"

"We will." His shoulders relaxed ever-so-slightly. "As soon as we're outside."

Grayson led the way back into the main part of the warehouse. Lia and Markus were just finishing gathering items from the tables when we joined them, then followed us outside without a word.

I shared a look with Lia, nodding in confirmation that things were as okay as they could be. She had seemed to know a lot about Grayson when we'd first found her, so she might have already known about his sister. I'd still want to talk to him about it more later, because he'd been loose with the details before and I hadn't wanted to pry on such a sensitive subject.

We exited the building the same way we'd come in and stood a few yards away when I began to sense energy pulsing from Grayson. His normally ochre skin was darkening as if it were being burnt from the inside out, but he didn't seem to be in any pain. Instead, a glint was growing in his eyes.

His hands raised just before he thrusted them forward. Dark flames that seemed black at first grew in size, climbing up the sides of the building. When the sun hit them, I could see hints of the forest-green color I was used to seeing in Grayson's eyes.

The metal siding of the building began to warp from the rapidly rising temperatures, and the rest of us had to back up to avoid the heat from burning even us.

Grayson, however, stayed right where he was with his hands still directed toward the building. Each time he moved them, the flames changed directions, staying confined to the building that we sought to destroy.

Minutes ticked by as we watched the structure start to collapse and turn to rubble. Lia joined my side and leaned her head on my shoulder. "He's a little pissed off."

I lightly snorted. "I'd say that's an understatement."

"He needed this," she said more solemnly. "None of us should have to hide who we are. Not any longer."

While I knew she was right, I also knew there would be ramifications to these revelations.

The Houses were about to find out not only that a unicorn still lived, but that there was a blood heir who was staking a claim to Fire and Fluorite, and her mate was a demon-wolf hybrid.

Putting it all together, it sounded as if we had the upper hand, but I wasn't that naïve.

I knew that only made the target on our backs bigger, but we'd be ready for anyone that wanted to come for us.

I hadn't spent my whole life wishing for a real home and family, only to find just that and have it ripped away from me.

Nobody would take what was mine.

My mate, my friend, my brother, and my House.

Right then, I knew.

I knew I'd fight to the death for each of them.

CHAPTER TWENTY-SIX

GRAYSON

A week of eerie silence passed after we returned from No Man's Land. We should have used that time to act against the third faction and to be sure the second one was backing down now that their leader had been killed, but instead, I'd listened to my gut.

I'd convinced Kinsley and the others to remain quiet until we had confirmation that news of our group had been spread.

That had been confirmed only the day before by Markus when he'd gotten in touch with Danni, the Queen to Blood and Beryl and a former member of Fire and Fluorite.

While that had been what I'd been waiting for, there were other pressing matters to take care of before we acted against the other factions.

Like my mate's heat.

Her scent had been calling to me for days, but now it was damn near irresistible. Tonight would mark two full weeks since the new moon, and I had hardly been able to keep my hands to myself.

Even Lia and Markus had to leave, because just having him be in the same room as Kinsley drove my inner beasts to the brink of insanity—regardless of their relation or logic.

All I could focus on was Kinsley and knowing that for the next couple of days, she would be all mine to please, devour, and claim.

My wolf was ravenous for our mate, and the demon side of me—that I was no longer keeping on a tight leash—was eager to see what kind of pleasure-pain we could inflict on her.

And the man in me wanted to ravage her body for hours on end.

I hoped she was ready for that, because as the moon rose higher in the sky, I knew soon that there would be little to stop either of our needs.

Kinsley was sitting at the counter, eating a cold sandwich on my advice. She was going to need sustenance to survive the following days.

When she finished, I was nearly panting with need. It was a foreign feeling for me, but then again, I'd never allowed myself to care for someone as I did for Kinsley.

It wasn't only that she was my mate. She was strong and intelligent and kind. She was everything I'd long ago stopped searching for, but now that I had her, I realized that I'd just been waiting.

Waiting for her.

Kinsley walked around the counter and sauntered toward me. My eyes watched the sway of her hips, and when she was close enough, my hands jerked her against my heaving chest.

Her pupils were a minuscule speck within the ocean depths of her eyes, and her cheeks were stained crimson. I traced my tongue over her plump lips, then picked her up, cradling her in my arms.

"You're mine," I murmured, scraping my teeth over her already burning skin

Her hand rose and cupped my cheek. "I'm yours always."

Fuck. Her words pierced my chest while I walked us to the bedroom. The moonlight shining in through the window only briefly captured my attention before I threw her on the bed.

"I hope you're not fond of these clothes," I said only seconds before reaching forward and ripping the white shirt from her upper body.

Her shorts and underwear quickly followed, and I lost all sense of control when I took in her submissive form.

She'd lain on the mattress with her arms settled loosely above her head and her legs spread just for me.

Knowing that I was the only man to ever touch her so intimately had my wolf surging to the surface, wanting to claim her in his own way. To sink his teeth into her, leaving a permanent mark on our mate.

As Kinsley's chest began to rise and fall with rapid succession, I pushed him back for the moment. I knew our focus needed to be on her needs and getting her through this first heat. I'd been told it wasn't an easy feat, but I was more than up for the challenge.

My index finger tilted her chin up as I leaned over her naked body and claimed her mouth. She moaned loudly into the kiss before grabbing my other hand and placing it over her pussy.

That was one of the things I admired most about my mate. She wasn't afraid to say or do what she wanted, and being in the bedroom was no different.

I swept my tongue across her lips while I slipped one, then two fingers inside her slick heat. She contracted around them, and I began to pump them in and out of her, moderately surprised when her breathing became strangled and her nails dug into my sides so quickly.

Within seconds, she was screaming my name and already claiming her first orgasm of what I assumed would be the best, yet longest night of my life.

"Fuck," she panted. "I didn't mean to do that."

I smirked at her. "That's only the beginning."

Her eyes flashed with emotions I couldn't quite decipher, but they seemed to be a mixture of anticipation and something like trepidation.

I'd known she'd asked Lia about what to expect, but unicorns didn't go through the same kind of heats as wolves, thanks to their mixed races. Lia wasn't able to ease any uncertainties besides saying the "throes of passion" would be worth feeling like her body was on fire from the increased temperatures.

Now, it was up to me to make sure my mate wasn't in a constant state of pain and orgasmed as much as she needed to for however long it took for the heat to subside.

Basically, I was one lucky mother fucker.

Kinsley pushed me onto my back and practically growled at me as she did. "I need your cock inside me right the fuck now."

The feral look in her eyes had my dick becoming painfully hard, and I didn't object to her taking the lead. I knew better if I wanted to keep all my body parts attached.

I was surprised that my wolf was also okay with it. He was an alpha at heart. Even if we'd been in agreement about not trying to lead our own pack, we'd never backed down to anyone. Until Kinsley.

Her strength was equal to ours, and I had no qualms about kneeling for her. Not now that I'd tasted her and knew her heart.

My head sank into the pillows as she clawed at my clothes, ripping them from my body just as I'd done to hers.

By the time my cock sprang free from its constraints, Kinsley was practically salivating with eagerness.

She positioned herself over me, pressing her hands onto my chest to prop her body up before slamming down onto my waiting dick.

"Mother fucking hell," she moaned, nearly coming again from the hard thrust.

I reached my hands up as she began to ride my cock, grinding over me with abandon. My fingers pinched her nipples, and her head dropped back.

Her long, nearly white hair moved over my thighs, tickling them until I reached around her and wrapped the strands around my hand.

I pushed her forward and rolled my hips until she gasped from the deepened position. My thrusts moved in time with hers and I pounded into her even when her eyes squeezed tight.

"I can't stop it," she muttered, clenching tightly around my cock.

My hands cupped her ass cheeks hard. "Don't fight the releases. You'll only cause yourself more pain."

She nodded briefly until her lips parted and she cried out once more.

I kept moving inside her, stretching out her orgasm to hopefully offer her more relief. Her nails dug into my ribs, leaving crescent shapes in their wake but not drawing blood.

I reveled in watching her fall apart on top of me, taking what she needed only from me. Only ever from me. For the rest of our lives.

Nearly three weeks had passed since I'd first laid eyes on Kinsley, but that didn't matter now that we'd completed the bond. It was as if I'd known her all my life, and there would never be a point in the future that I would tire of showing her how much I wanted every part of her body, mind, and soul.

Her shoulders drooped forward, but only for a few seconds before the next wave started to crest within her.

"I've got you, Mate," I said when I rolled us back over so that she could rest.

She nodded. Or at least attempted to as her head lolled to the side.

We'd only just gotten started, but I knew she'd get through this. Just like she had everything else before.

Instead of leaving my hard cock pulsing inside her, I pulled out, much to her apparent dismay, then I closed my mouth around her dripping pussy, using my tongue to lap at the evidence from her previous release.

"You fucking stop and I will cut your balls off," she threatened, but the warning seemed thinly veiled, given how breathily she gave it.

Still, I didn't intend to stop. Not when her thighs squeezed around my head and her fingers had a strong hold on my hair, pressing my face down.

I sucked hard on her clit before swirling my tongue over the throbbing nub and dragging it in a straight line all the way down to her ass.

She cried out from the unexpected contact, and I gladly repeated the action until she was coming over my face.

Using one hand, I wiped my chin and mouth clean, then kissed my way up her body until she was coherent enough to look at me again.

Her eyes glanced between our bodies, and she raised a brow. "You still haven't come."

"But I will," I said confidently. "Don't you worry about that."

Though, it wouldn't be inside her. At least, not during this heat. I wasn't going to risk getting her pregnant when there was so much uncertainty around us.

She groaned and rubbed both hands over her flushed face. "I don't think I'm capable of worrying about anything when my skin feels like it's going to turn to ash at any moment."

"That's not going to happen," I promised. "Just listen to your body."

Kinsley fought a smirk as she peeked at me again. "She's a horny, demanding bitch right now."

A shudder rocked through her, and I knew it wouldn't be long before the agony of needing to come overtook her again.

I reached for one of the bottles of water that I'd set on the nightstand and handed it to her. "Drink up. I don't need you getting dehydrated on me."

Her responding growl made me grin while she gulped down half the contents in one go.

Once she'd had a brief rest, she reached for my cock and squeezed the base hard. "Let's see how long I can last this time."

She was insane if she thought I was going to let her delay the orgasms that only made both of us feel better, but I kept that thought to myself while I flipped her over until she was propped up on her elbows and knees.

My hand pressed over her spine, slowly pushing down until her ass moved higher in the air. She trembled beneath my gentle touch, and I rubbed the head of my dick between her ass cheeks.

Her responding moan was giving me ideas, but tonight wasn't the time to try something new. Not when she wasn't in complete control of her thoughts.

Instead, I surged forward and was fully seated inside her throbbing pussy in the next second.

She clenched hard around me, and her head fell forward onto the pillows. I let her stay as relaxed as she could be while I pounded against her, enjoying the sound of our slapping skin echoing through the bedroom.

She gripped the pillow underneath her and pushed against me in time with my movements, taking what she needed from me just as I'd hoped she'd do.

My fingers held tightly to Kinsley's hips until I felt her inner tremors begin again. I reached a hand around to her front, then pressed a finger over her swollen clit.

She tried to object, holding back as I suspected the stubborn woman might do, but I wasn't going to be stopped.

Kinsley would have a release every five minutes if she needed to, and I was going to make sure her body was taken care of.

"Grayson," she moaned, her voice already starting to go hoarse.

I kissed her spine. "I told you…I've got you."

With those words, she growled and twisted back around until we were both on our knees, facing each other. There was a shift in her eyes. A brightness within the blue depths that showed less of her human side and more of the feral wolf buried deep within.

Her tongue swept over her gums, and when she leaned closer to me, I saw elongated canine teeth peeking out from between her slightly parted lips.

My wolf surged forward, but before I could claim her first, Kinsley grabbed my shoulders and brought my neck to her mouth.

Sharp points punctured my skin, and I saw stars.

Fuck. Her bite consumed my every thought while she pushed me back onto my ass and straddled my lap until my dick was buried inside her again.

My hands held her tightly, rocking her against me until I couldn't hold back from claiming my mate in the same way. My mouth salivated as it moved closer to the thrumming pulse in Kinsley's neck. I licked over her salty skin, then pierced her skin just like she had mine.

As soon as her blood began to spill into my mouth, my mate fell apart within my arms. Her head fell to the side, and she cried out my name.

Slowly, I traced my tongue over the marks I'd left behind, glad to see they were healing already, then laid her back onto the mattress, enjoying the rapid rise and fall of her chest as she tried to get her bearings once more.

When her eyes finally fluttered back open, she glared at me. "How the fuck haven't you gotten off yet? I thought this heat was supposed to affect you, too?"

"Oh, it is." A smile of satisfaction rose on my lips, and I reached down, brushing back hair that was stuck to her cheek. "Just not in the same way it affects you. If you think I could stand to be away from you tonight just because I'm in control right now, you'd be sorely mistaken."

Her eyes darkened and she licked her lips. "What would you do if I weren't with you right now?"

"Do you really want to know?" I asked darkly, and she nodded quickly in response. "I guess it depends on the exact situation, but there isn't a building or spell that could keep me locked away from you and there isn't a supernatural who could endure my wrath if they tried to stop me from getting to you. I'd burn buildings, remove heads, and scour the lands, leaving a trail of blood in my wake, to find you."

As her breathing stuttered, I continued. "And not just tonight or because of the heat, but every day, for the rest of our lives. Nothing and no one will ever take you from me."

That might have been too much too soon, but I hadn't lied to her yet and I didn't intend to start.

She grabbed my cheeks and pulled me forward until our mouths smashed together. "I'd fucking do the same for you," she murmured against my lips.

I knew then that fate might have taken away my family for reasons unknown, but the mate it had given me was more than I could have ever hoped for.

Kinsley was my equal in every way, and there wasn't a single fucking thing I wouldn't do to keep her safe.

CHAPTER TWENTY-SEVEN

KINSLEY

Three days later, I wasn't sure I'd ever walk right again.

Okay. That was maybe me being a bit dramatic, but the heat lasted just over two days and even the sixteen hours of sleep I'd gotten after the seemingly endless orgasms didn't seem like enough. Not when every time I moved, I remembered the way Grayson had cared for me and bit me and made me feel like a damn queen.

By the end, I was convinced my heart might explode from the elation filling my body, but then reality came crashing back and I knew that our time for lying low was over.

Lia and Markus had returned to the house, and they weren't alone. Ryder and Tuck were with them, dressed in combat gear. Dark circles hung under their eyes, as if they hadn't slept in a couple of days.

"What happened?" I asked as soon as I'd opened the door for them to come in.

Guilt assaulted me from having spent the extra time alone with Grayson, but I quickly reminded myself that I'd have been useless to the faction—and the House as a whole—if I'd ignored the heat or my need for rest afterward.

"Ethan's faction has joined with Dylan's," Ryder said. "Well, at least those still left who don't want to see a woman leading their House."

"Have they made any attempts to attack?" I asked, ignoring the chauvinistic comment. I wasn't going to validate the idiocy of it.

Tuck shook his head and handed me a tablet. "But there has been chatter that we've picked up on."

I scanned the contents, but I didn't see what I was looking for. "Have you heard anything about Johnathon?"

After what we'd seen in the warehouse, I had a feeling that fucker was going to be working with anyone who wished to see me fail to become Alpha Supreme. Whether that was because he wanted the position for himself or because he had a hard-on for my bloodline remained to be seen. Either way, I'd do whatever it took to make sure he never got what he wanted.

"Johnathon and the witch you mentioned before seem to have disappeared," Ryder answered. "Though I doubt that will last for long."

I glanced at Grayson. "We need to be out there. We can't stay hidden any longer." Then I directed my attention to Lia and Markus. "This might get messy quickly. You two have done more than I could have asked for and I won't blame you for walking away now if that's what you choose."

They shared a look of mutual confirmation before Markus spoke. "You're my family, Kinsley. Even if we didn't grow up together, I won't turn my back on you now that I know you. We're in this together." He lightly grinned. "Plus, it would be nice to know that our little brother has somewhere safe to grow up without me needing to smuggle him into Blood and Beryl."

I wanted that, too, even though I'd yet to meet Triton. Hell, I wanted that for everyone inside of Fire and Fluorite.

"We'll do a quick training session and make our first appearance tonight," Grayson said. "Your people can come with us, or it can be just the four of us. Either way, we'll leave at dark and be back whenever we decide we've had enough."

Ryder and Tuck stayed silent a beat before the former nodded. "I'll be joining you while Tuck stays behind and keeps an eye on the more vulnerable members of our faction."

I assumed that primarily meant Ryder's son, but I also knew that they lived in an apartment surrounded by other families who were doing their best to stay alive without having to run away from the only home they'd ever known.

"That works for us," I said, eager to get outside now that Grayson had mentioned a training session.

I hadn't shifted since before the heat, but I could feel the restlessness setting in, making my skin itchy again.

Lia nudged me, a growing smirk on her face. "Are you ready for the horn?"

Markus groaned. "Please don't ever say that to my sister again."

His agony made me smile. "I can handle whatever you want to throw at me," I replied to Lia.

"Good." She grabbed my hand and pulled me past the group of men, then out the door without saying another word.

I glanced back at Grayson before I was pulled outside, but he smiled encouragingly at me.

"What are we doing?" I asked with a chuckle after her pace increased.

She glanced back at the house that was almost out of view. "Having some girl time. Don't get me wrong, I'm already more than in love with Markus, but I feel like I haven't talked to you in forever. Please don't tell me I'm the only one who feels that way."

"Sorry, but I'm not in love with my brother," I joked with a wink.

Lia let go of my hand and shoved me lightly. "You know what I mean, damn it."

That I did, and I also understood what she was saying, except my mind hadn't thought the same way until she'd said something.

I'd been okay with all the alone time I'd been having with Grayson. More than okay, in fact. I'd been thriving from our bond, feeling stronger and more capable with every day that passed. The well of energy inside me seemed to grow with every hour I spent with my mate.

It seemed selfish, but very necessary at the same time.

We got to the park, and she headed straight for a big oak in the middle that would provide us some shade from the midday sun.

Once we were both settled on the ground, her foot kicked mine. "So, are you ready to dish about all the amazing sex? I mean, one of us should, and since Markus is your brother, it probably shouldn't be me."

I choked a little at that. As much as I already considered Markus family, I hadn't yet been grossed out by him being mated to my first and only friend. That small mercy was now completely shattered.

Though, I wouldn't deny I was glad on some level to have confirmation of their bond. They both deserved the kind of joy I was currently experiencing with Grayson.

"Yeah…" I said flatly. "Let's not talk about you. Please."

She smirked and tossed her midnight-colored hair to one side. "Then, please, tell me all the things that have happened to *you*."

I glanced around to make sure we hadn't been joined by anyone yet, then sighed like a fool. "If I'd known sex could be that…energizing, I would have found a way to get laid much sooner." My face contorted as the words left a sour taste in my mouth. "On second thought, maybe I wouldn't have changed a thing, even if I'd known."

"There's nothing wrong with having waited for your mate, even if you hadn't realized that was what would happen," Lia said with a swoony sigh. "So, you're happy with him? The bond isn't forcing you to do anything you're not okay with?"

Her question made my chest ache. Mostly because when she'd said "the bond," I assumed she'd really meant Grayson and while he might have been scary as fuck at times, he'd never once made me feel pressured to do anything I hadn't wanted to.

She waved a hand between us. "Sorry. I didn't mean to overstep. I just had to be sure."

I reached for her, softly squeezing her hand. "I appreciate the concern, but I promise, I haven't done anything I didn't want. Badly."

Lia laughed, the sound ringing around us like soft bells. "That's what I want to hear. Tell me more."

My head shook, and I grinned widely. "I didn't come out here to talk about my sex life…or yours. How about you tell me how you're feeling with all this? People know you exist now after however many years you've worked to keep your identity a secret. That can't be easy to process."

Her face tilted up toward the sky, and a peaceful smile appeared on her umber face. "You know, I didn't think it would be easy, either, but it has been. At least so far. I haven't done anything that I regret. Maybe it's time for the world to change again. For the people who have remained hidden to show the rest of the supernaturals that there isn't anything to be feared."

Since meeting Lia, Grayson had told me how the unicorns had been hunted for their unique powers. When the groups realized they couldn't control the shifters, they'd decided the beautiful creatures shouldn't exist. They'd had no right to make that decision, but fear made a lot of people do stupid shit sometimes.

"I hope you're right," I said. "But more importantly, I just hope you're okay with your choice. I'm more than thankful that you've saved me numerous times now, but I don't want the price of those actions to be too high for you, either."

"Just like you, I haven't done anything I didn't want to," she said while standing back up. "Now, if we're not going to talk about the good stuff, I'm going to kick your ass instead."

Laughter bubbled up from deep within me as I followed her movements. "That's, uh, quite the threat."

Light-silver energy began to shimmer around her. "I'm quite the unicorn."

Before she launched herself at me, I stepped back and shifted into my wolf. The transition came easier than ever before, and when I landed on all fours, there was a white magical charge around me.

"Holy shit," Lia murmured as she tiptoed closer. "What... I don't even know what I should be asking."

She and I both. All I could see were my paws and tail, but that was enough to have my chest tightening as I wished more than ever that Grayson was with me.

Lia reached for my fur, and when she touched me, the magic around me slid up her arm briefly before retreating back.

"Fascinating," Lia whispered.

My wolf yipped, needing her to elaborate.

"I have a theory," she said, circling me. "One I'm not sure how to test, but it's intriguing nonetheless."

This time, I rumbled, wanting her to get to the mother fucking point.

Lia winked, then kneeled before me, lightly touching me again. "You're a wolf shifter, through and through—there's no doubt about that—but you were raised in a coven with your wolf suppressed, surrounded by magic. That may have changed your natural born supernatural abilities, something that bond magic could have triggered."

I couldn't stand having a one-sided conversation anymore. My wolf moved back, and I shifted to two feet again. "What the hell does that mean, Lia?"

"If I'm right," she said pointedly, "it means that your wolf has a magical charge nobody else has ever seen from a pure-blooded shifter."

A part of me felt like I should have been thrilled with this revelation, but the only thing I felt in that moment was dread.

Pure fucking dread, because I'd thought I had left the coven behind. This felt like a step back into the life I wanted badly to forget.

CHAPTER TWENTY-EIGHT

GRAYSON

Watching Kinsley be pulled away by Lia made my thoughts darken, but I did my best to hide that reaction from my mate.

I'd had her locked away for days, and I didn't want her to have any regrets about tying herself to me. She needed that time away with her friend, and I needed to learn to be okay with that.

"If I can be frank," Ryder said after Kinsley and Lia had headed out of the yard, "the bond between the two of you is quite powerful now that you've completed it."

I hadn't realized that the energy was identifiable, but that didn't bother me.

"As should be expected with two alphas," I answered, wondering what his point was.

Ryder and Tuck shared a look again, and I snarled before either could speak. "If you think it's okay to talk about my mate and me behind our backs, then you're sorely mistaken. Say what you think if you've already said it out loud to one another."

Tuck took a step back, which was when I noticed my hands were clenched and I'd moved closer to them. "We didn't mean anything by it. We're just curious how well things will go with an Alpha Supreme mated to another alpha. This House has already been through so much. We don't want there to be more tension if your wolves aren't okay with hierarchy."

"He's right," Ryder said. "I want to back Kinsley, but not if the House is going to be in the same position it is now, even with her leading."

My wolf had never once challenged Kinsley's, but that wasn't something they got to know. Instead, I took another step closer, towering over both men. "Our bond might be new, but it's as solid as they come. The House and the supernaturals here only need to worry about the threats that come against us. Kinsley and I won't have any problems with each other. Not now or ever."

They each stiffened as I spoke, then nodded.

"Noted," Ryder said. "Would you like me to send some wolves to the park for practice?"

I shook my head. "Markus, Lia, and I can handle things today."

More importantly, I didn't need any new males around my mate. Not when their leaders had just pissed me the fuck off.

Ryder and Tuck quickly departed after that, closing the door behind them.

Markus moved to my side and asked, "Do you need a shot of whiskey or something?"

I chuckled darkly and shook my head. "Why don't we go join our mates instead?"

"Yeah, that's a much better idea," he said, then he paused at the door, looking over at me. "I really do care about Kinsley like family. I'm not like my father."

My hand closed over his shoulder. "I know."

He snorted and nodded. "Of course, you do."

"But it's nice to hear you say the words out loud," I said. "Kinsley has been through enough, and I'll do whatever I can to minimize the things that hurt her moving forward."

Markus seemed to ponder his next words carefully as we headed outside, but then all he said was, "I'm glad she has you."

Him and me both, but really, I was more glad that I had her.

With our bond complete, the realization of how many decades I'd gone without letting people in my life really set in.

It wasn't that I regretted my past choices, but I knew without a doubt that things moving forward would need to be different.

They had to be, because Kinsley deserved better than the life I'd chosen up to this point. I wouldn't make that same choice for us.

We walked the rest of the way to the park in silence, and when we turned the corner, my steps faltered. I could see a glowing wolf next to Lia that I swore was my mate, but that was the first time I'd seen her entire body covered in shimmering, white magic like that.

"What the…?" Markus's voice trailed off while my speed increased.

Before we got to them, Kinsley had already shifted back to her human form with a prominent crease formed between her brows.

"I still don't understand how this is fucking possible," Kinsley grumbled when I got to her side.

My arm wrapped around her waist, and I pulled her snug against my side. "What was that?"

She looked up at me with wide eyes. "You saw my wolf?"

I grimaced. "I don't think anyone outside and near the park missed your glowing wolf."

"Fuck," she muttered, kicking at the grass. "Lia thinks it's aftereffects from having my wolf suppressed for so long by magical means and living with the witches. That I might have somehow had magic embedded into me, even though both of my parents are wolf shifters. At least, we assume they are."

I squeezed her hip tightly. "We'll figure out who your mom is just as soon as we can, but I'm sure she's a wolf shifter as well. When Lia removed the cloaking spell from you, there was no denying you were pure wolf."

Lia nodded eagerly as I spoke. "You have too much alpha in you to be anything besides a pureblood."

Yeah, the unicorn wasn't wrong about that, but it would still be good to one day figure out who Kinsley's birth mother was. Someone who—for Kinsley's sake—I hoped was still alive somewhere and could give her answers to why she was placed with the witches to begin with.

"How did you feel when you were shifted just now?" I asked, glancing down at my mate.

She bit her lower lip. "I don't know. I was so panicked when I saw the magic around me and by Lia's response that I didn't pay close attention."

Markus stepped forward and tilted his head. "Why don't you shift again, so we can all get a better feel for your magic?"

Kinsley nodded but didn't pull immediately away from me. She took a steadying breath and closed her eyes first. When she reopened them, she lifted her head and there was renewed determination set in her face.

I stepped back, giving her some room, and I nearly missed the shift when I blinked. Fuck, that was fast. Faster than any other shifter I'd ever seen.

Sure enough, she was again covered in a pulsing, white energy. The color nearly matched her hair while she was human, and I wondered briefly if that was a coincidence or not.

Her wolf's piercing eyes landed on me, and I moved forward, quickly closing the distance between us. I kneeled before her without thinking twice, even though we had company. Her wolf's head pressed against mine and she let out a deep, low rumble.

My fingers intertwined with her fur, and the magic surrounding her thrummed through me, lighting our connection on fire, but not the kind that sought to destroy. No, this was a blaze that made my wolf want to leap from my skin and run for miles beside her.

"Stunning," I whispered to her.

I continued to soak up the magic, and then stared directly into her eyes. "Can you control the power inside you?"

I hadn't seen it happen after her first shift. I'd never told Kinsley that I'd seen these same flickers around her before, but on a much smaller scale. So, whatever this was, it wasn't new. The energy had just grown more powerful. Likely from our bonding, her heat, or both events.

Kinsley's wolf eyes closed, and a tremor rolled through her. Briefly, the energy faded, but it didn't completely disappear.

"Oh, that was awesome," Lia cheered, distracting Kinsley. She winced as the wolf grumbled. "Sorry."

Markus grabbed Lia's hand and pulled her back a few feet.

I stayed right there with my mate, softly encouraging her to try again.

She closed her eyes again. This time, instead of her body trembling, Kinsley took several deep inhales and lowered her head.

I waited patiently in front of her, staying on my knees and keeping my hands to myself so as to not break her concentration.

Finally, the magic around her charcoal fur began to fade. With each subsequent breath that Kinsley took, the power lessened until she looked just like she had before.

Her eyes reopened, and her head twisted to glance back at her body while I spoke proudly and stood back up. "You did it."

I took a better look at her, and now that I wasn't so distracted by the new energy, I noticed her wolf was several inches bigger than before. Possibly even the same size as mine.

"Want to go for a run?" I asked, curious to know if she was faster as well.

She nodded and turned toward the city blocks. There wasn't a lot of room for our wolves to run here without going beyond Ryder's territory, but there were enough streets to circle a few times before we'd get bored.

I shifted into my wolf, who immediately nudged Kinsley's, nipping at her neck and nudging her around. They played together like that for several moments before Kinsley's wolf straightened and yipped.

I took that to mean it was time to run, which I was more than ready for.

"Don't worry about us," Lia said flatly. "We'll be right here, just waiting on the two of you."

We ignored her unspoken complaint and took off. Well, Kinsley did.

She was a blur of dark fur and crackling energy as she raced ahead of me. It took more effort than I'd anticipated to keep up with her, but even as she jumped over dumpsters, dodged cars, and avoided fences, I stayed right on her tail.

Though I was breathing hard, she seemed to barely be getting started.

We did a few laps that covered about a dozen blocks each before we stopped back at the park. This time when we arrived, there were more people around, including Ryder, Sammy, Tuck, and several of their men.

Kinsley shifted back first, and when she shook out her hair and arms, the men with Ryder bowed their heads to her, murmuring, "Alpha Supreme."

Not only did that seem to shock the hell out of Kinsley, but I was also taken aback. I'd known Ryder was supporting Kinsley, but given the amount of times that we'd all disagreed, I wasn't sure what information he was passing along to his people.

This showed us—well, at least me—that maybe I'd been too hard on him, regardless of the surprises he'd thrown our way.

Kinsley stood tall, and I adjusted my stance so that I could stand by her side. She took my hand in hers as she gracefully accepted the show of respect from these wolves.

"Thank you," she said quietly, then she turned to Ryder. "Did you see my wolf?"

He nodded and gestured to the group in front of us. "We all did."

"We'd like some privacy to train for the rest of the afternoon," she said. "Only because this is new and I'd rather nobody get hurt in case there are any other new developments with my wolf."

"Understandable," Ryder said, and then the other wolves began to disperse. "Use the building behind us. I'll make sure it remains empty until you're done."

"You're welcome to join us if you'd like," I said to Ryder, hiding my smirk when I noticed how wide his eyes had become.

He glanced down at Sammy, who was still staring at Kinsley with his mouth open. "I promised my son that we would spend today together since I'll be gone tonight. You four enjoy."

Sammy tugged on his dad's pant leg. "Can we watch them?"

Kinsley lowered herself to the boy's level. "How about I call your dad when we have something exciting to show you, and then you can join us?"

He grinned widely. "That would be super cool."

Kinsley held out a fist to the boy. "Then, I'll make sure it happens."

Ryder took his son and headed in the direction I knew their apartments to be, then I gave Kinsley my full attention. "How did that feel?"

"Empowering," she replied quickly with a spark in her eyes. "I felt like I was home for the first time ever. The way the land called to me, and having you there with me... It was like all my wishes had come true. I know that's cheesy, but I don't know how else to describe it. Then, when they called me 'Alpha Supreme'?" She sighed, her eyes bright, but there was also a frown forming on her face. "I don't know what I'll do if things don't go like we hope."

I pulled her into my arms and held her tightly against me. "You're going to have that position. I won't stop fighting until you do."

"None of us will," Markus said as I released my mate. "My father raised me to take the position one day, but my heart never truly wanted it. I only wanted to please a man who didn't deserve the respect I gave him. But you? You were born for this without needing any conditioning."

Kinsley's eyes glazed over, and she leaned her head on my shoulder. "Thank you. Thank you all."

I nudged her lightly. "Let's see if you're still saying that in a few hours."

Even the reminder that we were about to push her and her wolf to their limits didn't diminish the natural glow about my mate.

"Give me your best," she taunted me with a sly grin.

Lia snorted. "Pretty sure he gave you plenty already."

"I'm beginning to see that's not possible," Kinsley replied without missing a beat. She pulled me toward the warehouse we'd be training in, seeming more eager than ever to get started.

I didn't presume that meant anything good for the rest of us.

CHAPTER TWENTY-NINE

KINSLEY

The euphoric rush that was still swirling inside me was unreal. I still wasn't even sure if I was awake or dreaming, but when we got into the warehouse to start training, I had no doubts about anything anymore. Even if I didn't win against Dylan, the third faction leader, this was where I belonged.

I knew it with every fiber of my being.

Though, that was only until Lia blasted me with icy energy then shifted into her unicorn form. Her horn, which was nearly two feet in length, glinted under the lights inside the building, and she dragged her hoof over the concrete ground before charging me.

I jumped over her, shifting as I did, then swiped behind me with my paw, minus the claws, as soon as I landed on four feet.

All I caught was her tail, but even that quickly disappeared when she swiftly swung her ass around and turned to face me again.

"If you stab my mate with that horn, not even Markus will be able to stop the wrath I'll unleash on you," Grayson warned from where he and Markus were waiting near the door.

Markus jabbed him and said something that I didn't catch, because Lia was coming for me again.

This time while in my wolf form, I could easily identify the new power inside me. I hoped that I'd get to the point where I could shift and already have the energy contained, but as long as I could control the magic, I didn't much care about hiding it.

The glow around me increased when I focused on the pulsing sensation at my core, something I'd always wished for while living in the coven. I'd hated being different and weaker than everyone else.

If I'd only known that was the furthest thing from the truth...

Lia's horn came dangerously close to my throat, and I let out a warning growl, to which she responded with her own saucy whinny.

That bitch. She was totally trying to stab me.

I still loved her, but things were about to get aggressive.

Instead of leaving my claws retracted, I extended them, then ran for the wall behind us and used it as leverage.

My paws pushed off the drywall there, leaving cracks in their wake, and I leapt over Lia until I could grab her around her long neck.

The attempt at taking her down didn't go quite as I planned, but she also couldn't stab me if I was on her back.

My wolf scrambled to stay where I was when she didn't fall to the ground as I hoped, but the damn unicorn began to buck, and we had to jump off, barely escaping the hoof that tried to stomp our head.

My only friend was trying to kill me.

So not cool.

I charged her once again, this time going straight at her. She lowered her head, the intent clear in her turquoise eyes, but I wasn't stupid.

I jumped high above her when she swooped her head lower, seeming to be attempting to skewer my stomach.

My teeth bit down on her horn and an electrical current ran through my body, making my jaw clamp down tighter instead of letting go like I'd wanted.

Fuck! I screamed in my head, and I heard Grayson's roar follow, but nobody interfered as I fell limply to the ground.

Deciding to change my tactics, I stayed on the ground until she came for me, surprisingly falling for my act. Well, my sort-of act.

Her nose nudged my front flank, and I used her closeness against her. My paw with extended claws slammed into her legs and forced her front to fall forward. Without missing a beat, I was up on my feet and ramming her further onto the ground before I laid over her, biting lightly into her neck.

She dropped her head down and stopped fighting against me, which I took to mean she was tapping out.

I jumped off her and shifted back to my human form, surprised I didn't have any visible bruises on me as I crossed my arms. "You fight dirty."

Lia's midnight-colored hair and umber skin came back into appearance, and she grinned. "So do you, which is what I was hoping. I wanted to make sure that when it came down to it, you'd do whatever it took to win."

I reached forward and shoved her shoulder. "You know, none of my other opponents are going to have a horn that can electrocute me."

"Maybe not, but they might have potions or enhanced powers gifted to them by a certain witch," Lia said, and I caught her eyes moving to stare behind me. "So don't you plot my murder, Demon-Wolf. I was doing your mate a favor."

I glanced to find Grayson with his arms crossed and jaw clenched tightly. He didn't reply to Lia's comment, but I still chose to walk toward him.

"She shocked the shit out of me," I said with a light smile, then added, "literally." Except he didn't find my words as funny as I did. "I promise I'm okay."

His glare slowly softened as his eyes stared into mine. "Doesn't mean I like seeing someone try to skewer you." He gripped my hand and lightly kissed the top of my head. "Can we get back to normal training now?"

I patted his chest and grinned. "Sure thing, Mate."

He pulled away from me, seeming less upset, but then he shoulder-bumped Lia when he walked past her.

Yep. The next few hours were going to be loads of fun.

As expected, Grayson was extra hard on me, but I'd needed it. With the new energy pumping through me, the extra exertion helped me control the magic I wasn't sure what to do with.

We'd practiced a few things, but other than making my wolf bigger, faster, and stronger, there was nothing new that I seemed to be able to do.

Sammy and Ryder had also rejoined us just before we'd finished, and my favorite little boy played with my wolf with ease while his father sat rigidly by, unable to do anything about it without facing the six-year-old's wrath.

After that, we headed back to the house for dinner, but now that the sun had set, it was time for our first late-night stroll through Fire and Fluorite.

We'd only been outside of Ryder's territory twice since arriving—first when we'd fought Ethan and second when we'd made it to No Man's Land. I wasn't nervous about going out, but I was on my guard. There was also excitement at the prospect of getting to see more of my House.

Even if the people didn't really know who I was or even accept me, I'd already begun to think of this place as home, which I hoped was a good thing and not something that could possibly add to future disappointment if things didn't go as well as I hoped.

"Are you ready?" Ryder asked us when he got to the house.

I nodded and answered first. "More than."

"Good, because it should be an eventful night," Ryder said. "There are no doubts that you'll be fighting tonight."

"I'd have been disappointed otherwise," I replied confidently.

Grayson stepped forward and stopped at my side. "Am I right to assume these fights don't have rules? If someone challenges her and others step in, there'll be no stopping me from doing the same."

"There haven't been proper rules for anything in this House for years," Ryder answered. "You're welcome to do whatever you want. Just remember, the more help Kinsley has, the less respect she'll garner."

Lia scoffed, joining us along with Markus. "Or it'll be the other way around. It's not as if we're just any ordinary help."

Ryder grimaced. "You're right about that."

I pulled Grayson toward the door, moving past Ryder. "Let's go, then."

We walked as a group of five toward the center of town. A first for me since arriving. As we continued, everything looked the same. More rundown buildings, more graffiti, broken glass in the streets, and scorch marks from past fires or spells being thrown at structures.

I knew then that, once the people of the House accepted me, the first thing I wanted to do was clean up the chaos—literally. The streets shouldn't have cracks in them, and the buildings should all be livable by at least basic standards.

A distaste for my sperm donor gathered inside me. I'd never met the man, and I'd been devastated about that for many years, but not any longer.

From the sounds of it, I wouldn't have ever wanted to be influenced by Mathis's selfishness or tyranny. Though I did still wonder about my mother.

Was she still alive? Why hadn't she kept me with her? Did she still live here in Fire and Fluorite? So many questions, and there wasn't a single place I could think to start looking for answers without going back to the coven.

Going back was something I didn't want to do. It seemed stupid, considering all the changes I'd gone through, but after waiting twenty-eight years to escape that place...going back seemed more daunting than fighting for the Alpha Supreme position.

Maybe I could conquer those fears once this was all over. Not only for myself, but for my mother. I didn't want to believe that she'd hidden me for any other reason than to protect me.

Though, there was nothing that I could do about those thoughts at the moment. I pushed them to the dark corners of my mind to worry about another day and focused on the streets again.

More people were out this time. I wasn't sure if that was because of the section we were in or because it was nighttime or maybe a combination of both.

There seemed to be some sort of club or bar up ahead where most people were gathered. "Which faction are we in?" I asked Ryder quietly.

"None," he answered. "The center of town is open to all who want to come. That's why I came here first. The people who haven't chosen a side between the three factions deserve to know who you are as well."

Ryder really was a good leader and shifter. He wasn't an alpha by any means, but he was smart, and that went a long way. I could see why he'd chosen to start his faction, but I was also certain that if we hadn't shown up, he might not have been leading for as long as it would have taken to make things right within Fire and Fluorite.

A group of young guys came stumbling out of the bar. One of them was shouting and laughing but barely staying upright.

We paused, and I watched them intently, curious why anyone would choose to indulge in something so heavily that it hindered their ability to keep themselves alive.

The intoxicated blond pointed at us, his hand unable to stay still as he leaned against one of his friends. "Yo, Ryder. How goes it, man? Did you bring me and my boys some presents?"

His brows waggled, and I nearly vomited in my mouth.

Grayson's chest rumbled, but Markus grabbed his arm. "Let Kinsley handle this," he whispered.

The blond held a hand over his eyes. "Is that you, Markus? What the fuck is your pathetic ass doing here?"

The three guys behind him snickered, then Ryder nodded his head at me. It was showtime.

I sauntered forward, pretending to be facetious. "He's here showing me around," I said softly.

His light-green eyes trailed over my body that was thankfully clothed in flexible jeans, a T-shirt, and combat boots. Perfect fighting attire while also trying to blend in.

"Well, sweetheart," he drawled, "I could show you a much better time."

I was within reaching distance of the guy and was tempted to just punch him in the balls like he deserved, but instead, I reached up, acting as if I was about to gently stroke the side of his face before I changed directions and tightly grabbed the back of his neck.

Using his inebriation against him, I jerked him forward, letting my knee meet his face before I bent down and spoke sternly in his ear. "Don't ever fucking call me 'sweetheart' again."

I threw him onto the dirty road and backed up as the shifter began to throw up. "Pathetic," I said, then I glanced at his friends. "Does anyone else want to show me a good time?"

They shook their heads, then abandoned the dumbass now lying in his own bodily fluids.

I moved to rejoin Grayson's side since I knew he wouldn't be too happy, but when I was only half-turned, a voice called out.

"I'd be up for the challenge," a man from the alley next to the bar said.

Slowly, I swiveled in the direction of the voice and watched as a man with short dark hair came toward us, dressed in all black. His hands hung loosely at his sides, but there was a tension in his stubble-covered jaw that I hadn't missed.

"Kinsley, right? I've heard quite a bit about you this week." His grey eyes appraised me. "Seems there were a few exaggerations."

I smirked, not falling for his attempt at getting under my skin. "Pity. Too bad I don't give a damn."

Our eyes locked in a stare-down that had my wolf perking up in interest. The drunk idiots had held no interest to her, but whoever this asshole was, he was a challenge that could get our blood pumping.

"What do you want, Dylan?" Ryder asked, and I was honestly a little surprised this guy was the third faction leader.

Dylan glanced around me. "Don't play stupid, Ryder. It's not a good look on you." He met my gaze again. "You're here for a position you have no right to. Just because Mathis's blood runs through your veins doesn't mean you have a claim to our House."

I stepped closer to him and squared my shoulders. "You're right. Mathis has nothing to do with this, but that doesn't mean I don't have a claim here. I'll be the Alpha Supreme of this House before long, and I'll do whatever I have to in order to make that happen."

He shook his head slowly and smirked. "You're so out of your league here that I almost feel bad for this."

Dylan moved to strike, and Grayson tried to warn me, but I didn't need the assist. I was prepared for an underhanded move and easily dodged the first punch.

"So, you're quick on your feet," Dylan taunted. "That doesn't mean you can beat me. How about we settle the matter right now?"

"I think that can be arranged," I replied calmly. "And when I win, you'll shut down your faction and I'll claim Alpha Supreme."

He threw his head back and laughed hauntingly. "So much confidence for a naïve woman who didn't even know she was a wolf shifter until a few weeks ago."

I nearly flinched at the comment. I hadn't realized anyone would know where I'd come from, but I managed to hold in my reaction. Though, Dylan wasn't done trying to get a rise out of me.

"Did you think people wouldn't talk about a female showing up here and trying to lay claim to a land she's never been in before?" he goaded. "When I win, there are no options for you. You'll be dead, and that will be the end of this absurdity."

"Are you requesting a fight to the death, then?" Ryder asked.

Dylan's hardened gaze didn't move from my face. "If you need formalities, then yes. I am. Right now."

We'd barely made it into town, and I was already getting what I wanted. Well, sort of. I didn't want to kill Dylan. I hadn't wanted to kill Ethan, either. But that didn't mean I wouldn't take Dylan's life if it meant keeping myself alive.

"I accept your challenge," I said confidently. "A fight to the death at a location of your choosing."

There was a flutter of hesitation I could sense from him. I doubted that he'd expected me to agree so easily, but being underestimated was more than okay with me.

I glanced back at Grayson, Lia, and Markus. My mate was standing completely still, almost as if he'd stopped breathing entirely. His eyes were nearly black, aside from the dark-green flickers I could see within them.

Lia and Markus both nodded tensely at me. Hopefully, they'd keep an eye on Grayson for me. I needed to beat Dylan on my own, or I was going to continue being challenged for Alpha Supreme, wasting time and lives.

When I gave Dylan my attention again, his eyes were stuck on Grayson and a vein was now pulsing in his neck. "Nobody interferes. This is just about you and me."

I smiled triumphantly at the sound of unease in his voice. "I agree."

"Follow me," he said gruffly, then he turned, shifting into an espresso-colored wolf that nearly rivaled me in size. Still, I wasn't worried.

This was why I'd been led to Fire and Fluorite. I would beat Dylan, give him the option to surrender, or end him if he chose to remain stubborn.

Nothing more, nothing less.

CHAPTER THIRTY

KINSLEY

Instead of immediately following Dylan, I reached for Grayson, pulling him close and needing to feel him once more before the impending fight. "Shift with me?"

He nodded stiffly. "Whatever you need, Mate."

His support was something I wouldn't take for granted, and it also fueled my confidence. If he wasn't trying to convince me to back down, then I knew he believed in me as well. Something I hadn't realized I'd needed until that moment.

We both transformed into our wolves, and I ignored the gasps while people I hadn't noticed gathering stood and pointed at my glowing wolf.

"What is she?"

"Maybe she really is meant to be the Alpha Supreme."

"She's not a true wolf. A hybrid should never be allowed to rule over our land."

Varying tones and inflections were spoken by each House member who had circled around us, but I ignored them with Grayson at my side. We followed after Dylan, who had headed back down the alley.

The group of curious shifters followed us, including Lia, Markus, and Ryder, who stayed ahead of everyone else. We went another four blocks before we saw Dylan stopped at a smaller park than the one that I was used to in Ryder's faction.

Dylan was still in wolf form, so I stayed the same. Grayson's wolf pressed his head against mine, and a charge rolled through me.

Our bond, I thought.

Grayson definitely played a part in increasing my strength.

A menacing growl echoed behind us, then I heard Dylan's voice, surprised he'd wasted energy changing again so soon. "No magic during this fight. You didn't say you were a hybrid."

Grayson shifted before my opponent had even finished speaking, and I gladly let my mate have this moment.

He stalked toward Dylan, his rage palpable. "If you're as strong of a wolf as you say, then look at her," Grayson pointed at me, "and confidently tell me she's anything other than pure wolf."

Dylan's hardened stare narrowed at me, and his chest rumbled. "What is that magic, then?"

"Something your *research* clearly didn't tell you about," Grayson snarled.

Dylan shook his shoulders and arms out while bouncing on his feet. "Whatever. It doesn't change anything. I'm still going to kill your mate."

The menacing smile that appeared on Grayson's sculpted face made even me shiver. "Right." He backed up, kneeled before me, and kissed the top of my wolf's head. "Rip his fucking throat out."

His words were a mere whisper, but they echoed loudly through my mind as he walked away.

I would if I had to.

While Grayson rejoined our small group, other members of Fire and Fluorite circled around us. This was exactly what we needed. It wasn't just the faction leaders who needed to know I wasn't backing down, but more importantly, it was the members of the House that needed to know I deserved the title I was seeking.

My wolf moved forward, and I readied myself mentally for the fight, but Dylan didn't give me much time for that.

He shifted back to his wolf and hadn't even let his front paws touch the dying grass before he swiped at me. His claws caught my tail, but no blood was drawn and nothing about the energy pulsing from me hurt him.

Just like it hadn't for Lia, Grayson, or Markus when we'd been practicing earlier.

I had surmised that was because, just as Grayson had said, I was a pure wolf. The extra power I had didn't give me special abilities, but it did enhance what I'd already worked hard to hone.

Dylan leapt for me again, but by the time he landed, I was already two feet away. He snarled, snapping his jaw.

I wasn't afraid of him. I countered his move. Instead of trying to keep a distance, I rammed my head into his side, sending us both tumbling a good ten feet.

The gathered crowd parted for our wolves while we clawed and tried to bite each other. There wasn't a moment of reprieve once I was on him. I ripped fur from his front flank as his claws shredded my right side, drawing the first blood.

My accelerated healing was already kicking in, attempting to staunch the blood, but that didn't mean the wound burned any less.

I focused on the adrenaline instead of the pain, then slammed my head against his jaw.

The cracking sound gave me a boost of confidence and I went for his neck, but he must have seen the move coming and dropped his body before I could make a second contact.

Recovering, I went for his legs and locked my teeth onto his back leg, grinding the sharp points until I heard bones snap. Unfortunately, Dylan had the same plans as I did.

His bite cut into my right rear flank, tearing muscles I needed to fight at my best, but he at least hadn't broken any bones yet.

I managed to swipe at him with another paw, scratching his eye and forcing him to release my leg.

Within minutes, we were both in poor shape, and I honestly had no clue how Ryder had beaten this asshole before.

He was twice as strong as Ethan had been, and I was already tiring while I limped, keeping pressure off my back right leg.

Thankfully, Dylan was doing the same.

I briefly paused my forward momentum, searching deep within myself and finding my connection to Grayson.

I didn't dare look at him, but I pulled on the bond, knowing I needed to fight not only for this House and myself, but for my mate.

We needed each other, and I wouldn't be the one to send him back to the darkness by losing this fight.

Not on my fucking watch.

With renewed determination, I charged for Dylan again. My pace was slower since I couldn't put weight on my back paw, but that didn't make my intentions any less ferocious.

Dylan was one of the few things that stood in the way of what I wanted.

That was going to end tonight.

He was ready for me when I plowed into him, but I still put him on his side. His teeth snapped at me, but I was careful to position my body away from him, so he missed.

I, however, didn't.

While his wolf struggled to get back up, I didn't waste the opportunity. My front left claws hooked under his chin, tearing through fur and skin until they hit bone. I then jerked his head back to the ground and moved in for the kill shot.

My canines tore into his neck, and not gently. Once I had a solid hold on Dylan, I paused instead of biting down and taking his life.

His wolf whimpered, and I breathed heavily, wondering if the faction leader was actually going to surrender.

Only I'd fallen for a move I'd done myself so many times before.

Dylan's good back leg slammed into the side of my head, jarring me enough that I lost my advantage and rolled once away from him.

I was at least back on my feet and ready to go again before he was.

There was a new darkness in his eyes that confirmed what I should have already known. Dylan wasn't going to back down. If I wanted this over, I was going to have to take his life. Just like I'd had to do with Ethan.

Fucking arrogant wolves.

Voices from the crowd chanted around us. "Kill! Kill! Kill!"

There was something seriously wrong with these people if death excited them this much. Unfortunately, I seemed to have no other choice.

I was going to give them what they wanted.

Dylan came for me next, but I was ready for him.

My eyes followed him as he tried jumping for me, but he must have thought his leg had healed more than it had, because instead of landing on me, his body dropped to the side and I took advantage of his mistake.

Without thinking about my actions, I bit into his neck again, and this time, there was no hesitation.

My sharp teeth tore at his already-mangled skin, but just before I was ready to clamp down and break bones, his body began to shimmer.

The stupid fucker was shifting back to his human form.

If he expected to somehow survive, that was the last damn thing he should have been doing.

I backed up just a step while his naked and bruised body came into view. There were even puncture marks on his neck where I'd just been biting, and I didn't doubt for a moment that he had internal bleeding that would end him sooner rather than later.

He coughed up blood, confirming my previous thought, but then grinned wildly at me. "You might have won, but I'll still get the last laugh. You never should have left your faction tonight."

Dylan's eyes slowly closed and reopened while he seemed to be choking on his own blood. I watched for several seconds, trying to process what he'd just said, and then…his heartbeat stopped.

Cheers erupted around me, but there would be no celebrating tonight.

Not when a life had been taken.

But more importantly, what had his last words meant?

I painfully shifted back to my human form, thanking my wolf as we transformed for her strength that had kept the both of us alive. My aching body turned to where I'd last seen Grayson with Ryder, Lia, and Markus.

My eyes first saw Ryder on the phone and jogging away from the growing crowd while Grayson came forward, pushing through the other shifters who were closing in on me.

"What's wrong?" I asked through clenched teeth, trying to hide the true level of agony I was feeling. "Do you know what Dylan meant?"

"Ryder can't get a hold of Tuck and you can't fight anymore," Grayson said quietly yet sternly. "So we need to get out of here."

Fuck.

Did that mean Dylan's challenge had been more of a distraction than anything else? Had we left the people in the faction to die?

I hoped to hell not.

CHAPTER THIRTY-ONE

GRAYSON

Of course, it didn't fucking matter that Kinsley had several severe injuries. As soon as realization set in, she wanted to race back to the pack. Only she was in no condition to do so.

Lia came over to us and laid a hand on the center of Kinsley's chest. "This will speed up your healing, but you still can't fight again until at least tomorrow."

A silver glow emanated around my mate, and she shuddered but stood taller in the next second. "Can you teleport us back to Ryder's?"

I turned to call Ryder back over so he could go with us, but the faction leader was already gone. Hopefully, he'd gotten word from Tuck, but judging by his previous pacing, that didn't seem likely.

Without saying another word, Lia grabbed onto Kinsley while Markus reached for his mate and I held on to mine.

Holding her in my arms, even for the brief seconds it took to go from the dingy park to Ryder's apartment building, eased the frenzy I'd had pulsing through me ever since Kinsley had first shifted for Dylan's challenge.

Supporting her in fighting for her title had been an easy decision, but when it was unfolding right in front of me? That was something else entirely.

Watching another man lay hands on her and doing nothing about it had been one of the most painful things I'd ever had to endure. Second only to burying my sister, then mother.

When we appeared back at Ryder's faction, there were smoke plumes all around us and screaming families.

People were running from building to building, likely searching for whoever had done this or their loved ones.

"Fuck," Markus hissed. "This is bad. Really fucking bad."

Lia grabbed his hand. "Come on. We need to help."

Kinsley was vibrating next to me. She hadn't said a word or made a move, but there was a storm building inside her, that was certain.

Her chest rumbled, and I wrapped my arms around her. "You need to take a breath."

"*A breath*?" She slowly turned her head to look up at me. "A fucking breath? Are you seeing what I'm seeing?"

She took a step away from me, but I pulled her back flush against my chest. "This is what Dylan wanted. He wanted to tear us apart. Don't let him win now."

Her arms jerked within my hold, and I was barely keeping her contained. "We have to fucking kill them all. Every single shifter who hurt these people. They're all going to fucking burn."

The hoarseness of her voice, the agony I could sense within her…all of it made me want to rage on her behalf, but I knew that wouldn't solve anything.

Not for the people here.

They needed to see their potential new Alpha Supreme in control, not falling apart at the first sign of destruction.

I grabbed Kinsley's cheeks and forced her to look at me. "Who are you?"

"What does that have to do with anything right now?" she spat back.

"Everything." I tightened my grip. "Now answer the damn question."

Her eyes narrowed and her lip lifted in a quiet growl before she replied, "Kinsley Ash."

"And?" I pressed.

She took a trembling breath. "The future Alpha Supreme of Fire and Fluorite."

"That's right," I said, loosening my hold just slightly. "And what do you need to do right now?"

Her eyes fluttered closed, and she leaned forward, relaxing within my arms. "I need to calm the fuck down."

"You also need to be in control," I reminded her, lifting her chin back up. "Go help the people here in the way *they* need right now. We can rage on their behalf later. When they're safe and healing on their own."

She took another deep breath. "Thank you."

"There's no thanks needed," I said. "That's what I'm here for, and what I'm sure you'll do for me many times over."

Her hand pressed over my chest. "You know, I think you just might be someone I could fall in love with."

"I'm glad you're just now realizing that." My lips twitched upward. "Now let's go see how we can help."

She rolled her eyes and took my hand. "That wasn't the reply I expected."

"You won't usually get what you expect from me."

Kinsley matched my pace, and we walked swiftly toward the closest building. "I'm okay with that."

Good, because I wasn't going to give her a choice in the matter. Not now that we were officially mated. There was no going back after that.

Lia and Markus were nowhere to be seen, but I caught sight of Tuck and waved him down.

He jogged over, soot covering his ashy skin. "Are you okay?" he asked Kinsley first.

She nodded. "How can we help?"

"The group that showed up fled through a portal, so they had a witch helping them," Tuck replied. "Since we have no way to track them, we're just focusing on one family at a time. Lia and Markus are helping put the last of the fires out and clearing smoke, but people are going to need somewhere to sleep tonight. If you can direct those who've been displaced to the warehouse, Jenny is organizing beds."

I didn't know who Jenny was, but I was sure the other shifters would. "We'll start with helping search for people now and do that."

Kinsley stood up a little straighter. "Did anyone... Are there any bodies?"

"Not that I've seen, thankfully," Tuck answered. Even I lost some of the tension I'd been carrying since I'd figured out what was happening.

He continued. "We kept all of the guards here. None of them followed you all. Ryder was worried about the faction, and clearly his instincts were spot on. If they wouldn't have had the witch helping them, we wouldn't have had so many fires—"

Someone cried for help, stopping Tuck mid-sentence, and he ran to the left.

Kinsley's eyes followed him until he disappeared into the house closest to us. "Ryder is an even better wolf than we've given him credit for."

"I agree. Now let's see how we can repay the help he's given us." My hand pressed against her lower spine, and we headed toward the nearest column of smoke.

Almost six hours later, and just as the sun was beginning to rise, we'd finally all made it back to the house for some sleep.

Kinsley was battling immense amounts of agony while the rest of us were only fighting off exhaustion.

We didn't say a word to Lia and Markus before going to our room. I guided Kinsley to the bathroom before she could faceplant onto the bed.

After her battle with Dylan and then helping dozens of families find safe places to sleep, doing whatever we could to keep them calm, a shower was more than needed.

I was sure we'd both appreciate it later when we woke back up.

"I don't know what I would have done if we'd found anyone dead," Kinsley said quietly while I began to undress her.

"You would have mourned and then done what needed to be done, because that's what leaders do," I replied easily.

She shook her head. "I might have beaten Dylan, but *am* I a leader? If you hadn't been here, I would have lost my shit tonight. I would have gone after those assholes instead of being here for the people who needed us."

I stroked her soft cheek. "Nobody expects you to be perfect, Kinsley. There are going to be certain things you fail at, but what's most important, and what will matter to the members of this House, is that you learn from your mistakes and do better the next time."

"Who are you, and what did you do with my brooding mate?" she asked, leaning her head against my chest.

My arms wrapped tightly around her. "Oh, he's still here, but that's not who you needed tonight. Now let me get you clean so we can sleep. I can be 'brooding' again when we wake up."

That finally had her chuckling as I turned on the shower.

She stepped in first, barely staying up on her feet, and I did my best to ignore the bruises that covered her neck, back, and leg. Dylan had been a fair match for her, but he hadn't had the heart my mate did.

There was no scenario in which he would have ever beaten her.

Knowing that was the only thing that had kept me from getting involved. Especially when he'd drawn blood. Kinsley had done just what she'd needed to, and I was so fucking proud to call her mine.

Quickly, we washed and rinsed our bodies, then only managed to half dry off before making our way to the bed.

I tucked Kinsley against my side, but then she climbed on top of me, plastering herself to me.

"I need you," she murmured, peppering light kisses over my chest.

My lips pressed against her forehead. "You have me. All of me."

She shivered within my arms, and my hands roamed over her body as she moaned. "Make me forget the last eight hours."

I wasn't sure I could do that, but I also wasn't going to tell her *no*.

Not tonight at least.

CHAPTER THIRTY-TWO

KINSLEY

Later that afternoon, I woke up to find Grayson still sound asleep next to me. I'd lain next to him, watching him for a long while, enjoying the calmness in his face and hoping that one day he might feel that way more often and when he wasn't sleeping.

It wasn't until I heard someone in the kitchen that I decided to get out of bed.

I slipped into some pajama pants and pulled on one of Grayson's T-shirts. The hem fell just above my knees, but I didn't care. I was hungry and curious if there had been any updates about last night.

When I padded into the kitchen, I was surprised it was Markus there and not Lia cooking breakfast.

He was mixing up eggs when he glanced up at me. "Hey. Did you sleep okay?"

"Better than I expected to, at least," I replied, reaching into the fridge for some orange juice. "Want some?"

"Sure."

I glanced around but didn't hear or see anyone else. "Is Lia still sleeping?"

He nodded. "She used a lot of energy last night. More than she has in a long time."

"I know the faction appreciates her help," I replied. "We wouldn't have gotten everyone settled as quickly without her helping clear out the smoke."

He nodded again, taking the bowl of eggs and pouring them into the pan on the stove.

As awkward silence settled between us, I realized this was the first time we'd been alone. Either Lia or Grayson was always with us.

My fingers tapped on the counter, and I cleared my throat at the same time he did, causing both of us to laugh.

"Sorry," I said. "This shouldn't be so weird."

"And yet...it is," he said with another chuckle. "It's okay, though. I didn't expect us to become an instant family. Though, I did always wish I had an older sibling."

I raised a brow. "You did?"

"Sure," he said sheepishly. "Then I wouldn't have been the heir to the role of Alpha Supreme growing up. I wondered for a long time how different my life might have been."

I thought he was just referencing his relationship with our sperm donor, but then he continued, completely taking me by surprise.

"My first mate? I was cruel to her, and that led to her rejecting me. It took me a while to accept things fully, and then I was just sad. Not for Danni, because she found her second-chance mate immediately, but a part of me resented them and their happiness. If I hadn't been such a prick, that could have been me with her. But then, I met Lia, and I can see everything worked out the way it was supposed to, but for months? I'd had no clue."

Fuck. I couldn't imagine how Markus had felt before. Nor could I picture him being cruel since that wasn't the person I'd been slowly getting to know.

All I could see now was a man wanting to be better than the way he'd been raised, a man focused on the right things. That made me glad Lia had brought us together.

I'd found a family and a home here in Fire and Fluorite. Even if I was still what felt like a long way from being Alpha Supreme, there wasn't a part of me that intended to give up just because things would only get harder from here on out.

"What about you?" he asked. "How was life with the witches?"

My lips bunched as I thought about my answer. My thoughts on it always seemed to be conflicted. "It wasn't awful, but it was lonely. Some days, I wished they'd been mean to me just so people would talk to me, but instead, I was ignored most of my life, bounced from house to house before I was given my own place. I then spent my adult years training to at least be physically stronger if I wasn't going to be magically capable."

He frowned and stirred the eggs. "I'm sorry that you were alone, and I wish I could say you were better off, but maybe we both got the shit end of the stick in different ways."

I shrugged, finishing off my juice. "Nah, from the sounds of it, Mathis was way worse than the coven."

A dark look crossed over his now-sullen face. "Yeah, probably."

Without thinking too hard about what I was doing, I reached for Markus and, for the first time since meeting him, pulled him into a hug. He stiffened briefly then wrapped his arms tightly around me. "I'm glad I found you," I said.

He nodded over my shoulder and spoke gruffly. "Same."

We pulled apart, and both of our eyes glistened under the kitchen light.

"What can I help with?" I asked, pointing to the food he was making.

"How are you with pancakes?" He reached for the box of batter.

I cringed. "Um, I'm sure I can manage on my own."

His laughter had my chest warming. "We'll figure it out together."

Together. Like brother and sister.

I was good with that.

Not even five minutes later, I had egg yuck on my fingers and flour on my nose from sticking my face too close to the bowl as I'd dumped the ingredients in.

There also might have been more stuff on the counter than there was in the mixer, but we were having fun, and that was exactly what I'd needed after the previous night.

The night when I'd killed another person for the second time.

I was trying to keep the darker thoughts out, and Markus was definitely helping with that, but it was still harder than I would have liked.

When we finally finished plating all of the food we'd made, I started to head back toward the bedroom to check on Grayson, but Lia startled me before I could get too far.

"I had a vision," she said loudly and with wide eyes. "A really fucking big one."

Markus was at her side in half of a second. "What did you see?"

Lia shuddered, a crease forming between her brows while Markus guided her to one of the chairs at the table. "A lot. Where's Grayson?"

"I'll go get him," I said, but he was already coming out of the door by the time I'd turned around.

He joined me without saying anything, looking very much awake. Almost as if he'd known I'd been having a moment with my brother and had waited to come out.

I hadn't thought I could want him more, but he seemed to prove me wrong every single day.

We each took a seat around the table, the food long forgotten, and waited for Lia to tell us what she'd seen.

Her palms pressed over the table, and she took a deep breath. "I've never had one so vivid before. Normally, my visions come in small snippets that I have to put together before I know what they're saying, but this one spoke loud and clear."

I leaned forward in my chair. "What did you learn?"

"It's hard to describe what I see," she answered, "but what I translated from the images was huge. Johnathon and Hazel were working with Dylan. He was under strict orders to make himself known within the House, but not to take over until he was told it was time."

I was pretty sure he'd been told this week, given how quickly he'd challenged me.

Lia continued. "Hazel was here last night with the group that attacked Ryder's people. That's why nobody could track where the shifters went once Tuck knew they were there. Hazel must have teleported them."

"Fuck." Grayson growled. "Ryder is going to want to know about this."

"But that's not all," Lia said. "I know where they are, and I know what their plans are."

She paused for a second too long, and I snapped. "What the fuck are they?"

"First, they hoped Dylan would kill you, but Johnathon and Hazel wouldn't have been able to predict that you'd be mated or have extra strength from the magic you soaked up your whole life." Lia grinned like a proud momma. "Now, it seems as if they're scrambling, so I can't be sure of this last part, but what I gathered was that they're going to attack us head-on in three days' time. They want to kill Kinsley, and then Johnathon will do a hostile takeover with Hazel by his side. Given the weaknesses within Fire and Fluorite, his plan could work."

"Only if that fucker can get his hands on Kinsley," Markus spat, "but that's not going to happen."

Grayson grabbed my hand under the table and squeezed hard. "No, it's not. We need to attack them before they can come here again. Do you know where they are?"

My unicorn friend nodded triumphantly. "Their group moved back into the House once we found the warehouse. They're staying inside Dylan's faction, which has been combined with Ethan's in the last week, so they're going to have more people fighting on their behalf."

Grayson released his hold on me and stood abruptly. "They'll never have enough. No matter how many factions they join with."

I agreed with my mate. I hadn't suspected we'd be fighting Johnathon like this, but if that fucker wanted my House, he was going to be sorely disappointed.

I had no intention of giving up my claim to Fire and Fluorite, no matter how many dumbasses he'd convinced to fight for him.

Hell, Hazel could have spelled most of them for all we knew, but what was most important was that we knew their plan and we had time to make our own.

A plan that would include preparing our people today and attacking tomorrow.

I wasn't going to give Johnathon and Hazel any extra time to plot their next moves.

Not when so many lives were on the line.

"Let's go find Ryder and Tuck," I said, standing and joining Grayson, who was already halfway to the door.

"We're going to stay here," Lia said. "I want to stay as focused as I can today in case anything changes in my vision. It normally doesn't work like that, but I'd rather attempt to see something more than miss anything important."

I nodded and took Grayson's hand.

It was time to plan a war.

CHAPTER THIRTY-THREE

GRAYSON

We showed up at the building Ryder frequented for meetings and found him alone with his head in his hands. Either he hadn't slept or he'd gotten even more bad news. Possibly both, but hopefully learning that we knew where the cause to all these problems was would fix his mood.

He slowly glanced up at us, his hair in disarray. "What's going on?"

"Lia found Johnathon and Hazel," Kinsley said first. "She knows what their current plans are and that they've been encouraging Dylan's decisions. I would go as far as to guess that Ethan might have even been working with them, too."

Ryder's fist slammed down on the desk he sat behind. "I don't have fucking time for this."

I cocked my head to the side and stepped forward. "Did something else happen?"

Ryder's red-rimmed eyes narrowed at both of us in turn. "Tuck found two bodies when he did a second go-through on the burned buildings. One of our eldest mated pairs. They didn't have any family here and we don't keep a list of… We didn't know…"

Fuck. The heaviness of guilt weighed down around us.

We'd thought that the faction had gotten lucky with no casualties. I should have known better. Luck and war didn't often go hand in hand.

"I'm sorry, Ryder, but we don't have much time," Kinsley said with compassion. "They're going to attack again in three days if we don't make our move first."

"If you're not good to fight, you need to tell us now," I added. "After everything that's happened over the last few weeks, you have every right to be done with this, but we also have a right to be prepared. It's my mate's life on the line here."

Given all Ryder had done for us, I tried to keep the ire I felt out of my tone, but I wasn't positive I'd succeeded.

Ryder glanced down briefly and closed his eyes. When he reopened them, he stood and nodded. "We're going to finish this. Together. What do you want to do?"

There was the shifter I was hoping to see.

"We need to gather those who want to fight," Kinsley said. "But they need to be fully aware that this could be a fight to the death. Not everyone is going to make it back home. Not when the other side has a witch working for them."

He nodded and grimaced. "Let me see what I can do about countering Hazel. I've been stockpiling certain things for an emergency situation. I might have enough potions that I've traded for to make a difference."

His words reminded me that I had a whole house full of shit that I'd acquired over the years in my dealings.

I couldn't believe I hadn't thought of that before, but if Lia could get me there without having to make the several-hours-long drive, then we'd have an advantage Johnathon and Hazel wouldn't be expecting.

"Do you need help preparing your people?" Kinsley asked.

Ryder shook his head, his demeanor already back into fighting mode instead of grieving. There would be time for sorrow later. After we won.

"When do you want to leave?" he asked.

"At sunrise," I answered. "Let people rest tonight, but we gather in the morning and head toward Dylan's faction together."

"That will help keep people from getting too anxious," Ryder said. "I'm good with that plan."

I grabbed Kinsley's hand, wanting to fill her in on my own plans alone. "We'll check in with you later. Call if you need help with anything."

We turned to leave the building, moving swiftly, and when we exited, there were shifters standing around, staring at Kinsley as soon as we hit the sidewalk.

I tensed, thinking they were going to blame her for the attack that had cost two lives, but instead, they began to slowly bow their heads in her direction.

The action was brief and small, but I could see the way Kinsley's shoulders straightened and how she held her head a little taller.

She nodded and smiled in return before we continued toward the house.

"Where are we going?" she asked, a clear change in subject that I let her have.

"To the house. I need to ask Lia to take me back to my cabin," I replied. "I have things there that will help during the fight. Like enchanted weapons, potions, and other shit I can't recall."

She raised a brow. "All items you've acquired by killing people?"

I could hear the slight judgement in her voice, but I didn't blame her. "It wasn't often that I killed, and I always made sure I had proof of the crime. When I went after you, I'd seen pictures, thought I had my proof, and it didn't help that I'd been spelled without realizing it. Something that I'm rather positive has never happened before."

Her head rested against my arm. "Don't worry. I don't hold you trying to murder me against you."

The tone of her voice was light, and while I didn't think I deserved her forgiveness, I was fucking thankful for it.

We got back to the house to find Lia prone on the couch with her eyes closed. Fuck, I'd forgotten that she was trying to…do whatever she was doing to get more visions. Still, a quick trip to the cabin was just as important.

Markus came out of the kitchen—likely cleaning up the breakfast we didn't get the chance to eat—and put a finger over his lips before waving us toward him.

"She's meditating," he whispered.

I glanced back briefly. "Well, she needs to be done. I need her help."

Markus actually growled at me, and I was a little impressed. "You're going to have to wait."

"Fine, but not long," I snapped in return, then I headed toward the room I'd been sharing with Kinsley.

I heard her mutter an apology before she trailed after me, yanking hard on my arm after she'd closed the door behind us.

"Was that really necessary?" she demanded.

I shrugged. "Markus can handle me just fine."

She crossed her arms and glared at me. "But he shouldn't have to."

"This is who I am," I said without remorse. "Markus knows that. I *did* agree to wait, after all."

Kinsley seemed to consider my words, then threw her arms in the air. "Men are fucking crazy."

"And if you try to figure us out, we'll only confuse you more," I added just because I could.

She had already been headed toward the closet, but she turned around and pointed a finger at me. "You're not allowed to all of a sudden be a smartass."

I smirked and stalked toward her. "What can I say? You bring out *all* sides of me."

Her fist punched my chest, and I wrapped my arms around her before she could do it a second time. "I'm glad you're getting along with Markus."

She pulled her head back and half-smiled, half-glared at me. "Were you listening to us earlier?"

My thumb rubbed lightly over her bottom lip. "Only for a moment. When I realized you two were having a personal conversation, I decided to stay in the room until I heard Lia shout."

"I wasn't telling him anything I haven't already told you, anyway," she said, relaxing within my steady hold.

I'd already assumed that, and, while it wasn't necessary, it didn't go unnoticed that she was trying to make me feel better.

"How about you put on something similar to what you wore last night so you can come to my house prepared for anything?" I suggested. I didn't want to think we'd find trouble there, but I'd rather be overcautious than ambushed.

She nodded, tension filling her eyes again. "I'm going to be glad when this mess is over."

"Unfortunately, 'this mess' is only beginning," I reminded her. "Being Alpha Supreme of a House that has been through everything that Fire and Fluorite has over the last two-plus decades isn't going to be easy, but you'll learn who you can trust to handle some of the issues that come up. They won't always fall on you."

"Like you?" she asked with a small grin playing on her lips.

"As much as I haven't wanted to be part of a House in past years, I wouldn't be anywhere other than where you are," I said. "Plus, you'll have Ryder."

"And Lia and Markus," she said hopefully.

I wasn't so sure about that.

I stroked her back. "You might need to prepare yourself in accepting that there's a chance they'll go back to Blood and Beryl."

Her face jerked back as if that shouldn't have even been an option. "Why would they do that? This was Markus's home for most of his life."

"Exactly," I said.

She nibbled on her cheek, then sighed. "I see your point. It might be too much for him to stay here. Too many reminders of the person he used to be."

I nodded and kissed her forehead. "But that doesn't mean they won't visit frequently."

"Yeah." The word fell flat from her lips.

I turned her in the direction of the closet. "Get dressed so I can show you my cabin."

She brightened a little at that. "I better not find any clothing from other women there."

Without thinking, I jerked her back to me and she landed against my chest with an *oomph*. My eyes bored into hers, hoping she would not only hear my conviction, but see it in my face as well. "I've never brought another woman into my home, Kinsley. You'll be the first."

She swallowed thickly. "Good to know."

I smacked her ass. "Now hurry up."

Without another word, she disappeared to change, likely into the boots I'd peeled off her last night and some new jeans.

I'd only picked combat clothes when Ryder had offered us extra things to feel more comfortable, so I was ready, but I needed to check on Lia.

I left Kinsley in the room to finish preparing and headed back to the living room. Markus was nowhere to be seen, so I took the opportunity to disrupt Lia's meditation without him bitching about it.

My finger was an inch away from her arm, ready to poke, but her other hand snatched mine and she opened one eye. "What are you doing?"

"Getting you up," I answered while yanking my arm back. "I need you to teleport us to my house."

She groaned and sat up. "I thought my only job was trying to get another vision to confirm our plan will work?"

"That's one job. Not the only one," I said pointedly.

Markus came out of their bedroom and lifted a lip at me. "I told you to leave her alone."

"And I did. For a short time," I countered before glancing back at the unicorn. "Are you going to take us?"

She pushed off the couch and shoulder-checked me. "Of course I am."

Lia went to Markus and kissed his cheek. "Will you come?"

He was still glowering at me while he answered with a terse, "Yes."

"Are we ready to go, then?" Lia asked, back to her cheerful self.

Kinsley's footfalls could be heard coming from the bedroom, so I nodded and reached back for her before Lia could grab onto my arm.

"Do you know where you're going?" I asked the unicorn.

The smirk on her face didn't bode well for me. "Of course not. I'm not a stalker. I don't know where you live."

It wasn't like I had an address for my cabin in the middle of nowhere, so I wasn't sure how to give her directions. Just when I was about to say this was a lost cause, she spoke up again.

"I can get the location from your memories. I just need to take a little peek inside that head of yours."

"No," I immediately replied. There was no way I was going to let anyone poke around in my mind.

She rolled her eyes and stepped closer to me with her hand out. "If you're only thinking about your cabin, then I won't see anything else and it will be quick. I promise."

Lia spoke sincerely, and considering all we'd been through in the last few weeks, maybe giving her the benefit of the doubt wouldn't be so bad.

"Don't make me regret this," I warned before closing my eyes and picturing the outside of my home, the roads I traveled to get there with my jeep, and the areas surrounding it.

A small shock rolled through my mind when Lia pressed two fingers to my temple, and just as she promised, she pulled away quickly. "Got it. Let's go."

My shoulders shook, and Kinsley stroked my arm. "I'm proud of you."

Before I could respond to my mate, Lia latched on to me, then Markus and teleported us out of the room. The air left my lungs, and everything went dark, but that only lasted for a moment before we reappeared between my living room and kitchen.

Lia glanced quickly around and smirked. "I'm not the least bit surprised this is what you call home."

I didn't validate her comment with a response. Instead, I took a deep inhale, then stiffened when I scented something foreign. "Be quiet."

I closed my eyes and focused on my one-bedroom home. I knew every corner and crevice in the place and there was something off. A sour taste of energy that didn't belong.

Someone had been here while I'd been gone.

I didn't hear anything else, which was good, but that didn't mean everything was okay. I glanced at the others. "We need to be quick.

Markus, go into the kitchen and rip up the floorboards. There's a chest hidden there."

Without waiting to hear his response, I grabbed Kinsley's hand and pulled her to my room, which had already been ransacked. "Fuck," I muttered.

Thankfully, I wasn't a moron and had hidden most of my more important items, but still, we'd only be taking back half of what I'd hoped for.

My dresser was toppled over, and the drawers were all broken. The closet door had been ripped from the hinges, and all my clothes were shredded and lying on the floor or on my bed, which had been overturned.

Kinsley gasped next to me, taking in the destruction. "I'm so sorry, Grayson."

"They're just things," I said as I shoved the box spring and mattress out of my way.

When I'd tracked down someone's runaway teenager and only asked for cloaking spells in return, they'd thought I was crazy, but they'd sure the hell come in handy now.

Quickly, I ripped the wooden slats up from the floor and unearthed three chests. One smaller and the most important, the other two larger and filled with weapons and other potions.

I handed the smallest to Kinsley. "Protect that as best you can."

I'd almost said *with her life*, but as important as the contents were, nothing was more important than my mate still living.

She cradled the wooden chest to her stomach. "Of course."

With effort, I hauled the other two boxes from their hiding spot and stacked them on top of one another. My stomach churned as soon as I stood up. "We need to go."

Kinsley headed for the kitchen, where Markus thankfully already had the trunk I'd hidden there in his arms. "Is this it?" he asked.

A blast of power rocked the outside of the cabin. "It's going to have to be," Lia answered as she reached for Markus and Kinsley. My arms were full, but Kinsley was able to grab on to me.

Unfortunately, not before a crazed woman with long, midnight-colored hair floating around her kicked in my front door and shot an electric blue orb at us.

"Shit," Lia muttered just before she teleported us back to Fire and Fluorite, but it was too late.

Markus had been hit in the back with the witch's magic, and when we appeared in the living room of our borrowed house, he fell to the floor, dropping the box onto his feet, adding insult to injury.

Kinsley set the chest I'd given her down on the table and moved to help him while Lia inspected his back.

"How the hell did they know we were there?" the unicorn snapped.

I was setting my boxes on the ground as I answered, "There was residual magic left behind from whoever went through there before us. That's why I said to hurry. I figured you knew what that meant."

She sneered at me. "Next time, be fucking specific."

Markus getting hurt had quickly turned Lia into someone none of us had seen yet. Kinsley helped as best she could, but by the time Lia had him lying down the way she wanted, we realized it was better to leave her alone.

Markus at least had gone unconscious, so whatever the gaping wound on his back was doing to him, he wasn't aware of the pain.

Small favors.

Kinsley and I took the trunks to our room while Lia did her thing with Markus. I caught Kinsley looking back several times.

"He's going to be okay," I promised. "Lia is just as powerful, if not more, than the witch."

"I'm pretty sure that was Hazel," she said, surprising me. "I didn't get a good look at her face, but she had the dark-purple hair I've always known her to have. It's part of her signature."

That last part was said with thick irritation.

"She must have been the witch in my house the first time and left something behind to alert her if anyone came. Though, if she didn't sense the cloaking spells on these"—I gestured toward the chests—"then she's not as powerful as I thought."

"Or she'd left them as bait so you'd be there long enough, searching for stuff, allowing her time to return." Kinsley shrugged, making a solid point, then handed me the smaller box she was still holding onto. "What's in this one?"

"Let me show you." I flipped the latch and turned the chest back toward her.

Inside were pictures of me, my mother, and sister before the world had become a much darker place. Along with those, there were baby items like our first pairs of shoes—something my mom had insisted had been important to keep—and locks of our baby hair, including Mom's.

Kinsley teared up. "This is what you deemed important enough to protect with my life? I mean, I know you didn't say that, but I heard the implication and mentally rolled my eyes because I thought it was some sort of weapon." She sniffled and chuckled. "I think your asshole-ness is rubbing off on me."

Her light laughter made me grin, and I wiped a fresh teardrop from her cheek. "Maybe, but I don't think that's a bad thing. Plus, you didn't know me before I lost them. I was a different person then. Keeping these items safe is my way of honoring my mother."

She looked up with admiration I didn't expect. "I'm sure she's proud of the man you've become."

I wasn't sure about that, but there were other things we needed to be discussing instead of diving back into my past.

"You should pick your weapon of choice," I said, nodding to the other trunks sitting on the floor next to us.

While Kinsley opened the first, I took the memento box and tucked it in the attached bathroom behind the pipes under the sink. It was as good a place as any for now.

When I came back into the room, Kinsley was wielding a sword. It was one that required two hands to handle, but she didn't seem to have any problems keeping it upright.

"You want that one?" I asked as I opened the second chest.

She peeked inside, then set the sword on the bed. "It's a contender."

I handed her a set of matching daggers that she set next to the sword after swiping them through the air a few times. Then she tried out throwing stars that ended back in the box along with the nunchucks, a flail, a sickle, and lastly, a boomerang with deadly points at its ends.

"So, the daggers or the sword?" I asked her when we were done.

She tapped a finger over her lips. "As much as I love the sword, I think the daggers will be better, assuming they will disappear and reappear with my clothes. I could strap them to my thighs."

Picturing her with weapons strapped anywhere on her body had me thinking very conflicting thoughts.

"They'll be safe when you shift, just like your clothes, thanks to the necklace Lia gave you," I said. "The daggers are a good choice." I picked up the sword and winked at her. "I'll take this one."

She glared at me. "I see how you work, Grayson Barrett."

I leaned forward and captured her lips. "I wasn't trying to hide it."

Lia opened the door, putting off much calmer vibes than she had been when we'd left her. "Markus is resting in bed. He'll be good by morning." She peeked at the boxes. "Are you sharing?"

I waved a hand over the remaining boxes. "Pick your favorite. I'll have Ryder take these when we have what we want." I put the sword back on the bed and grabbed one of Kinsley's daggers, squeezing the handle hard. "As a reminder, none of these are ordinary weapons."

The tip of the blade flickered with a blue flame that traveled down to the hilt and I held it out in front of me. "These will cut through any spell or armor, so be careful with them while they have this flame."

As soon as I released my hold and let the dagger balance in my palm, the flames extinguished.

Kinsley stole the dagger back and grabbed the other, her jaw agape. "That's fucking badass."

Lia chuckled at her enthused friend, and I smiled softly.

My mate was smart and strong, but when she showed her innocence, it was one of the most endearing things I'd ever seen.

And it was something I intended to protect with my life.

CHAPTER THIRTY-FOUR

KINSLEY

We'd spent the previous evening preparing for the battle and had gone to bed early. Well, we had headed to our room early. Sleep was hard to come by when we knew we were going to war in the morning. At least, it was for me.

I knew Grayson was worried about me, but I also knew he believed in my capabilities and strengths. That went a long way in helping me feel confident in what we were about to do.

The sun hadn't risen yet, but our house had been up for almost an hour. When Ryder and Tuck had come over to get the trunks from Grayson the night before, they'd brought more clothes with them, including black pants that were supposed to be "teeth" resistant, per Ryder's explanation.

When I put them on, they felt more like supple leather, and I was headed to test them with one of the kitchen knives when Grayson stopped me.

"Where are you going?" he asked.

"To the kitchen."

He raised a brow. "Are you still hungry?"

I was overly full from the breakfast Lia had cooked, so I shook my head. "I just want to try something."

Just as I assumed he would, Grayson followed me and instead of telling him what I was doing, I thought I'd start my day with a laugh.

I grabbed the biggest knife from the kitchen drawer and quickly sliced it over my thigh.

"What the hell, Kinsley?" Grayson shouted, tearing the blade from my hand. "Are you fucking crazy?"

I chuckled. "Nope. I just wanted to be sure these were really 'teeth' resistant."

"And you didn't think to test them when you *weren't* wearing them?" he said with obvious annoyance.

He had a point, but instead, I shrugged. "I didn't think of testing them until I was already dressed. Getting undressed seemed like a waste of time."

"Fucking hell, woman." He threw the knife onto the counter and stormed off down the hallway as Lia came into the kitchen.

"What the hell crawled up his ass and died?" she asked with a frown.

I pointed to myself. "I tried to slice through the pants."

"With them on?" Her eyes were wide.

"Yep."

She shook her head and laughed. "Savage, girl."

"Now we know they work," I said with a wink. "Are you guys about ready? How's Markus this morning?"

I'd already checked on him myself several times before we'd gone to bed, but he'd been sleeping every time. Lia had assured me he was going to be fine, just as Grayson had, but seeing that with my own eyes was the only thing I'd known would ease my concerns.

"He's up and ready for a fight," Markus answered instead of Lia as he came around the corner from the living room. "How about you?"

I smiled and let out a small sigh. "I'm about the same."

"Let's go, then," Grayson said as he rejoined us.

The sword he'd picked last night was resting across his back with the handle up. That, combined with his black pants and charcoal shirt that formed nicely around his defined muscles, easily increased his sex appeal by a thousand percent.

Basically, he was the definition of sex on a stick. Even better, he was all mine.

Grayson strode to my side and whispered in my ear, "Keep looking at me like that and we're not leaving this house."

Nodding, I gulped then attempted to distract myself by double-checking that my twin daggers were strapped to my thighs over the tight, black pants.

They were as secure as they could get in the sheaths Grayson had given me, and there wasn't anything left for us to do except meet up with the others.

Lia and Markus had already opened the front door, and when I moved to exit ahead of Grayson, a loud explosion sounded around us, vibrating the floor I still stood on.

"What the fuck was that?" I seethed.

"Seems like the fight came to us," Grayson answered, pushing me forward. "We need to see where the blast hit and make sure everyone not fighting already made it to the hidden bunker."

Ryder had made contingencies for those staying behind. Nobody would be in the houses or buildings like before. They were supposed to all be gathered in underground bunkers for the duration of the fight in case anyone slipped past us to attack.

There were still maybe twenty minutes until sunrise, though, which meant there was a chance innocent people had still been in their homes, saying their goodbyes.

The four of us ran, opting to stay on foot in case anyone needed our help while we searched for the others. When we arrived at the park, which was basically the center of Ryder's faction, the warehouse we frequented for training was on fire, and wolves were fighting each other on the grass.

Fuck. This wasn't good.

Lia stood ramrod straight, a silver energy shimmering around her. "I didn't see this. How could I have not seen this?"

Markus tried to hold her, but whatever power she was emanating didn't allow that to happen.

"This isn't your fault," he said sternly. "The heads-up you did give them will have helped, and so can we."

"Oh, yes. We're going to fucking help. Help unlike anything they've ever seen." With those final words, Lia charged forward, shifting into her pearl-colored unicorn as she ran.

Markus ran after her, his hickory-colored wolf quickly coming into appearance as he gave chase.

I glanced at Grayson once more. "Should we join them or search for Johnathon and Hazel?"

"Join them," he answered, then added, "for now."

Before we took off after our friends, his hand wrapped tightly around the back of my neck, jerking me forward until I was pressed flush against his chest. Our eyes locked in a battle of mixed emotions.

"Be fucking careful," he demanded before his mouth crashed down onto mine.

My fingers gripped his shirt tightly, bunching the fabric until my hands began to hurt.

I pulled back first, knowing we didn't have time on our side. "You, too."

He nodded stiffly, and then we ran.

Right into the middle of a war.

Even though I still had the daggers strapped to my thighs, I opted to let my wolf loose first. She seemed just as eager as I was to end this chaos, and I was glad to let her exert the pent-up rage we'd both been holding on to.

A russet wolf I recognized was being pinned down by an ebony one I'd never seen before and that I felt confident wasn't one of Ryder's. My wolf's head rammed right into his side, sending him in the other direction and giving the prone wolf time to get up.

Then the attacker circled back, revealing that he had crimson eyes and was salivating at the mouth.

A quick glance told me that more than half of these wolves had similar eyes, which would at least help us know who we needed to be fighting against, but it also meant that they were magically enhanced.

Ryder was supposed to have given the potions that we'd brought back to the wolves, but I doubted they'd been used yet, meaning we weren't fighting on an even playing field.

The opposing shifter charged for me this time, and I was quick to use my glowing paw and claws to hit him in his head, knocking him unconscious with ease.

The wolf who'd just been on the ground clearly wasn't satisfied with this one merely being knocked out. He dove for the guy's throat, ripping it open with one bite.

I moved on, trying not to think too hard about all the deaths that were happening around us, and searched for Grayson. He was fighting two wolves but had the upper hand, so I moved on.

As I turned around, sharp teeth clamped down on my tail, and I snarled loudly.

Fucker.

A tan, red-eyed wolf with brown patches on his sides stared me down, then came at me with teeth and claws at the ready.

I tumbled to the ground with the beast, using my advantage of magically charged strength to overpower him.

When I pinned the bastard down, I went for his throat, but his back legs slammed into my stomach, not only forcing me off of him, but cutting into my skin.

Blood dripped slowly from the wounds, but I didn't let that stop me.

From the corner of my eye, I saw the attacking wolf leap for me, so instead of getting up, I stayed prone until he was closer. Then I opened my jowls as far as they would go and closed them when he landed.

My teeth clamped down on his snout, and while the idea of tearing his face in half repulsed me, I acted on adrenaline and jerked my head to the left before spitting his nose onto the ground.

The howl that ripped from his chest almost allowed me to feel bad for the fucker, but then he raked his claws over my shoulder, thankfully not cutting through my fur.

I got up and put him out of his misery. My bite was quick and efficient, breaking the bones in his neck and ending the suffering. Not that he deserved any mercy, but I had other people to save.

My wolf spit out the blood, and I took a step toward Grayson but froze when I heard someone scream, "Dad! Dad, where are you?"

Fuck. It was Sammy. He hadn't made it to the bunker.

It took two glances at the building to my right to finally spot his blond hair poking out from behind a short wooden fence.

I wanted to tell Grayson what I was doing, but there was no time for that.

If I'd heard the boy, then others would have, too, and I was the only one between opponents.

Making a snap decision, I raced for Sammy and shifted back to my human form when his eyes went wide at my arrival.

"What are you still doing here?" I chastised.

His chin trembled. "I just wanted to help."

Damn it. This kid was something else.

"Can you shift?" I asked, hoping we could make a quick escape through the trees.

Tears fell down his cheeks, and he looked down at his shoes. "I tried, but it's not working." He hiccupped. "I'm sorry, Kinsley."

"It's okay," I promised, thinking of the best way to keep the boy safe.

Water-filled eyes looked up at me. "Where's my dad?"

"I don't know, but I know he'll feel a lot better if he knows you're away from the fight. I'm going to get you out of here." Without waiting for him to respond, I picked him up and slid him around my back. "Hold on as tightly as you can, bud, and watch my back. I'm going to need both of my hands."

He whimpered as his heels pressed themselves deeply against my stomach. I flinched from the pressure on my wounds that still ached there but kept moving.

I pulled the daggers out of their sheaths and squeezed the hilts until blue flames covered the blades.

"Whoa," Sammy whispered.

"Watch our backs," I reminded him, and then I began to sprint in the direction of the bunker.

CHAPTER THIRTY-FIVE

KINSLEY

It wasn't long before we caught the attention of the red-eyed wolves, as well as Grayson. He let out a menacing howl that made me think he wanted me to stop, but I couldn't. I had to get Sammy to safety. If anything happened to him…

I couldn't even finish the thought. This kid was going to be okay. Just like I'd promised.

"Left," Sammy shouted, and I swung my hand in that direction.

The dagger still flaming in my hand slid cleanly through the silver wolf with crimson eyes, taking his head right off.

"Hell yeah!" Sammy said.

I chuckled but still reprimanded him. "Language, bud."

The other wolves slowed in their attacks once they'd seen what I'd done to the first, but that didn't mean we were going to be left alone.

I assumed I was the specific target that they'd been told to kill, which meant I should have handed Sammy off to someone else, but I'd only just thought of that, and none of our wolves were coming to help me.

They were all being stopped by the attacking pack.

I should have realized that wasn't a good thing, but in the moment, all I could think about was getting the boy on my back away from the fight.

I heard footsteps behind us and slowed my pace a little. "Don't let go, Sammy."

My airways were almost crushed with how tightly he held on, but that didn't stop my movements.

I forced my body forward, rolling over Sammy with as little pressure on him as possible, and shoved both daggers in the air.

The wolf I'd heard behind us jumped just as I'd hoped he would, so instead of crashing into Sammy on my back, the chocolate-colored wolf flew over us and his guts fell from his stomach, thanks to my perfectly timed cut.

I rolled to the side but didn't exactly miss the mess I'd made. My arm was covered in blood and things I didn't want to look at too closely, but there wasn't time to be disgusted. Though, based on Sammy's gagging, he thought otherwise.

Scrambling back to my feet, I doubled-checked that the kid was still secure. "Are you good back there?"

I felt his head nod against my shoulder. "That was…"

"Let's not talk about it," I said gruffly as I resumed my running.

This time, there was no one behind us, and the sound of snarling wolves grew fainter.

My chest constricted as I ran farther from Grayson, but I knew he'd be okay. He was probably flamed out by now, burning those other fuckers to ash.

At least, that was what I was going to picture as I ran past the last of the residential areas and into the trees.

The bunker was only another fifty yards ahead. I could see the boulder that it was hidden under. We were so fucking close.

Until we weren't.

Hazel and a man I assumed to be Johnathon—based on his similarities to the picture I'd seen of him—shimmered into view, right in our way.

I skidded to a stop, raising both flaming daggers in front of me.

If these assholes thought they were going to get to Sammy, they were going to be quickly proven wrong.

Hazel's familiar emerald eyes wrinkled at the sides as she smirked. "It's lovely to see you again, Kinsley. It's been a long time."

Her long, dark, almost-black, purple hair draped over her shoulders, covering most of the red corset she wore over what I assumed to be a one-piece black leather number that covered her arms, torso, and legs.

"Not long enough," I easily replied.

Sammy stayed quiet behind me, keeping his head tucked tightly against the back of my neck.

Hazel tsked. "Now, that's not any way to greet one of the women who helped raise you. I only wanted to introduce you to my friend here."

She gestured to Johnathon. His hair had more grey than black in it like the picture we'd seen and the scar along his forehead wrinkled heavily around the edges, but it was the glow of his silver eyes that captured my attention most.

"I've been searching for you for some time now, Kinsley," he said inquisitively. "Though, I had been looking for someone named Bethany. Not Kinsley. It's a pity the coven took the name your mother gave you away when that was the only thing you had left from her."

He was trying to fuck with my mind, but it wasn't going to work. He might have thought he knew who I was, thanks to whatever Hazel had told him, but poking at my past and how I'd been abandoned was not a blow that would break me.

Not anymore. Especially now that I'd found my family.

I took a step to the right, keeping both of my hands out still. "Yep. Such a pity. Now, what the fuck do you want?"

Johnathon glowered. "Apparently, the coven didn't teach you any manners."

"I only reserve those for people who deserve them." I took another step to the right and a quick glance at the boulder. My eyes briefly caught movement that I hoped would be someone who could take Sammy from me.

My wolf was dying to escape and rip these fuckers to shreds, but I couldn't until I no longer had the boy to protect.

"So, what do you want from me?" I asked again, hoping to buy myself some time. Plus, it would be nice to know why this fucker framed me for murder.

His chin lifted slightly. "You were supposed to be mine."

My stomach churned, taking his words one way, but Johnathon continued before I could verbally react.

"Your mother was my fated mate," he said hauntingly. "She was my life, and when she'd told me she was pregnant, I was the happiest man in the world."

Except I wasn't his. I was Mathis's child.

"But my Rosy wasn't far enough along for me to be the father." His eyes darkened as he stared at me with malice. "I'd been gone for a couple of months, working further south per Mathis's demands. Rosy hadn't told me she was feeling the signs of the heat. I didn't get home in time, and another decided it was his job to help ease her through the pain."

Maybe my mother hadn't been hiding me from Mathis. Maybe she was hiding me from this psychopath. The look in his eyes was feral, and his voice grew deeper as he spoke.

"I wanted her to get rid of you." He laughed darkly. "Of course, she wouldn't, so I had to get rid of her. No mate of mine would disrespect me like she had. But then she disappeared. It wasn't until I met Hazel here that I scented my Rosy." He sighed, inhaling the air around us "Her sweet aroma is one I'll never forget. Only it wasn't her. It was you."

The sneer he was sending my way had my grip tightening on Sammy. The boy was making me proud as hell of him for staying so quiet and calm while this madman rattled on way more than I'd expected.

"So, I began to dig," he continued. "I figured out who your father was. I tried to end him for ruining my life, but that didn't quite go as planned. Once Mathis was out of the picture, I knew I needed you to be as well. It was the only way for me to get my Rosy back."

Fated mate or not, I hoped my mother wouldn't have been stupid enough to ever go back to this man.

"You think killing her daughter is the way to a woman's heart?" I asked.

His chest rumbled. "I think—"

Hazel gagged and cut him off. "Enough with this bullshit. I've heard enough, and I didn't agree to help you to hear about your pitiful life. I want my spot as queen as promised, so let's end this."

Queen? Did she expect to lead Fire and Fluorite, or maybe Earth and Emerald somehow? I didn't know, but she was right about one thing. It was time for this nightmare to be over.

Johnathon turned and grabbed Hazel by the throat. "You'll get what was promised as soon as you locate my Rosy and remind her that being with her fated mate is the only thing she should concern herself with any longer."

The witch slammed her hand down on his arm, forcefully removing his hold from her. "And I need the blood of her child to do that, so let me do my damn job."

So, that was what I was to them. A means to an end. Well, too bad for them. I had no intentions of playing along.

Johnathon said something, but I missed it. Then, Hazel pointed at me. Or at least I'd thought she did. "That's Ryder's pup. I want him to use as leverage to get the last faction in line, then we kill her as planned."

The more the pieces began to fit together, the more I realized our guesses had been close, yet so far from the truth about this whole fucked-up situation. Though, that didn't matter now.

"You're not going to touch the boy," I said, taking a step back. "And you're definitely not going to kill me."

Hazel chuckled. "Is that so?" Before she'd even finished speaking, she sent an orb of dark energy toward us.

I dropped to the ground and rolled on top of Sammy, squishing the hell out of him, but it was the only way to shield him.

The magic scorched my shoulder, and I let out a string of obscenities while trying to get up before she could hit me again.

Sammy didn't keep his hold on me this time, so I had to lift him from the ground before picking my daggers back up, then nudged him behind me with my hip as soon as I was steady on my feet again.

I caught more movement in the trees. Fuck, whoever that was had better be friendly, and they needed to hurry the hell up.

"You're fast, but that will only keep you alive for so long," Johnathon taunted.

Didn't I fucking know it.

My shoulder was burning as if the muscles there were being disintegrated by whatever that bitch had hit me with. Still, I gritted my teeth and hoped my hyped-up healing energy would do its thing quickly.

A twig snapped behind us, and I decided it was time to hope fate was done being a fickle bitch, because I really needed this to go my way.

I briefly gave Hazel and Johnathon my back and pushed Sammy away from me with my booted foot. "Run for the trees. Now."

The brave kid didn't hesitate, and he did just as I'd told him to do. By the time I faced my enemies again, Hazel was sending another orb at me, but this time, I didn't have a kid to protect on my back. I only needed to make sure he didn't get hit with any magic.

I swiped the still-flaming blade through the air, sliced through the dark sphere, and then winced when the fucker exploded.

Tiny flickers of dark magic landed on my arms and chest, but thankfully, my legs were covered by the teeth—and apparently magic —resistant pants.

Fuck this. I was never going to get close enough to Hazel on two feet to use the daggers. It was time to show them what a true wolf was capable of.

The weapons went back to their sheaths, and I could hear several sets of feet running away from us. Ones that I hoped were currently rushing Sammy to safety.

My shift came fast and painlessly, then my wolf roared with ferocity as we landed on four flickering paws.

Based on the widening eyes of Johnathon, he either hadn't heard about my magical wolf or he had assumed the details to be exaggerated.

"Kill her," he spat, shoving Hazel forward.

I still wasn't sure what the entirety of Johnathon's endgame was, but if he sought to be Alpha Supreme and wasn't willing to fight me himself, he'd already failed.

This House would chew him up and spit him back out. Again.

Stupid fucker for thinking otherwise.

Hazel's circling hands brought my focus back to her, but I wasn't afraid of her magic.

I charged forward, my stride lengthening until I was only a few feet away from the bitch.

She lashed out with tendrils of ebony and charcoal magic, but the lighter energy around me blocked the worst of whatever she was doing.

Shit. If I'd known my wolf had been capable of that, I'd have shifted as soon as I'd seen them, but it wasn't like we'd had magic to hit me with while testing the capabilities of my wolf.

She screeched in frustration as she backed up, but I wasn't stopping.

I swiped a paw out, cutting through her thigh and destroying her femoral artery.

Survive that, bitch, I thought.

Hazel fell to the ground in a heap, and her darkening eyes went to Johnathon, but he wasn't looking at her. His silver eyes were focused solely on me.

My wolf growled, baring her teeth at the fucker as if to say, "Come and get me."

"I'll end you myself, then," he said before shifting into a pewter-colored wolf with black paws.

I felt rather confident there was little chance of that happening… until his wolf began to grow in size then plowed right into me.

Damn it! That had hurt like a mother fucker.

I was pretty sure that hit had broken a bone or two, but my wolf wasn't easily deterred. We got up and refocused on Johnathon. So what if he was nearly the size of a car by the time he'd stopped increasing in size? We were fast and smart and motivated.

Highly fucking motivated.

His large paws echoed over the forest floor when he came for me again, but this time, I wasn't distracted by the hulking wolf.

I ducked and slid beneath his underbelly, digging my claws into his stomach. However, given his ridiculous size, I'd barely drawn blood.

The asshole must have been spelled. There was no way his natural wolf was that big, but there was no time to overanalyze things that were trying to kill me.

I just had to figure out where his weakness was.

He moved around me, foaming at the mouth while his glance moved between me and Hazel.

She was still alive, and she wasn't actively bleeding anymore, but the witch hadn't healed herself, either.

I found that rather fucking interesting until Johnathon came for me again.

My wolf jumped back, then ran for one of the trees before using our claws to climb about ten feet up the trunk. She bounced off the hard surface and landed on top of Johnathon.

Her mouth opened wide and pointed canines punctured his skin, but his neck was so fucking large that it wouldn't be possible to kill him this way.

We were going to have to keep injuring him enough to slow his big ass down and come up with a Plan B.

Johnathon jerked his body left to right, hard enough that my wolf lost her hold on him and went flying into the trunk of a nearby tree.

A solid *thud* sounded around me, and there was a slight ringing in my head, but I wasn't down for the count. Not even close.

I encouraged my wolf to get back onto her feet and snarled up at the bastard before us.

He lifted his right front paw and tried to take my head off, but even injured, I was faster than the big fucker.

My wolf lowered to the ground, then we ran just far enough away to be out of striking distance for the moment.

I took a deep breath and tried to focus on the situation.

Johnathon was huge, but he was slow.

Hazel wasn't using any more of her magic and was currently swaying against a rock with her eyes closed.

I hadn't heard Sammy scream for help, and whoever had hopefully saved him hadn't come back.

Not surprising, given the weakest of the pack faction were out here, but I wouldn't have turned down help in any form.

Johnathon also wasn't tiring easily. Not even the small injuries I'd made seemed to faze him.

I needed to go for weaker spots. Like his eyes. Hell, maybe even his balls. Just because I couldn't kick him in the jewels didn't mean I couldn't still hurt him there.

His thunder paws reverberated through the thinning forest when he came at me again.

With a new plan in mind, I did my best to ignore the searing pain in my front flank where my shoulder had been burned with magic and the soreness in my stomach from the early hit that was only just beginning to fade.

All four feet of mine pushed off the ground, and I leapt as far right as I could. My teeth clamped down on Johnathon's furry tail, knowing full well that this wasn't going to hurt him, but I needed him distracted.

Sure enough, he whipped around too quickly for his size and got his own feet tangled.

The mess he'd made of himself gave me the opening I'd been looking for, and I went for his eyes.

My wolf jumped onto his back, then clawed her way to the top of his head. Her sharp nails raked across one eye with precision. Though, before we could take out the other, Johnathon had recovered and sat as if he was going to itch his head with his back foot, but instead, the asshole launched us into the air.

His front paw then swatted at my wolf with claws extended while we were still in the air. Thankfully, his aim was off, so we didn't get skewered, but we were still slammed much harder into the ground than I'd been prepared for.

The impact was so severe that the earth around us cracked, and there was a small crater beneath my wolf that hadn't been there before.

Fuckity fuck!

I tried to get up, but exhaustion was taking over. I had broken bones, likely internal bleeding, and who-knew-what-else wrong with me.

My eyes fluttered closed briefly, but then I saw Grayson's face in my mind and remembered that I'd only just begun to really live my life. Was I really going to let this fucker take that away from me?

No, I wasn't.

Come on, Wolf, I said mentally. *We need to fight just a little harder.*

She growled in response, working to get back up just as we heard a familiar howl.

Grayson.

Our mate was coming to help, but would he get here in time?

I couldn't be sure, but either way, we still had to fight for our life. For the one we deserved.

CHAPTER THIRTY-SIX

GRAYSON

When Kinsley had run toward the forest with Sammy on her back, I'd known exactly what she was doing, but I hadn't been able to stop her in time. Not that I didn't want the boy safe, but I'd rather she hadn't gone off alone.

Instead, I'd stayed behind and focused on ending the battle in the park, so I could join her without worrying about bringing the fight to where people were supposed to be safe in the bunker.

That was really fucking hard for me to do, but it wasn't about me. It was about Kinsley and what she would want.

I hadn't brought out my demon side yet, because I didn't want to hurt innocent wolves, but now that the circumstances had changed, there was no holding back.

The other wolves needed to move the fuck out of my way or get burned.

My wolf's size grew as his coat darkened to the color of burnt charcoal and forest-green flames licked over his fur.

I searched for more crimson eyes and charged forward, growling loudly as I moved to warn people out of my way.

Most did, but some weren't quick enough and yelped when they were singed. Still, I stayed focused and targeted the attacking pack.

The first red-eyed wolf stupidly came for me, and all it took was one light bite to his neck to end his life.

The chestnut-colored wolf tried to fight back in the split second he had before his body became engulfed in flames, but his claws and teeth couldn't hurt me, not with my demon power on full display.

Others began to retreat, but in this state, I was bigger and faster than them. I easily took one after another down. Lia and Markus were on the opposite side of the park now doing the same, but I could see even from several dozen yards away that the unicorn was tiring.

Her power wasn't endless, and there would only be so much Markus could do to protect her when she was tapped.

I still hadn't seen Johnathon or the witch, even though I knew all of these wolves had some sort of magical enchantment coursing through them.

More and more of them kept coming from the alleyways, and the longer I fought, the sooner I expected Kinsley to return to the fight.

Nearly ten minutes later, Lia and Markus were nowhere to be seen, and the wolf who had been coming for me dropped to the ground before I even touched him.

The crimson glow that had been in his eyes disappeared, and his body twitched in place.

One quick glance showed me that was the same for the rest of the wolves.

Hazel.

She must have been linked to them all and needed her power back, which had to mean only one thing.

They'd found my mate, and she was alone.

Ryder came racing toward me in his human form, but I didn't stay to answer his questions. Hell, I didn't even know where he'd been this whole time, but I didn't have time to care.

I let out a rageful howl, then raced through the forest to find my mate. As we ran, and the closer we got to Kinsley, the more my flames began to diminish. My wolf easily picked up on our mate's scent, and the farther into the trees we went, the more magic we could sense.

Painstakingly, I slowed my wolf so that we could sneak into whatever was going on.

I could hear something loud echoing up ahead, and when we finally saw what was happening, I couldn't fucking believe it.

The wolf Kinsley was fighting was fucking huge. Unnaturally so.

One glance behind them, and I found Hazel leaning against a rock with her eyes closed. Magic flickered off of her, but she was barely moving.

That dumb bitch was giving the energy she needed to live to the wolf I presumed to be Johnathon. That was the only scenario that made sense for what I was seeing, but I was quickly going to end this madness.

Or at least help Kinsley to do so.

Her wolf was glowing like normal, but the white sparks around her weren't as bright as I was used to seeing, which told me she was far more injured than I could see from where I stood.

Without wasting any more time, I shifted back to my human form and pulled the sword out from the sheath on my back.

The blade was magically enhanced like Kinsley's daggers, but not with flames. No, this weapon had tendrils of electric power that moved along the steel surface while I held the hilt with two hands.

Noiselessly, I crept through the trees and approached Hazel. She didn't even flinch when I was right behind her. Though, her vulnerability didn't deter me from what I needed to do.

Two-handed, I lifted the sword up and then quickly brought it down, the blade slicing through Hazel's neck with ease.

Her eyes widened from the impact, but no sound came from her open lips.

Wisps of magic rose from her body and then headed straight for my sword that eagerly soaked up the energy while her head tilted and rolled to the ground.

Blood pooled around her neck and shoulders, but I didn't look long enough to be elated by the death.

Instead, my stare moved to my mate and the fucker who was trying to kill her.

I thought to help her more directly, but when I saw Kinsley's opponent start to shrink in size, I forced myself to stay put. If she was meant to be Alpha Supreme, she had to try to finish this fight herself. She had to show this House that she was capable of protecting them in the ways I knew she was.

If I thought for one second that she was too injured to end Johnathon on her own, though, I'd gladly step in. Alpha Supreme position be damned.

It wasn't worth her life.

The pewter-colored wolf trembled as the magic that had been charging him swiftly left his body. Kinsley moved to attack while he was distracted, but thankfully, she paused. Neither of us had any idea what the power might do to her if she got too close before it was done returning to the earth.

Within a minute, Johnathon was nothing more than a scraggly wolf, several inches smaller than Kinsley and not even close to her mass.

I saw the hesitation in Kinsley's wolf. She didn't want to kill him now that it was too easy of a death, but if she didn't, she would be sending a message in the worst way possible.

Before I could verbalize that, Johnathon lurched forward, trying to bite her face off, but even with a limp, Kinsley was faster than he was.

Mercifully, she whipped around and clamped down on the wolf's neck, biting down until the cracking of bones sounded around us and the wolf went limp in her hold.

She released Johnathon, letting him fall to the ground in a heap. Her wolf took several steps toward me, but I was already running for her.

With the sword back in its sheath, I dropped to my knees and gently held the head of Kinsley's wolf. She blinked slowly, once then twice.

"Kinsley?" The world felt as if it had dropped out from underneath me as she wavered, then fell to the ground.

I had a good enough hold on her head that I was able to help lower her, but when I saw that her chest was hardly moving, all air inside me became lodged in my throat.

No. This wasn't happening. She'd won. Johnathon was dead.

My hand stroked over her wolf. "Kinsley, open your eyes," I demanded, but her wolf only whimpered in reply.

In the distance, I could hear people, or possibly wolves, coming, but my eyes wouldn't move from my mate's face.

Her breathing grew shallower by the second, and I didn't know how to fucking fix her.

How could I have not seen how hurt she was when I'd first arrived?

"Fuck!" I screamed into the forest.

I should have stepped in. What did it matter who delivered the final blow? I shouldn't have given a shit about this House or what they'd think of her.

She was mine to protect, and I'd failed.

A shadow passed over me, and I nearly pulled my sword back out until I caught Lia being carried by Markus, who set her on the other side of Kinsley. His jaw was tight, and it seemed like a forced effort for him to release her.

Lia looked up at him. "She's your sister. I have to try."

I didn't know what was going on, but if Lia still had enough magic in her to heal my mate, I needed her to fucking do it now.

"Save her," I ordered, unable to conjure any other words over my fears.

Markus reached over Kinsley's prone form and grabbed my shirt by the collar, his eyes dark with unfiltered fury. "She'll fucking do it when she's ready and not a moment sooner."

I ripped his hand from my clothes. "Kinsley's brother or not, touch me again like that and I'll fucking end you."

"I might just ask you to," he muttered as his gaze went back to Lia and I released him.

The unicorn was barely holding herself up, and I tried to force myself to empathize with him.

Both of our mates were in bad shape. If Lia gave too much to heal Kinsley, she could die and yet...I was a big enough asshole that I didn't speak up. I didn't try to stop her, because Kinsley dying wasn't an option I was willing to live with.

I couldn't lose her.

"What the hell happened here?" Ryder asked, but nobody answered him.

My focus was on my mate, and that was where it would stay until she opened her eyes for me.

I wrapped my fingers around her limp paw while I watched Lia press her palms over the wolf's chest.

"Don't you fucking die," Markus whispered in Lia's ear when her faint magic began to cover my mate.

Lia didn't respond to him. Instead, she closed her eyes and slumped forward so limply that Markus needed to hold her up while she worked on Kinsley.

I watched with strangled breath, helpless to do anything other than sit there and hope my reason for living didn't stop breathing when I'd only just found her.

Lia groaned, and Markus tried to pull her back, but she at least had the strength to keep her hands pressed over Kinsley. "I need to save her. It's why I'm here."

I was certain Markus disagreed with that, but this time, he kept quiet. Just like I selfishly was.

I hadn't noticed him leave, but Ryder's wolf came running back toward us, then skidded to a stop next to me, carrying a brown leather bag in his mouth, which he dropped next to my feet.

My lips parted so I could tell him what I thought about his wolf kicking dirt up over my unconscious mate, but he shifted back first and kicked the bag closer to me. "Pour that into Kinsley's mouth."

"What is it?" I asked while grabbing the bag and opening it.

Inside was a glass vial filled with some sort of green liquid.

"Magic that will save her life without killing Lia," Ryder answered.

Before I'd even taken a second to inspect the vial, Markus snatched the potion from my hands. "I'll fucking do it if you won't."

My growl gave him pause and I gently, so as not to crack the glass, took the potion back. "You won't fucking touch her."

"Will the two of you shut the fuck up and help her already?" Lia grumbled, eyeing the green liquid that I noticed also had orange flecks of something inside. "I've seen that before. It will work."

She slumped back against Markus, and I kneeled forward, ripping the top of the bottle off with my teeth as my other hand reached for my mate. My fingers carefully parted her muzzle before inserting the vial as far back into her mouth as I could.

The contents dripped out slowly, seeming thicker than I'd first thought, but within thirty seconds, every drop was inside the wolf's mouth.

I kept a hand lightly over her throat until I felt movement that I hoped confirmed she'd swallowed everything. Seconds later, the wolf's fur took on a burnt-orange hue, then faded back to the normal charcoal color.

Her wolf sounded as if she were choking briefly, but then she quieted. My hands moved over her, confirming her breathing had evened out, but still, she hadn't woken back up.

My hardened gaze cut to Ryder, but he was apparently already prepared for my wrath. "It's not a cure-all. Kinsley still needs time to heal internally. Take her back to the house."

"She was out here alone because she was saving your son," I said in case he didn't already know.

He nodded stiffly. "I heard, which is why I gave her that potion. It was the last one I had that I'd saved in case I needed it for Sammy one day. I figured I owed Kinsley that much."

I watched him walk away with tense shoulders and his head slightly drooped.

The battle was over, but our fight was far from done.

CHAPTER THIRTY-SEVEN

KINSLEY

I didn't want to believe that I'd fought against a giant wolf and had gotten my ass kicked. Except, when I woke up in my room to three unknown women standing over me and a very menacing-looking Grayson looming behind them, I realized none of it had been just a nightmare. At least I'd won.

"Hi," I croaked, my voice hoarse. I wasn't sure if that was from injury or lack of use. Hell, I hadn't even remembered shifting back to my current form, and someone must have cleaned me up because I was wearing one of Grayson's shirts and what felt like shorts under the blankets.

"Hello, Kinsley Ash," the eldest of the three said. "Do you know who we are?"

I tried to shake my head, but the action hurt. "No."

The first one with silver hair, bright blue eyes, and faint wrinkles over her alabaster skin gestured to herself, then the two next to her. "We are the Crone, the Mother, and the Maiden."

Holy. Fuckity. Fuck.

I'd heard of them growing up. The Triarchy. They were *the* witches. Like, you didn't get more badass than these three women. I had even dreamt of being one of them when I'd been a child, wishing I could have been powerful enough to leave the coven I'd resented.

"We heard you were here and had figured out your true nature," the Mother said, her emerald eyes narrowing at me as if I'd done something wrong. Like I shouldn't have been able to learn who I was on my own.

Then again, I hadn't. I'd had Lia's help and the bond with Grayson to make me see the truth buried deep beneath the lies.

"Twenty-eight years was long enough to go without knowing who I truly was, don't you think?" I said snarkily, then I realized I should probably have just kept my mouth shut.

I was under no assumption that these three couldn't pulverize me in an instant.

The Crone nodded curtly. "We were asked to keep you hidden, and that is what we did. Nobody ever said we had to lift the spell by a certain age."

My eyes cast back to Grayson. He was remaining awfully quiet, and I briefly wondered if something had happened before I'd woken, but since I wasn't sure how long these witches were going to be around, I wanted to learn what I could from them.

"Who told you to hide me?" I asked, wondering if they were who my mother had run off to, but also why she'd have gone to witches instead of another pack.

The Mother flicked ebony hair behind her shoulder and lightly chuckled. "Nobody *told* us to do anything. We were asked for a favor and chose to grant it."

Right. That made more sense.

"Your mother came to us, offering her life in exchange for your protection," the Maiden said, her voice almost ethereal and garnering my full attention. She wore a white linen dress that probably meant to highlight some sort of innocence. Her long, dark brown hair stood out in contrast over the linen material and her chestnut eyes blinked expectantly at me.

My heart instantly dropped into my stomach, and tears burned at the back of my eyes for a woman I'd never known but had always longed for.

"She's…" I couldn't even say the words.

The Crone sighed. "Your mother lives. At least, last we heard. We did not take her first offering of her life. Instead, we concealed your true form and her mate bond with Johnathon."

I glanced at Grayson again, hope blossoming in me for the briefest of seconds until a realization hit me. If she were still alive, why hadn't she come for me? After nearly three decades, why hadn't my mother wanted me? Had Mathis and Johnathon terrified her *that* much?

Grayson finally pushed through the three witches and kneeled beside my bed. Still, he said nothing, but his touch eased some of the aching in my chest.

His eyes filled with flames when I stared into them. "Are you okay?" I asked, trying harder to sit up in the bed that felt like it had formed to my body.

He shook his head, and my eyes immediately cut to the three witches.

"What did you do to my mate?" I demanded.

The Mother looked at her nails casually. "He wouldn't stop yelling, so we silenced him."

"Well, *un*silence him," I practically growled, no longer caring how powerful they were. We'd already been through enough shit. I didn't have time for theirs.

The Crone placed her hand on Grayson's shoulder, and he quaked, closing his eyes briefly until she pulled her faintly glowing fingers away.

His forehead pressed against mine. "I'm so fucking glad you're awake."

"How long have I been out?" I asked with trepidation.

"Three days." The sorrow in his voice nearly broke me.

Fuck. I'd been worse off than I'd realized. "I'm so sorry, Grayson."

His head shook sharply. "Don't apologize."

"We didn't come here for a casual visit," the Crone said. "We only needed to make sure none of our magic was left inside you. Meeting your mate weakened the spell as it was intended to, and the unicorn helped you to see your true nature, but it wasn't until you accepted your bond to Grayson that our spell was completely shattered. Now that we've confirmed what we needed to, it's time for us to leave."

As they turned around, I called out. "Wait."

Only the Maiden turned around with a raised brow.

"Do you know where my mother is now? Or why she left me behind instead of taking me with her when she ran?" I practically begged, even though I'd just been a bitch to them.

The Maiden glanced at the Crone, who nodded tersely before walking away with the Mother. Once the two older witches were gone, the Maiden's voice became softer, and her eyes glistened, almost as if she could feel the tears I was holding back.

"Your mom's name is Rosella Moreno, and your birth name was Bethany," the Maiden said. "We did not keep track of where she went after she left you with us, but she was hiding you from your father Mathis Del Reyes, as well as from her mate Johnathon. We foresaw what would become of the men and understood why she was running with you. We left you with the most inconspicuous coven we could find that had witches with good intentions. That's all we needed to know."

"Thank you," I said earnestly, considering I hadn't thought they would share even that much.

Still, I wondered why my mother hadn't returned at some point.

The Maiden paused at the door to our room. "She would have come for you, but we warned her that our protection was a one-time deal. If she interfered in any way, the consequences were on her."

A sob built in my throat as Grayson squeezed my hand tightly. Words wouldn't come with the tears, so I nodded instead.

The witch disappeared into the hall, and I tried to get my shit together, but the moment Grayson wrapped his arms around me, I lost all sense of control.

My head pressed against his chest, and my fingers dug into his back as I held him, needing his closeness to anchor me back to the world. Needing his touch to soothe the agony storming through me.

"It's okay," he promised. "I've found hundreds of people before, and I can find your mom if you want me to."

My muscles tensed. Did I want that? What if things weren't as they seemed? What if she didn't want me to find her after all this time? She could have a new family and be happy somewhere else. I couldn't stand the thought of being disappointed.

"Let me think about it," I finally said once the tears had begun to subside.

Grayson pulled back, his eyes their normal cognac color again. "Whatever you want."

I glanced at the door, needing a change of conversation for the time being. "Is Sammy okay? Where are Lia and Markus? How are *you*?"

He lightly smiled at me. "Sammy is fine, all thanks to you and the two elder men who snuck out of the bunker to grab him from you. Lia and Markus are helping with the cleanup. I promised to call them if you woke, but given I was silenced when that happened…"

I lifted his hand and kissed the back. "I'd have died trying, but I would have done my best to hurt them if they didn't give your voice back."

Grayson lifted me up until I was sitting in his lap and cradled in his arms. "Let's not talk any more about you dying."

It hadn't gone unnoticed that he didn't answer my question about how he was doing, but I didn't need his words to know.

I could imagine the torment I'd have felt if it were him in this bed instead of me. Then, I'd multiply that rage by a hundred to get to Grayson's level.

He at least seemed okay physically, and that was enough. For now.

"How is everyone else?" I asked, knowing there would have been casualties but hoping not many.

Grayson stared ahead at the wall, and I instantly knew something worse had happened.

"Is Ryder…?" I let my voice trail off.

"He's fine," Grayson answered. "It was Tuck, along with more than a dozen others we didn't really get to know."

Damn it. I'd hardly known Tuck, but he'd helped us and he'd been a close friend of Ryder's, along with being Sammy's "Uncle Tuck." My heart ached for their losses and for the grief felt by the rest of the families.

I started to pull Grayson's arms away from me so I could get out of bed, but his hold tightened. "What do you think you're doing?"

"I'm going to take a shower and then we're going to go help," I said sternly. "This was our fight, and we need to face the consequences."

His lips thinned. "This fight was coming, with or without us."

"Maybe, but it happened *with* us and it needs to be finished with us as well." Sure, I was still sore as fuck, but I could walk—at least I was pretty sure I could—and that meant I needed to be out there, showing the House members I hadn't abandoned them.

Even if I'd gotten my ass kicked and they possibly didn't want me as their Alpha Supreme, I still felt a sense of duty to them, and I was going to follow through on that.

I forced my way out of Grayson's hold, and he glowered at me. "You're a stubborn woman."

"Tell me something we don't already know," I teased as I carefully headed for the bathroom to shower off the days I'd spent in bed.

Within the hour, we made it to the area with the worst of the destruction, which was where the initial blast had been and where four of the men had died.

Markers and flowers had already been set out to remember each of the men and another four were out in the park, where I assumed some of the others had died, but the numbers didn't quite add up to what Grayson had mentioned earlier.

"Was there fighting in other places?" I asked softly while we walked toward where someone had said Ryder was.

Grayson nodded toward the right. "That's where Lia and Markus had gone before I went to find you. They were working with another group of Ryder's faction to keep the fight split up. It worked well, but there were still losses there, too. Like Tuck."

His response answered my unspoken question, which again tore at my chest. It didn't matter that we'd known people would die.

Knowing and accepting our consequences were two completely different things.

When we approached Ryder, he was lifting fallen debris that was too large for him to be handling on his own.

Before I could step in, Grayson did for me.

The two men moved the massive piece of steel that I assumed had come from one of the warehouses that had been blasted into.

Once it was placed onto the street, Ryder quickly began searching beneath the rubble, and I realized they were still looking for bodies.

Fuck.

"How many more?" I asked as I bent down to help.

"Two," Ryder replied gruffly.

And that was two more too many.

"Dad?" Sammy's voice came from around the corner.

Ryder stood, holding his hand up. "Don't step inside this building, Son."

He nodded, then his eyes landed on me and welled up with tears. "Kinsley."

"Hey, bud." I lifted myself back up—slowly—and made my way over to where he stood.

I was surprised when he didn't hug me, but instead, began to cry. "I'm sorry I didn't listen."

My fingers stroked his soft cheek. "It's okay, Sammy."

His lower lip jutted out. "But you were really hurt."

"I was, but I'm getting better even as we stand here," I promised.

"Can I hug you now?" Sammy asked. "Dad took me to see you, but they said I wasn't allowed to touch you."

His words felt like a dagger to my chest. "Of course. Just be gentle with me or you'll have to carry me back to my house."

He wiped the back of his arm under his nose and snorted. "You're funny." He hugged me softly, and I knew then that the world could have swallowed me up whole and I still would have chosen to save that boy.

Ryder pulled Sammy back and gestured toward me with a wave of his hand. "It's good to see you up."

"How can I help?" I asked, because that was why we'd come out here.

He glanced over at Grayson and then back at me. "Your mate didn't tell you?"

I glared at the man in question. "Tell me what?"

"You're the queen!" Sammy shouted while throwing his arms in the air in excitement.

Grayson moved to my side, wrapping an arm around my waist. "I was waiting until Lia and Markus came back. I thought you might want to celebrate together. The factions all met, and it was decided that you are welcome to the Alpha Supreme position and won't be challenged further by anyone here."

Holy shit.

I'd honestly expected the wolves to consider me a failure with how badly I'd been hurt. This was… It was something else entirely.

"That doesn't mean wolves from the outlying packs in Fire and Fluorite won't come sniffing around eventually, but the position is yours if you still want to stay here." Ryder smiled proudly. "You've earned it."

I snorted very un-queen-like. "Of course, I still fucking want it."

Sammy gasped. "Language, Kinsley."

His response had me laughing until my sides ached, and I had to lean into Grayson to keep upright.

This was really happening.

I was home, and I had a family, and I was going to rule an entire fucking House.

As hard as some of that was to grasp, I couldn't have been happier in that moment.

"You told her without us?" Lia gaped with her fists on her hips. She and Markus were standing behind Ryder, and I hadn't even seen them approach.

Sammy flinched. "Sorry."

I reached forward and patted him on the head, still grinning like a fool. "It's okay, bud. Isn't it, Lia?"

She leaned her cheek against Markus's shoulder and smiled. "Of course."

Markus nodded at me. "Congratulations, Sis."

I glanced at everyone before bringing my gaze back to my brother. "I couldn't have done it without all of you."

Grayson kissed the top of my head. "And we wouldn't have come together without you."

Even with the losses, my heart was so fucking full, I thought it might explode.

It might have taken longer than I'd expected to get here, but, staring at my found family, I knew everything I'd gone through had led me to right here and that was something I could never regret.

EPILOGUE

ONE MONTH LATER

KINSLEY

After several weeks of cleanup, I was finally waking up in the new-to-us house that I intended to share with Grayson for many, many years to come.

Once my injuries had healed, I'd gotten right to work on bringing this part of Fire and Fluorite back together. It hadn't been easy, and we were still a long way from where I hoped to see this House, but I knew we'd get there. One day at a time.

Plus, there was still plenty of other territory that I needed to visit now that things were more stable right here. I needed the other areas of Fire and Fluorite to see their new Alpha Supreme and know that I wouldn't forget about them, that their needs were just as important as the House members who lived nearest to me.

That would likely take me months to accomplish, but I wasn't going to be doing anything on my own, which made the tasks seem much less daunting.

Grayson had been right by my side, and I knew he would continue to be, helping however he could, even when he didn't want to. Given that *peopling* wasn't his forte, I'd figured out rather quickly that I needed even more help after the first week.

That was where Ryder had come back in. He was the perfect Beta. I'd known all along that there was a deeper connection that I'd felt to him, one that hadn't clicked into place until he'd accepted my offer as Beta.

Then there was Sammy. We'd just celebrated his seventh birthday last week, and he wished to one day be my assistant like his dad was.

"Assistant" wasn't the right word, but I gladly made his wish come true, and he was now my unofficial helper around the house. On a serious note, having coffee brought to me by a very proud seven-year-old was a joy unlike anything else.

"How's my mate this morning?" Grayson asked when he exited the bathroom wearing only a white towel around his waist.

I, however, was still in bed since the sun was barely up. "Awake but wishing she weren't alone under this blanket."

He chuckled. "We have a lot to do today."

I already knew that and didn't want to deal with it. Well, at least one of the things.

Today, I had to say goodbye to my brother and Lia.

Realistically, I knew it wasn't a real goodbye, but the thought of them going to Blood and Beryl to live broke my heart a little. Okay, a lot.

I hadn't been above begging them to stay until Grayson had kindly reminded me of the previous assumptions we'd already had, ones that Markus hadn't ever confirmed himself. Though, his eyes said a lot for him when he spoke of Blood and Beryl. That was his home now, and I respected that.

The only issue we hadn't tackled between us was telling his mother about me, which meant our little brother didn't know, either.

We'd both agreed to leave Triton out of what we'd learned, so that he didn't have to try to keep things from their mom, something he apparently wasn't great at.

That didn't mean I hadn't checked in on them in my own ways, and I would continue to do so until Markus and I decided to share the truth. For now, they were safe in Fire and Fluorite and would remain that way for years to come.

I was apparently lost in thought for too long, because the next thing I knew, Grayson was wrapping his arms around my waist. He hauled my naked ass out of bed by throwing me over his shoulder like a caveman. "Come on, Mate. You need to get ready or they're going to leave without saying goodbye."

I gasped. "They'd never. Lia and Markus love me too much to do that."

"And you love them too much to make this any harder on them," he countered.

Damn it. I hated it when he was right.

He set me down next to the tile shower and turned the water on before his darkening gaze started to roam over my body.

Within an instant, this man took away all my worries and made me want only him.

His allure and intensity drove me to the brink of the best kind of insanity. He was my safe place to fall apart and feel whatever I needed to feel.

He balanced me out on my bad days and kept me humble on the good ones.

He could ignite me in ways I'd never thought possible.

"Shower, Mate," he said gruffly, but at the same time, his arms boxed me in against the wall and his warm breath covered my neck, sending shivers through my body.

"Only if you join me," I quipped, sliding my hands over his chiseled chest and farther down until I shoved his towel down to the ground and gripped his growing erection.

"I just got out of the shower," he replied, moving his mouth lightly over my collarbone.

I unashamedly panted. "And yet you're still a dirty boy."

His head lifted and he cocked a brow. "'Boy'?"

With my hand still around his hard cock, I squeezed. "Oops. Maybe you need to remind me just how *manly* you are again."

"Or maybe I need to punish you for forgetting." He bit into my shoulder. Not enough to break the skin, but enough that I'd be feeling reminders of his touch for the rest of the day.

I was tempted to beg him for whatever punishment he wanted to give me, but I'd learned the hard way that only led to him denying me for longer than I liked. So I kept my mouth shut while he kissed over the bite mark, then back up my neck.

His fingers pinched my chin until my lips bunched together. "Naughty, naughty woman."

I smirked when he released me. "But I'm *your* naughty woman."

"All fucking mine." He growled before reaching between my legs and slipping one, then two fingers inside my throbbing pussy. "All of you. Every curve and crevice. You are mine, Kinsley Ash."

His words melted me from the inside out as I wrapped my legs around his waist and he carried me into the shower, pressing me against the tile wall. "Show me again," I challenged.

"I'll show you as many times as you want or need," he murmured against my lips.

And I knew he would.

For the rest of our long lives, Grayson was mine just as much as I was his, and together, there wasn't anything that we couldn't do.

"Don't you fucking cry." Lia pointed at me with a glare on her face as we stood outside my and Grayson's house.

I held my hands up innocently. "I wouldn't dream of it, especially when you promised to just appear anytime I called."

"And *only* when she calls," Grayson cut in, making the rest of us laugh.

Lia patted his arm, and she winked at him. "Of course. I wouldn't want to 'walk in' on anything that might cause me nightmares."

My mate stiffened and jerked his arm back. "What did I say about touching me?"

Lia shook her head and grinned at me. "Some things will never change."

"No, they won't," I responded. "And there's nothing wrong with that."

I loved Grayson just the way he was, and I had no problems being the only one he showed his softer side to.

Markus wrapped an arm loosely around Lia's waist. "We should get going. Elias and Danni are expecting us."

Lia was the first to sniffle. "Damn it," she muttered, then stepped out of Markus's embrace.

I met her in the middle, and we threw our arms around each other. "We can have coffee tomorrow," I reminded her.

She nodded against my shoulder. "I know, but it's not the same as living with you and not needing a reason to see you."

I knew exactly what she meant, but I had a feeling we'd find plenty of reasons to see each other every week. At least, that was what I kept telling myself so that I didn't make this any harder on them.

"Alright, my turn," Markus said, grinning at me.

Lia backed up, and I hugged my brother. We'd been hugging more often, which had felt weird at first, but only because hugs weren't part of my upbringing. Now, I didn't think I could ever go without them again.

"You're going to do great things here, Sis," Markus said to me once we pulled apart.

"Thank you for believing in me," I replied earnestly.

He chuckled. "It was easy to do."

"Alright," Lia sighed heavily. "We're not making this a thing. We'll see you in a day or two. Everything is totally fine."

Markus backed up and kissed the top of Lia's head. "Then, let's go home."

I leaned into Grayson as we waved goodbye to our family, and within seconds, they were gone. Teleported to another House.

"That wasn't so bad," Grayson said as we turned to head back into our home.

I shrugged, not really ready to talk about it, but he stopped me at the door, turning my body until I faced him and lifted my chin. "It's okay to be sad even if you can see her anytime."

I took a shuddering breath. "Good, because I'm really fucking sad."

He grinned and gathered me into his arms. "It's going to be…"

His words trailed off, and I jerked back. "What?"

Grayson wasn't looking at me. His eyes were facing the sidewalk we'd just left.

I turned my head, expecting to see Lia and Markus there for some reason—maybe a second goodbye—but it wasn't them.

It was a woman. One I'd never met before, but I knew her the moment our stares met.

Holy fuckity fuck.

It was my mother.

She had the same white hair as I did. Her skin was a few shades darker than mine, but her smile reminded me of my own.

Her lighter blue eyes blinked, and she lifted a hand to wave awkwardly. "Beth—Kinsley?"

I nodded, unable to form any words while I stayed frozen in front of our door.

"I'm Rosella," she said quietly, then added, "Your mother."

I glanced up at Grayson, and his eyes softened as he nudged me lightly forward. "Go."

My feet hesitantly carried me back toward the sidewalk. I wasn't sure what to think, especially since I hadn't yet decided if I'd wanted Grayson to look for this woman. I knew deep down that my resistance to finding her had mostly been because I was afraid that she'd have moved on, not wanting to be found.

She twisted her hands in front of her stomach. "I've wanted to find you for so long, but I was so scared. Then, the Maiden sent me a message. She told me that there was a new Alpha Supreme in Fire and Fluorite I might be curious to know. I just couldn't believe…"

Tears welled in my eyes, and I was certain there was a vice trying to break my ribs with how tight my chest was.

"I found my way home," I finally said, voice thick with emotions.

She nodded and grinned widely, her hand reaching up to touch me but stopping before she got too close. "Yes, you did."

Grayson joined us, and he offered a hand to…my mother. "I'm Grayson. Her mate."

She accepted his gesture. "I'm Rosella. Her…"

"My mom," I finished for her as more tears fell down my cheeks.

"Would you like to come inside?" Grayson asked, nodding toward the house.

Her eyes met mine again. "Only if that's okay with you."

I swallowed thickly. "It is. Go on in, and we'll be right behind you."

I needed a minute to breathe before we sat down for whatever conversation was about to happen.

She smiled and dipped her head. "Of course."

Once she opened our door on her own, I fell into Grayson's arms and let my emotions run rampant. "She came for me."

His hands rubbed over my back. "But she doesn't have to stay."

"I know, but I think I want her to."

He squeezed me tighter, and I could hear the smile in his voice. "I had a feeling."

I took a few calming breaths before pulling back and looking up at my mate. "Is this all real? Or am I going to wake up alone back in my apartment any moment now?"

His lips pressed against my forehead, and he squeezed my hips. "This is very real, and you're *never* going to be alone again."

A shudder rolled through me at the intensity of truth I felt from his words.

It might have taken me longer than I'd have liked, but I'd found my family and my home. I wouldn't ever stop being grateful for everyone who helped me to get here.

Especially the man beside me who knew just when to hold me up and when to stand by my side.

If you've enjoyed Kinsley and Grayson's story, it would mean the world to me if you could leave a review on Amazon or Goodreads. Thank you so much for reading!

Corrupt Me by Everly Frost is the next standalone release in this world and will feature the Triarchy, the three powerful witches that you just met at the end of this book. Flip the page to see the full line up!

Want to know about future releases without having to follow the authors everywhere? Text **"IMMORTAL"** to **(844) 506-1510**

IMMORTAL VICES AND VIRTUES

Want to read more from this world? Great news! Ten other authors
have and / or are writing stories in the world!
Here is the recommended reading order for your enjoyment:

Reject Me by Kel Carpenter and Aurelia Jane
(where Markus first appears)
Queen Me by Amber Lynn Natusch
(Myra and The Riff-Raff bar are in this one)
Haunt Me by Amanda Pillar
Crave Me by Lexi C Foss
Expose Me by Kaydence Snow
Ruin Me by Jenna Wolfhart
Ignite Me by Heather Renee
Corrupt Me by Everly Frost *(the Triarchy witches are here)*
Burn Me by KA Knight and Kendra Moreno
Slay Me by Jessica Wayne *(D from the circus will be here)*

Each story is a complete stand alone and they can be read in any order,
but they're best consumed consecutively.
If you love spicy paranormal romance, angst, feisty heroines, and the
darkly delicious men who sweep them off their feet,
you're going to devour this world!

STAY IN TOUCH

Find Heather on Facebook:
Reader Group:
Want to talk all things books and get updates before anyone else?
Come hang with me in my reader group:
Heather Renee's Book Warriors

Author Page:
Teaser and big updates are also posted here:
Heather Renee Author

Newsletter:
I only send this out sporadically, so don't worry. You won't ever be
spammed by me and you get a couple goodies when you sign up!
http://smarturl.it/HeatherReneeNL

ALSO BY HEATHER RENEE

Mystics and Mayhem Series

Fated to the Wolf

A complete New Adult Witch and Wolf series (dual POV) featuring an abandoned witch, a rogue wolf, and their broken bond.

Scorned by Blood

A complete New Adult Vampire series featuring a supernatural hunter and the sexy vampire bound to protect her no matter the cost.

Luna Marked

A complete New Adult wolf shifter series (dual POV) featuring a strong-willed leading lady and a patient, yet fierce alpha male.

Broken Court

A complete New Adult Urban Fantasy series featuring an unconventional and anti-heroine leading lady, a broody love interest, and a fae kingdom with a vile king.

Individual Series

Raven Point Pack Series

A complete Upper Young Adult Paranormal Romance series featuring wolves, witches, vengeance, and fated mates.

Shadow Veil Academy

A complete Upper Young Adult Urban Fantasy Academy series featuring shifters, elves, witches, and more.

Elite Supernatural Trackers

A complete New Adult Urban Fantasy series featuring witches, demons, a smart-mouthed female lead, alpha males, and a snarky fairy sidekick.

Royal Fae Guardians

A complete Young Adult Urban Fantasy series featuring fae, magic users, a sweet romance, along with snark and humor.

Blood of the Sea Series

A complete Young Adult Paranormal Romance series featuring vampires, open seas adventures, and the occasional pirate.

Standalone Books

Ignite Me - A spicy wolf shifter story featuring a lost heir, the mate who doesn't want her, and the enemies who wish them dead.

Marked Paradox - A Young Adult fae story about a realm divided and one fae to bring them back together.

ABOUT THE AUTHOR

Heather Renee is a USA Today Bestselling author who lives in Oregon. She writes Paranormal Romance and Urban Fantasy novels with a mixture of romance, humor, and sass. Her love of reading eventually led to her passion of writing and giving the gift of escapism. When Heather's not writing, she's spending time with her loving husband and beautiful daughter, going on their own adventures. She loves to hear from her fans, so visit her website: www.HeatherReneeAuthor.com and check out the Contact Me page for ways to connect.